CW00499314

PAINLESS

A novel about Chronic Pain
and the Mind-Body Connection

Chana Studley

Cover design by Chana Studley
Back cover photograph by Andrea Brownstein
Edited by Sarah Rosenbaum
Formatting by Heather Osborne

ISBN 9798569311156

Chana Studley
www.chanastudley.com

Praise for *Painless*

Chana Studley has written an engrossing novel that explains the mind-body connection in scientific, as well as spiritual terms. Some of the characters may be fictional but the results are not. I have witnessed astounding outcomes, since 1985, for people experiencing emotional pain, as they also came to understand the true nature of the human experience. It makes sense that it would work the same for physical pain. The author writes from her own experience with traumatic physical pain and a depth of understanding that will unleash your own insights into the formless workings of the mind which represents a paradigm shift, across the board, for humanity, bringing enormous hope for all. Painless is a must-read for anyone experiencing physical or emotional pain, regardless of age or circumstance.

- Lori Carpenos M.Ed., LMFT co-author: "The Secret of Love; Unlock the Mystery, Unleash the Magic and author of "It's an Inside-Out World."

As doctors, we are missing out on an essential ingredient if we do not understand how people's thinking and beliefs affect their illnesses. Modern science has made so much progress, yet most diseases are still idiopathic, which is a polite way to say "we have no idea.
Chana Studley has bridged a huge gap between a perceived scientific subject of illness with the spiritual aspect of Mind, Thought, and Consciousness. Chana shows us that not only are we not our thoughts but that we have innate well-being and wisdom and we can tap into it whenever we need.

- Helen Ching, MD. Family physician, Hospital Authority of Hong Kong.

Painless is a book on two levels. On one level it is a sweet, gripping page-turner about a courageous woman embarking on an amazing journey that results in impacting the lives of so many people. I was moved and intrigued by what might happen next, and even cried!

On a deeper level, this book has an important message of hope for those who find themselves in chronic pain. The author was one of those people who lived with pain daily and thought that would be her lot in life. Chana shows us that the body has an innate ability to heal itself. She shares story after story of incredible recoveries and liberation from endless pain through this tale of people who became free of their suffering through a simple understanding of the mind. I know this is a book that I would turn to if I were in pain and I am sure she will liberate many from their pain by sharing what helped her become pain-free.

As a Natural Healthcare Practitioner, I have seen how people can get stuck with their physical issues and feel hopeless. Chana offers us a way through and out the other side. We all know the power of the mind and how it can hold us stuck. Through her engaging tale, Chana shows us there is a way to become free of our usual thinking and our usual stories so that our healthier self can emerge.

- Susan Marmot, Homeopath and Faculty Member of The One Thought Institute.

Chana Studley has done a great job with "Painless." Chana has referenced all the big names in Pain Science and has managed to integrate their ideas in both an informative and easy-to-read way. "Painless" is inspiring and a must-read for any health practitioner interested in chronic pain.

- Ryan Green BAppSc, MA Physiotherapist, Exercise Physiologist, Clinical Pilates Instructor.

Painless is a story of the freedom that can be found despite your pain and in many cases, this same freedom is the path to reducing and even eliminating symptoms.

With wit, clarity, hard science, and a lovable cast of eccentric characters, Chana Studley expertly addresses the common misunderstandings around the cause of chronic pain and the road to healing. Time and time again she demonstrates how a never-ending list of tools, techniques, and specialists often exacerbate our pain. She guides us to realize how a true understanding of the human experience will mean you can weather life's inevitable storms and access your innate health, resilience, wisdom, and peace.

It is from this space that healing and recovery are possible.

I consider it vitally important that this message of hope reach sufferers, their loved ones, and medical professionals around the world.

- Flick Hardingham, Chronic Pain at Work Consultant, and Managing Director.

Praise for Chana Studley's first novel,

The Myth of Low Self-Esteem

Chana Studley has written a powerful novel about how we can use the power of our mind to heal us from the negative messages that cause us to feel anxious, enraged, and depressed. Her book provides hope to people who have been diagnosed with various disorders, showing how, by letting go of their self-limiting inner narratives, they live a life of unlimited joy and inner peace. I heartily recommend this book to those who want to free themselves of negative mental constructs.

- Dr. Miriam Adahan Ph.D. Teacher, author, and spiritual guide

As I read your book, I realize the truth is so simple. It's our desire to create a story to live by rather than living our lives truthfully that complicates life.

- Justice Milton Joseph Simon

I just want to tell you how much I loved reading your book. I took it with me over winter vacation and couldn't put it down. It is now my favorite 3P book: love the novel style, well-written, easy to read and relate to, love your honesty, your journey, how you smash all myths, not just the one related to self-esteem. I have been recommending it to whomever I speak to.

- Aviva Barnett, MSW

Foreword

Recently a longtime friend and fellow Three Principles sharer related to me that she had been deeply touched and impacted by reading the manuscript of Chana Studley's second novel, *Painless*, and urged me to do the same with a view to writing this foreword.

I first met Chana in person when I attended one of her presentations at the annual Three Principles conference in London. She shared with eloquence, clarity, and gratitude her journey from experiencing overwhelming emotional and physical pain subsequent to multiple traumatic assaults to an ever-increasing level of inner peace. She indicated that this remarkable transformation of her experience had accompanied her having incremental insights into the spiritual nature of the Three Universal Principles of Mind, Consciousness, and Thought as uncovered by Sydney Banks.

Chana has a gift both as a storyteller and teacher. In reading the book I often felt like an invisible companion as she deftly presented profound questions and paradigm-changing solutions with a gentleness that minimized reactiveness both in the participants in the novel and in the reader.

Painless has the potential to awaken fresh hope to the millions of people worldwide who spend the majority of every day enveloped and overwhelmed by their experience of pain. This state, when left unabated, often results in permanent disability and, all too often, in suicide.

Utilizing her novel as a vessel, Chana points to the formless (spiritual) Universal Principles behind life that permeate the soma (the body) and the psyche (spirit, soul, mind). Chana does this with a clarity and certainty that would make Candace Pert Ph.D., the late pioneer in the oneness of the body-mind phenomenon, proud.

In doing so, I believe Chana's book and the sharing of

the Universal Principles presented will be substantial elements in facilitating a speedy amelioration of, and, in time, awaken hope of an eradication of the opioid crisis, which is gripping so many countries and resulting in the untimely deaths of so many people who are struggling to come to peace with their thinking.

And yes, I also recommend reading Chana's first novel, *The Myth of Low Self-Esteem*, in the very near future.

William F. Pettit Jr., M.D.

Retired Psychiatrist, now full-time student and mentor of the 3 Principles; with fifty-plus years of clinical and teaching experience and past recipient of Board Certification in Psychosomatic Medicine.

Contents

1
Westwood

Deborah had recently turned down a big project with Columbia Pictures. She just couldn't do it anymore. It was strange, after a lifetime of creating incredible and fantastical special effects with her hands for top British theater productions and Hollywood movies, she was done. She had worked with the best in the business, A-list actors and directors, and seen the world whilst filming on location. She had been part of an Academy Award-winning team and set the standard high for those who were to follow. This last job was what she had been working toward her whole career; she had been asked to be the supervisor of all the animatronic effects for the movie Stuart Little. The script was really good, but she knew it was time to stop. It had been an amazing rollercoaster of a career, and even though she was certain it was the right decision, she had stared at the phone for a few minutes before calling the producer, knowing that this would be the end…the end of her Hollywood career.

This wasn't the hardest call she had ever had to make, but it was certainly a significant one. So now that she had taken herself out of a cherished career, she needed to think about what to do next. Deborah loved the counseling work she had been doing for the last several years and was beginning to write and teach, so things were already changing. She felt more purpose and less pressure, as if she knew what she wanted her life to look like, she just didn't know how it was going to happen yet. This kind of uncertainty had rarely bothered Deborah; she was used to it from being self-employed her whole life, but being okay with not *trying* to make it happen, that was new. Deborah knew intuitively that it would unfold. The question was, how and from where?

Deborah finished up with one of her regular clients at the Santa Monica Drop-in Center on the Westside of Los Angeles, where she volunteered as a counselor, and stepped into Bob's office for what she thought was going to be a quick chat with the director.

"Hey, Debs, come in. How are you doing now that you aren't hobnobbing with Hollywood stars anymore?"

"Fine. Relieved, I guess. Why? Do you think I need some readjustment counseling? Some of my friends think I need my head examined for leaving the film biz!"

"Nah, although I don't quite understand why, when you worked so hard to get to the top, or why you couldn't keep doing both like you did before, but, hey, what do I know? I don't understand a lot of what most people do! No, I actually have a paying client for you, if you are interested."

"Wow, sure!"

"It's a bit delicate, which is why I would appreciate your discretion. One of my old colleagues at UCLA called me to ask for help with a student. This girl is just finishing her first year and she attempted suicide. It was a lame attempt—just 10 Wellbutrin—but, of course, the parents are freaked out and the school has to be proactive in providing care for her."

"Are the parents coming to get her?"

"Nope, they are in Sydney. She only has one final left and then she will go home. But the school will only let her stay if she has supervision. She is seeing a psychiatrist and they have her on all kinds of meds. Stan says she is quite remorseful and wants to finish her degree."

"So, like glorified babysitting, then?"

"Yeah, I guess. She's okay during the day, as she has extra classes and a study partner who is in on the whole story, so it's just evenings and weekends. At $30 an hour plus expenses, I wouldn't mind doing it myself! But that probably wouldn't be appropriate. You are going to need to stay with her overnight."

"Wow, really? That'll be…uh…where? Where will I be earning this $30 an hour for sleeping?"

"Ah, so that's the other thing. The school can't let her stay in the dorms, it's not fair to the other kids. The parents are putting her up in a small boutique hotel in Westwood near campus, so you'll have a shared suite situation with her."

"Okay, let me get this straight: they are going to pay me 30 bucks an hour to hang out and stay in a hotel for two weeks?"

"Yeah, plus expenses. Is that okay?" They both laughed. "Sorry, but I thought you might enjoy it! I have no idea what she is like, or what the problem is. I'm hoping you will be able to help her."

Deborah paused. "No problemo, just send me all the

rich spoiled brats you have and I'll do my best. When do I start?"

"Today. I mean, you won't have any night life for a couple of weeks, but I imagine you are used to dropping everything and going on location—only this time, it's just across town. You will have most of your days free, and on the weekend she is going to some family down in San Diego, I think. Can you go meet her and her student advisor, who is overseeing this whole thing, this afternoon to get acquainted?"

Deborah drove home, not quite sure what to make of it. The family must be loaded to afford her plus the hotel, the doctors, and not to mention UCLA for school. She wondered what she was studying, would they get on, and what the cry for help was all about.

She parked on a side street in Westwood and walked onto the campus to find the student advisor's room. It was late on a hot June afternoon and there were still plenty of students hurrying to class or on their phones, talking to friends and doing some last-minute cramming for the end-of-semester exams. She found the room and knocked gently. The door was opened by a casually dressed woman who invited her in and offered her a glass of water.

"Here, it's pretty warm today. Julia will be here shortly. Do you know much about the case?"

"Not really, only that she made a suicide attempt and needs to be…supervised?"

"Yeah, she isn't really talking much so don't expect a lot of interaction. This is more procedural than anything else."

"Okay."

There was a light knock on the door and the advisor got up to let Julia in. She was in her early twenties, attractive and alert. She came in and perched on the edge of a folding chair as if she was ready to make a quick getaway.

"Julia, this is Deborah. Deborah, Julia."

The two women looked at each other.

"Nice to meet you," offered Deborah with a smile. Julia glared and looked away.

"Okay, so you two will be spending a lot of time together in the next two weeks. Do you have any questions or concerns?"

There was a pause while Deborah waited for Julia to speak up, but she continued to look away. Then suddenly she said, "I don't want any of my friends knowing about you."

"Of course. So…let's think of a story to explain who I am."

"No need, you aren't going to meet any of them."

"Sure, but just in case we bump into someone, how about…uh…we could say I'm an old friend of your mom's?"

Julia shrugged her shoulders and looked away again.

"Okay, so you two will work that out. Here are the details of the hotel, Julia's study and exam schedule, contact information for me, doctors, and the parents." Deborah looked over the schedule. "We got Julia checked in to the hotel this morning. I see you are done at 6 p.m. tonight… I guess you guys should meet then, say, at the library, and then make plans for your evening?"

"Sure, sounds good to me," replied Deborah. Julia shrugged her shoulders again. "Okay then, see you later. You have my number in case you need me before then."

"I don't need anything, thanks," snapped Julia, as she grabbed her purse and left.

"Bye, Julia, we'll speak soon," called the advisor, but

she was gone. "See, not very communicative."

"I don't blame her. I mean, I don't think I would like to be followed around all the time even if I was feeling great."

"Yep, me too. So when she goes out, just sit at another table, or you can be down the block. You don't have to be on top of her the whole time. I think the family just wants to make sure she is okay and that she can make it to the end of school in one piece. There are no knives allowed in the hotel room and you will have to keep all her meds with you and dish them out, she knows what to take when…and, I guess…good luck!"

Deborah came back in the late afternoon and parked in the hotel parking lot. She walked over to the UCLA library, which was much quieter now. Julia was sitting on the steps with her study partner. Her hoodie was up, even though it was really warm, and she was smoking a cigarette.

"Hi!"

Julia didn't respond but just picked up her books and started walking. The study partner walked off too, so Deborah followed Julia. *Ugh, this is going to be fun,* she thought, and caught up with her as they walked out of the campus for the five-minute walk to the hotel.

"I just need to get my bags out of the car, can you wait for me in the lobby?"

Julia stopped and put her cigarette out on the sidewalk.

"Okay then, I'll be right back."

They went to the front desk for Deborah to get her own key, and then upstairs to the room. It was a one-bedroom suite with a small kitchen, bathroom, and sitting room. There was a small table, two chairs, and a sofa bed that had already been pulled out and made up.

"That's yours," said Julia, and slammed the bedroom

door behind her in frustration.

It was very modern, very clean. The kitchen was already stocked with groceries and paper goods. There was a big flat-screen TV and a view of the street below. Deborah could see a café, a corner market, and hairdressers. *Now what?* she wondered. She had brought some books and her laptop to do some work and decided to do her own thing until something else became obvious. About an hour later, Julia came out of her room and headed for the door.

"I'm meeting some friends for dinner. There's another restaurant next door so you can eat there, or…wherever you want, I don't care."

"Okay, but slow down a second. If we are going to make this work, you need to communicate your plans with me a little more. I'm hungry too, so this is good, but I would appreciate knowing what your plans are a little in advance, like, a five-minute warning that you are about to leave would be nice." Julia shrugged. "Are we coming back here after?"

"Maybe, dunno yet… I'll text you." With that, she walked off. Deborah grabbed her purse and followed.

Julia motioned to where she would be eating and walked on to meet her friends. Deborah hung back for a bit and then went in, sat at the furthest table, and ordered dinner. *How on earth is this going to work,* she thought to herself. What if I'm halfway through eating and they decide to leave? This is ridiculous! But hey, I'm just the babysitter.

After dinner, Julia texted to say they were going to a café to hang out and that Deborah could go home. Deborah texted back saying that this wasn't part of the deal and that she would be obligated to blow her cover if she didn't cooperate. So Julia walked with her friends and Deborah followed at a distance. She felt like she was in a spy movie, half expecting the LAPD to come screeching up in a cop car and take someone down. They hung out for a few hours in a coffee shop, then she said goodbye to her friends and started to walk back to the hotel. Deborah followed. Julia went straight into her room and shut the door.

Two weeks of this? thought Deborah. She texted Julia from the living room:

We need to talk.

In the morning.

Ok.

Ok.

2
LAX

The next morning, Deborah showered and sat down at the kitchen table. Julia soon followed. Deborah put out the meds that Julia needed for the day and paused to gather her thoughts.

"Look, I have no idea what you are going through, but *I'm* not the enemy. I actually think this whole thing is kinda ridiculous. If you really wanted to hurt yourself, I'm not going to be able to stop you."

"I *don't* want to hurt myself… I just, I was just tired of waking up, that's all."

"Okay." Deborah was trying to understand. "Let's try and do this together so that we can both have an okay time of it."

Julia shrugged and took her pills.

"Look, it's all a game," Deborah offered. "A game where you do what's asked of you now so everyone will start to trust you again and you get your freedom back. I'm sure it's not easy or fun to have me following you around, but it's the rules, and if you play by them now, it will be over quicker and you can get back to your regular routine."

Julia shook her head. "You have *no idea*."

"Maybe, maybe not, but if you don't talk to me, how could I know? I'm a counselor with a lot of experience, as well as being an overpaid babysitter. Try me?"

Julia got up and went back to her room, shutting the door hard, though not quite a slam.

Leaving in 5

This continued for a few more days: Julia doing the bare minimum and Deborah making the best of a very weird situation. She went about her usual daytime life of seeing clients, writing and hanging out with friends. In the evenings she was with Julia, either in the hotel with all the doors closed, or at some restaurant or café spying from a distance. Sometimes in Westwood, sometimes on the Third Street Promenade in Santa Monica or at the beach. Deborah couldn't get over how much money was going into this girl's well-being, which Julia didn't seem to appreciate at all. She let Julia know that the offer to talk was always there but got no response; in fact, she started to feel a bit like a drug pusher. The only time Julia would communicate at all was for the two minutes it took to take her pills, morning and night. When it came to Friday, Deborah gave her "customer" just enough to last until Sunday evening.

"You'll text me when you are on your way back from San Diego, right? I'll need at least an hour's notice on Sunday to pack up from where I am so I can meet you here."

"My uncle is bringing me back so I don't know when."

"Exactly, me neither, so please give me a heads up

when you leave San Diego and when you are about an hour away, okay?"

"Okay," replied Julia, with maybe a fraction less attitude this time.

On Monday morning Deborah got a call from the student advisor.

"You have a passport, right?"

"Yes, of course. I'm British and live here with a green card, why?"

"Well, Julia's parents don't want her flying home by herself. They have heard that she is getting on really well with you, so they are asking if you could fly to Sydney with her next Monday."

"*What?!*"

"I know, that's what I thought, but hey, you get to go to Sydney. Can you? Are you available? Do you even want to?"

Deborah took a deep breath. This was sooo weird, but no weirder than some of the other things that had happened in her life, so she accepted.

"But it's too far to go to just turn around and come back. What if I want to stay for longer, maybe a week?"

"Uh, yeah, let me ask them what that could look like and I'll get back to you, but email me your passport number and full name so they can start the bookings."

It had been a few years since Deborah was in Australia and she had always wanted to go back, but she never imagined it would be like this. Later that day, the advisor called back to say that they couldn't keep paying her once she arrived in Australia, but that they were happy for her to stay in their guest house and to change the date of the return ticket.

As the week went on, Julia seemed to get more agitated. There were some screamy phone calls with her mother and some very late nights. The final exam was Thursday, and that night, Deborah realized she still didn't even know what Julia was actually studying.

"So it looks like I'm coming to Sydney with you."

Julia rolled her eyes. "They treat me like a baby. If they think I'm so incapable, why did they let me come here in the first place?"

"I don't know… Maybe they want to be able to trust you, but got scared by what happened."

Julia got up from the kitchen table after swallowing her pills and went back into her room. *So that was a bit of progress*, Deborah congratulated herself. *Two actual sentences. I wonder where they got the idea that we get on so well?*

Monday night came and a taxi arrived to pick them up from the hotel. The Qantas nonstop flight was due to leave at 1 a.m. After the bags were loaded onto the trolleys at the curb, they made their way into the terminal to check in. Julia said nothing as they stood in line but was constantly looking around, scanning the crowd. Deborah hadn't given up trying to make conversation, but also knew not to push it, so they shuffled along in between the ropes in silence with all the other passengers. Once they had checked in, Deborah picked up her carry-on and started to walk toward security, but as she looked around, Julia was gone! *Oh no!* This was Deborah's last assignment, to get Julia on the plane and home safely! Where was she?!

Where are you?!

Don't worry, I'll be there in a few minutes

Not good enough, come back NOW!

12

At least she hadn't gone far…or had she? *Had she run off, was she in a taxi headed for Mexico?!* Deborah looked around frantically; there weren't that many people in the terminal, as it was late. Scanning the area she noticed what looked like Julia's legs poking out of the bottom of a photobooth and another pair of legs facing her! She ran over and banged loudly on the side. The curtain pulled back and Julia looked out, a young man holding her in an embrace.

"I said I'll be there in a few minutes!"

"If you wanted to say goodbye to someone why didn't you just say so?"

Julia pulled the curtain back and Deborah stepped back a few feet. Finally, they came out and said a final goodbye. The two women then walked in silence through security and immigration, got a drink each, and sat down near their gate in silence waiting to board.

The flight was excruciatingly long but thankfully uneventful. Boringly, peacefully uneventful. Eventually, Julia was able to message her parents that they had arrived so that by the time they were done with passports and luggage, they would be waiting.

"Where are they?" Deborah inquired as they emerged into the waiting crowd.

"Not here. You didn't think they would *actually* get out and come in, did you?"

"How would I know anything?"

Julia pushed her luggage trolley through the crowds and out the main door into the warm, fresh air. She looked up and down, then headed left toward a black limo.

"Darling, oh my poor darling!" A very well-dressed woman had jumped out of the back of the car and ran awkwardly in high heels toward Julia with her arms out. Julia hugged her, but it was soon over and they got into the limo. Deborah came up behind and stood with the luggage, quite bewildered. The limo driver opened the trunk and started to load up the bags.

"Welcome to the circus," mumbled the driver under his breath.

Deborah was confused…was she staff and should ride in the front with him, or was she now a guest and could get in the back?

Julia's mum jumped out of the car again apologizing profusely, introduced herself as Sylvie, and beckoned Deborah to come inside. She had been in a few limos in her time in Hollywood so it wasn't so unusual, but Deborah wasn't quite sure what to make of Julia's family.

"And this is my husband, Richard."

Richard was a stern-looking man, tanned and dressed like he had just come from a game of golf. He had his arm around Julia and she had her head on his shoulder.

"G'day, nice to meet you," offered Richard. "We are very grateful for everything you have done for our precious girl."

"Of course." Deborah smiled but was getting more and more confused. She tried to catch Julia's eye, but nothing. Julia was staring out the window as the limo smoothly pulled out toward the Sydney skyline.

Arriving at the house, the limo pulled into a long driveway up to the front door of a palatial-looking home. The driver got out and opened the doors.

"We are so happy that you wanted to stay. Make a vacation of it!" advised Sylvie. "Stay in the car and Lonnie will take you on to the guest house. Please let us know if you need anything." With that, Sylvie and Julia got out, but Richard stayed sitting in the limo…he didn't seem to be getting out either. Deborah was confused. She then noticed a young man hurrying out of the house pushing a wheelchair. He came right up to the limo, reached down to help Richard into the chair, and then wheeled him through the front door into the house.

Before she knew it, the doors were all closed again and Lonnie was driving back down the driveway. Deborah tapped on the glass. "Where are we going?" She was so confused.

"To the club."

"What club?"

"The Killarney Country Club and Golf Course. The Sharpes have a suite there, that's where you are staying. They didn't tell you?"

"Nope, nobody tells me anything."

"Sounds about right."

Deborah sat back and watched as the limo drove past more massive mansion-style homes and then into the driveway of the country club. He pulled up at the main entrance and the concierge directed someone to collect her bags.

"This way, Ms. Deborah."

Deborah turned to Lonnie, "Has there been some mistake or misunderstanding? I can't afford this. I thought I was staying in a guest house at their home?"

"It's okay, the Sharpes have a membership suite that is paid for year-round so it makes no difference to them if you stay here. Mr. Richard used to stay here a lot when he had golf tournaments but since his accident he doesn't play, so he doesn't use the room. Someone might as well take advantage of it. There is a pool and a game room you can use, and a little kitchen in the suite if you don't want to pay extra for the club dining room. Enjoy. And if you need anything, just get the front desk to call me." He jumped back in the limo and drove off.

Deborah was not sure what to make of any of it, but she followed the young woman who had put her bags on a trolley through the lobby, down a shady path, alongside the dining room and past a large function room. She saw signs to the pool and jacuzzi and, out in front of it all, spread the exclusive golf course garnished with palm trees, majestic cypress trees and beautiful, exotic flowers. They arrived at the suite which had a stunning view of the lake and fountain, with its own private patio. She stepped inside to find a small living room, kitchenette, bedroom and bathroom. It was all beautifully furnished.

"I hope you have a wonderful stay, please let us know if you need anything. Mrs. Sylvie said I should look after you."

"Thank you, what is your name?"

"Lucia, ma'am."

"Oh, please just call me Deborah. The only thing I need is to rent a car."

"Oh yes, they can help you at the front desk."

"Thank you so much."

Lucia left, and Deborah went out onto the patio, sat in a wicker chair with large, soft, inviting pillows, and put her feet up on a small wooden table. The weirdness was over, her mission accomplished, and now, she could finally relax.

3
Bowral

After Deborah had rented a car and bought some groceries, she decided to take a trip out to the town where she had stayed ten years before. She had done all the usual Sydney sightseeing when she was there last time, so going back to her old haunts seemed like a good idea. She and her movie colleagues had stayed in the small town of Bowral for six months while filming the movie *Babe*, so she bought a map and drove the two hours out into the bush. The countryside was lush and green, and she marveled at how enormous the sky was as memories started to float back about the time she had spent there all those years before. Bowral was a weekend getaway for Sydney-ites, a small, rural but sophisticated town south of the metropolis settled in Kangaroo Valley. She had met Steve there, which had led her to move to L.A. The relationship only lasted a few years, but she now had a life of her own and felt very settled in California. The town was much the same as before—the shops and cafés, hardware store, and bakery were all still there. She walked up and down the high street reminiscing as she took in the scene.

Deborah remembered how last time she was there she had experienced the most sudden, terrifying pain. She had woken up one morning to find her chin stuck down on her right collarbone totally unable to move, virtually paralyzed from her head to her waist. She had stumbled her way to a chiropractor in the next village who had given her an X-ray and the diagnosis of a broken neck! Deborah had been mugged two years before that first trip to Australia and had pulled herself out of the depths of PTSD. Her neck had always been sore and painful, but this was a huge shock. She also had three herniated discs in her lower back, and the chiropractor had done an amazing job of returning full movement and mobility to her spine. *Was the doctor still there*, she wondered... She got back in the car and made her way as best as she could remember to find the small clinic. Would he remember her after ten years?

She parked outside the building where she thought the chiropractor's office was but didn't see anything familiar. She had gone to see this doctor nearly every day, and then every other day, for weeks of treatment. She was sure it was on this corner, but a hair salon was now in residence. Deborah was disappointed, but as she had come so far, she thought she could at least ask, in case he had moved somewhere nearby. As she pushed open the door of Margie's Hair and Nail Parlor, the smell of hairspray and nail polish wafted through the air right up her nose.

"G'day, my lovely! What can we do for you? A trim? Wash and blow-dry?" A middle-aged lady with fabulously coiffed hair called over from the chair where she was putting in heated rollers for a customer. Behind her was a nail salon in the area where the examining rooms used to be.

"Hi. No, uh, I'm looking for the chiropractor who used to be here?"

"Oh, Dr. Dan? Gosh, so sorry luv, but he moved out about eight years ago. Went up to the city I think. Are you sick, my lovely? I have some aspirin in my desk somewhere if you are feeling a bit crook?" She put her comb down and bustled over to her desk.

"Oh no, not at all. He was very kind to me and I just wanted to tell him how I was doing, that's all."

"Oh, well sure, he was a lovely fellow, grew up here, you know. Now let me think, who would know…" She picked up her phone and dialed gingerly with her long painted nails. "Angie? G'day, my sweet… No, no, everything's just tip-top. Hey, do you have an address for Dr. Dan, you know his new place in the city? There's a Pommy girl here looking to catch up with him…Yes…yes…uh-huh, okay, thanks my lovely, you too." She wrote down an address and handed it to Deborah. "There you go, sweetheart, try that."

"Wow, amazing, thank you so much!"

"No worries, good luck and toodle pip as they say where you come from. You are a Pommy, right?"

Deborah laughed, "Yes, I'm a Pommy, and thank you."

As she got back in the rental car to drive back up to Sydney, Deborah started to think about how much pain she had been in back then, how frightening it was, and how the chiropractor had told her that she would have to have regular treatments for the rest of her life. She followed his directions and had seen a chiropractor every month for years after that just to keep from seizing up again, but there were always these really painful flare-ups. She would get such agonizing back spasms she would need to lie on the floor for days, and when they were off-the-charts bad, she would be doubled over in agony, unable to stand upright. There were at least two times when she was paralyzed from the chest down, unable to move her legs. Thank God they were only temporary, but at the time she didn't know this, so it had been a constant terrifying battle, never knowing when it would strike again. As she drove back through Kangaroo Valley, past signs for Mitagong and Wollongong, she thought about all the chiropractor visits in London and then L.A., being crunched and twisted, heated up and rolled over, whatever the latest treatment was for back and neck pain. She hated the thought of needles so she had never entertained the idea of acupuncture, and thankfully no one had ever suggested surgery. Sometimes the treatments would help and sometimes she despaired of ever walking again. But it would always pass until the next episode. Driving through the beautiful Australian countryside, she tried to remember her last bad episode… She thought back over the last few years and realized that she couldn't actually remember when it was… In fact, as she tried to remember, she couldn't think of a bad episode for about… *Hold on*, thought Deborah. She had cancelled her monthly chiropractic appointments when she had taken that trip to Israel… Funny how she never needed to make another one since, and that was a couple of years ago now. In fact, she couldn't remember having any pain in…well…since she had come across this new understanding of the mind that had led her to work as a counselor at the SMDC. *Wow!* thought Deborah. How could it be that by understanding how the mind works, her pain had gone away? This was unbelievable. She checked in with her back for a moment. No pain. Her neck and shoulders. No pain. In fact, her back felt strong, stronger than she had felt in years!

This was amazing! She felt excited at the realization that she hadn't done *anything* to get rid of the pain and yet it was all gone. She hadn't worked on it or applied her new understanding to it, it had…just…gone! Now she really wanted to see Dan Gieger, the chiropractor. She had so many questions. How can a herniated disc not hurt anymore? How could the numbness that she would feel in her arm sometimes have completely gone away? Her right leg was still longer than her left! She stepped on the gas a little more in the excitement of what this could all mean.

When she got back to the country club, there were some fresh flowers in a vase on the kitchen table and her groceries had all been put away. This made her feel a bit uneasy; she wasn't used to people being in her stuff, even if they were being nice. She looked around and everything was neatly folded or put away. *Huh?* She took out one of her books and spent the rest of the evening reading on the porch overlooking the fountain in the distant lake. Tomorrow she would find Dr. Dan and see what he had to say.

It was another perfect Aussie day. The sun was up and there was a slight breeze from the harbor as she made her way to the rental car. The concierge had told her that the address of the clinic was near the university hospital, which made sense, so she took the drive across the city to find the Sydney Pain Clinic. It was a new building, very modern-looking and quite imposing—nothing like the small, quaint country office near Bowral. *Dr. Dan must be doing okay for himself*, mused Deborah.

She walked into the main reception area, where there were two young women behind the desk and several people waiting in chairs.

"Can I help you?" one of the women kindly inquired.

"Uh, yes, I'm looking for Dr. Gieger?"

"Do you have an appointment?"

"No, I am an old patient of his and I just wanted to say hi." Deborah felt a bit foolish as the receptionist raised an eyebrow.

"Well, you will have to make an appointment. The earliest I can give you is in three weeks."

"Oh, no. I'm only here from L.A. for one week. I was here working on a movie ten years ago, you see, and I was partially paralyzed. Dr. Gieger did an amazing job to get full movement back in my neck. I was really hoping to see him. I guess…uh, could I leave him a note?"

Another young woman stepped forward. She had a much more helpful presence about her and gave Deborah a big, genuine smile. "Hi, I'm Melanie, Dr. Gieger's personal assistant. I can give it to him in a few minutes when his next patient goes in, if you like?"

"Oh, that would be amazing, thank you!" The receptionist handed Deborah a notepad and pen, and she wrote a few lines about the movie *Babe*, how he had treated her neck, that she was here for just a few days, and if he had time for a few questions.

"Take a seat and I'll see what I can do."

"Thank you, I really appreciate it!"

Deborah sat with the others waiting amongst the tropical plant displays. Some were reading magazines, others were hanging onto their chairs, clearly in pain, ever hopeful that relief was just on the other side of those doors. A few people were called by physios and massage therapists in white uniforms to the treatment rooms beyond. She waited, wondering if this was a mistake. He probably wouldn't even remember her.

"Deborah, please come this way." Melanie beckoned

her over. "He only has a few minutes but wants to say hello." She led Deborah around the corner and showed her into a spacious office. Light was streaming in from an ornate courtyard with a fountain and tropical greenery. Dr. Gieger came toward her, a big smile on his face. She could sense his genuine, warm surprise.

"How nice to see you again! I can't believe it's been ten years!"

"Yes! Things have changed for you too, I see!" Deborah looked admiringly around his office at the diplomas and certificates of achievement.

"Yes, I went to the States to be part of a research program after you left, and things just took off with all kinds of new treatments. And you? How are you doing?"

"Amazing, thank you. See, my neck moves just fine and I'm pain-free! I have so many questions for you, but I'm only here a week and then I'm back to L.A. I moved there after the movie came out."

"Wow, yes! The movie was amazing, my wife and kids and I went to see it! It was such a treat to see your hard work and Bowral in a big Hollywood movie! It's still our favorite film. Listen, I have a lunch meeting I can push off, would you join me for something to eat? I'll be done in about an hour. I want to hear all about what happened to you in the last ten years!"

"Yes, if you are sure you have time?"

"It's one of the perks of being the boss. I'll tell my assistant to change things and she'll tell you where you can hang out for a bit."

Deborah followed Melanie's advice and walked across the hospital courtyard to a small mall. There were some nice shops and a shady place to sit while she waited. She had picked up some of the pamphlets and brochures from the clinic and read up about the work that Dr. Dan Gieger was doing now. *At the Sydney Pain Clinic, we use the latest advances in state-of-the-art technology to give each patient a unique treatment program with the best specialists available.* It sounded fascinating, but she wondered why he was so keen to meet with her. Surely he had thousands of former patients in the last ten years and he must be so busy. She happily whiled away the hour and then went to the restaurant to get a table. The good doctor came in just a few minutes later.

"Thank you for waiting. I hope this doesn't take you too far off your plans for the day."

"Not at all, I'm on vacation. And besides, I'm curious why you would want to take the time to meet with me?"

"Ah, well, I do have an ulterior motive. But hey, not all my former patients are Academy Award winners, you know!"

Deborah blushed, "I was just part of the team."

They laughed and reminisced for a few minutes while they ordered lunch.

"If I'm correct, you had some broken vertebrae in your neck." Deborah nodded, amazed that he remembered. "And how is it now?"

"Well, it's so funny that you should ask. Ever since I left your office that last time up until about three years ago, I was in almost constant pain. I would have these episodes of agonizing back spasms that would have me on the floor for days. Several times I was rushed to the emergency room during work, and a couple of times I was paralyzed from the chest down. They said it was from the three herniated discs and the two broken vertebrae, C1 and C2. Sometimes I would wake up in the night with my arm numb, and I would get so scared that it would lose circulation while I was asleep and need to be amputated... Then at other times, the sciatic pain shot all the way down to my toes, and I would be terrified the feeling wouldn't come back to my legs!"

"Oh my, that is frightening, and exhausting too. But you say until recently? What happened?"

"Well, I have always been interested in self-development; I trained as a counselor back in London, and when I moved to L.A. I started to work in a community center as a counselor. About three or four years ago I came across some new ideas in understanding the mind. I was so taken by these ideas that I left the movie business and am now working as a coach and a counselor full time. In fact, that's how I came to be back in Sydney—I had to accompany a client here—but that's another story."

"Fascinating, go on." The food had arrived, but Deborah continued.

"Well, as I was driving back from Bowral yesterday, I started thinking about how I stopped my monthly chiropractic appointments about three years ago but I still don't have any pain… In fact, I haven't had a bad episode for about three years and not a *really* bad one in about five or six years! Nothing against chiropractors, I just don't have any pain anymore, and I feel stronger than ever!"

"This is amazing. I mean, not just your story, which is so good to hear, but the timing." The good doctor sprinkled some dressing on his salad. "I don't know if you noticed, but I don't do chiropractic anymore."

"Yes, I saw in your brochure that you taught for a few years at Chicago University. So, what happened? Are you a pain professor now?"

"Well, kind of. I had originally trained as a medical doctor and started out in family practice, but nearly every case I saw was stress-related; it's *the epidemic of the age*. I became so disillusioned with traditional medicine that I trained as a chiropractor, which is when I met you. I then had this chance to join a pain research team in the U.S., but my wife, Tali, and I wanted to raise our kids here, so after it ended, we came back and I started the clinic. We offer our clients an amazing multidisciplinary bio-psycho-social approach, which enables us to give each patient a unique, tailor-made treatment program with a highly qualified team of specialists. We treat the *whole person*."

Dan was understandably very proud of his work and the service he was now providing. "We are always looking into new therapies to offer chronic pain sufferers, as it's so clear that surgery doesn't work or isn't necessary most of the time and the overuse of opiates is already a crisis. When I suggested that you have adjustments for the rest of your life I really was trying to help, but I don't believe that continued chiropractic treatment is necessary now, and I'm so happy and amazed to see that you discovered that for yourself. I'm sorry I didn't give you better directions back then, I just didn't know better, I was doing what I was taught… It's funny, we were taught in chiro school that the body has an innate intelligence, and then we were taught that adjustments would help it heal. If anything, the treatment I gave you was probably as much placebo as it was actual. You were in so much pain, which is frightening, and along I came in a white coat and I made you feel better. My reassurance activated something in you that helped you heal, but you would have healed eventually anyway, I truly believe that."

"And so what therapies do you offer now?" Deborah was captivated!

"Well, the groundbreaking and pioneering work that is being done now is by helping the patient see that, A. either there isn't anything wrong with them structurally, or that their organic/structural condition is not the cause of the pain; and B. that although their pain is real, it's actually coming from suppressed anger. It's hidden in their subconscious." Deborah almost choked on her salad as she tried to stop herself from laughing. "What's so funny?" asked the good doctor innocently.

"*There's no such thing as the subconscious!*" Now it was Dr. Gieger's turn to almost choke on his salad. "I mean, sure, there is the autonomic nervous system, which takes care of things like breathing and digestion and temperature control, etc., and we unconsciously or subconsciously, if you insist, know how to drive a car, or we intuitively know what food or people we don't like without having to think too much about it, but that whole Freudian suppressed rage subconscious thing, sorry." She shook her head and laughed.

"Of course it's hidden in the subconscious, Freud proved it!"

"Proved it?! How?"

"Well, he did tons of research, and we all know that childhood stuff, trauma, and rage are stuffed down there in the subconscious, we've known this for years."

"And how do we know that it's '*stuffed*'...down there...in the *subconscious*?" Deborah pointed down, then up at her head and sideways as if to say, where exactly?

"Because we think it, of course!"

"Okay, but if you can only know it because you think about it, then it isn't *sub*-anything, is it? It's a conscious thought. You can only think thoughts in the moment; even memories or fears about the future are thought in the present moment. We can only be aware of them in this conscious moment. Look, I know people interchange unconscious and subconscious, but when I hear people talking about their subconscious, they are usually referring to fearful thinking, thinking that if they don't analyze or get some control over it, it is going to *get* them. The, uh…the *ghost in the machine*." She put her hands up like a scary monster.

"Dan, may I call you Dan? There is no *subconscious monster* under the bed, that's just thinking about fearful thinking! Look, we are always feeling our thinking, and if our state of mind is on a fairly okay to high level, then generally we feel good. If it's in the basement, then we are probably going to feel lousy. Oh, wow! I just realized why my pain went away! I began to understand how the mind really works, where our experience is actually coming from, and because I stopped scaring myself with my own thoughts, the pain…just went away!"

Dan thought for a second. "But it can't be that simple…"

"Maybe it can?" replied Deborah with a knowing smile.

They ate in silence for a minute and then he asked her to tell him more. Deborah relished the chance to tell him about this new understanding called the Three Principles, the work of Sydney Banks, and how it had revolutionized the way she saw the world and the human experience. Dr. Gieger was riveted.

"I really need to get back to the office, but this is too big for just a lunch and I want to hear more… Are you free tonight? I know Tali will want to hear about this too. Will you come over for dinner?"

"Sure, I'd love that."

4
Bondi Beach

Deborah drove back to the country club feeling elated. She had never expected to even find the chiropractor again, and here she was with an invitation for dinner at his house to talk about the Principles! As she walked thoughtfully toward the suite, she caught sight of someone sitting in the armchair on the patio outside her door. As she got closer she saw that it was Lucia…and she was crying. As soon as she saw Deborah, she jumped up.

"So sorry, madam, I'm so sorry."

"What's the matter?" Lucia looked very embarrassed. "Did something happen to you?"

Lucia looked down at the floor. "They say some money is missing and that they will be searching all the staff!"

"Did you take it?"

"No! No, miss!"

"Then why are you upset? If you didn't take it, then you have nothing to worry about." Lucia ran off and Deborah went into the suite. She lay down on the bed and thought she would rest for an hour or two.

At 7 p.m. she arrived at Dan's home in Bondi. It was a quaint, older house that had been done up much like the California Cottages back in Venice Beach, where she lived in L.A. The view of the famous beach was spectacular as she walked up to the front door.

"Come in, it's such a pleasure to have you here! I'm Tali."

"Thank you! I think we met for about five minutes ten years ago, you probably don't remember." Deborah was still confused by all the fuss.

"Yes, I do, of course! You guys put Bowral on the map and we loved your movie! Our kids watched it over and over. There is so much junk out there, I was so happy for them to be watching something with a bit of quality. Please, come through."

Deborah laughed, enjoying the compliments, and followed her through the beautiful family home to the large, bright kitchen, which opened up to a wooden deck overlooking the bay. Dan was drinking a beer with his feet up, and the kids were hanging out in the garden. "Wow, this is such a treat, thank you. You must be tired after a long day of seeing patients."

"Yes, so I sit here and watch the sun go down. What could be better? Now, tell me more about these ideas of yours, these Three Principles. Tali, come and listen, the salad can wait."

Tali invited Deborah to pull up a chair and joined Dan looking out at the view.

"I'm really telling you about the amazing insights that were put together by the man I told you about, Sydney Banks, back in the 1970's. He was on a retreat near Vancouver and had what you could call a 'spiritual enlightenment' experience. I'm not doing it justice, but he saw that we are always living in a moment-to-moment, thought-created world. He saw beyond thought and how we create reality for ourselves using the Principles of Mind, Thought, and Consciousness."

"Dan told me you guys had an interesting conversation at lunch. I did Psychology 101 in college, but I hear you don't agree with Freud? That's pretty brave of you. I mean, we were taught it like it was gospel, that the subconscious is as real as, say, the respiratory system and the gallbladder."

"Sure, but if you think about it, it's really just a concept, and concepts are made of thought. There is no scientific proof."

"I guess…but it's been regarded as true for so long."

"Only about a hundred years, which isn't that long when you think about it. People thought the world was flat for a lot longer!"

"And you Pommies thought it was a good idea to send starving children thousands of miles across the sea to Australia for stealing a loaf of bread!" laughed Tali.

Deborah waved an apology on behalf of Queen Victoria.

"So, you're saying that this is a new way to understand the mind, a shift in understanding? Like a…a paradigm shift? Like, we finally understood that washing our hands stops the spread of germs?" asked Dan.

"Yes, exactly!" Deborah took a sip of the fresh, homemade lemonade. "Ooh, that's good, thank you. Yes, this whole subconscious, submerged anger thing is *so* last century."

Dan laughed, "I guess that's one way to put it. I mean, a lot of people got well just from reading Dr. Sarno's[4-1] books about back pain; he originally used what he called 'knowledge therapy,' which, from what you are saying, would be like new thinking or insight?"

"Sure, by giving them 'knowledge,' they started having new thoughts. I imagine that took away the unknown, which, when you are in pain, is half the fear, and I'm guessing this calmed their thinking down, so they slept better and felt better."

Dan agreed. It had been his life's work to understand the connection of the mind and body. "Dr. Sarno explained that pain was coming from a dysregulated nervous system, which led to poor blood flow, meaning that not enough oxygen was getting to the muscles. And then with the brain-mapping research we did in Chicago about how chronic pain shows up in the emotional part of the brain…I mean…" Dan was battling with something. "But if the pain isn't coming from the herniated disc or the torn rotator cuff because it's actually being created by the amygdala, the fight-or-flight system, then lack of oxygen can't produce pain either! I mean, they are both physical, so why one and not the other, right? Hmm… This has always bothered me. And I've always been intrigued by how information could really transform so many people… Information doesn't guarantee transformation. Trust me, I have met plenty of Ph.D.'s who are full of knowledge and information but are also full of…well, who are very untransformed, to say it politely. Hey, are you familiar with Candace Pert[4-2]?"

"Don't think so…"

"I have her book here, somewhere." Dan jumped up, went into the living room, and quickly returned with a paperback. "Somewhere in here, she talks about the debate between William James and his student Walter Cannon when he was teaching at Harvard back in the late 1800's. Here, look. The debate was about the real source of emotions. One of them said it was physical and the other said it was psychological, and then Candace, a neuroscientist, comes along 100 years later and says it is simultaneous. But it seems you're saying that the whole debate is kind of a … a red herring?"

"Y..e..s…" smiled Deborah slowly, admiring Dan's deep perception. "When you have a shift in consciousness, when you see that it's not *what* you are thinking but that you just got caught up in thinking in a certain way, in seeing the world a certain way, which had a certain set of problems attached to it, then with a shift into new thought, you see it completely differently. You are right, information doesn't create transformation, but insight does. And with that shift, that insight, problems change. They can actually disappear simply by seeing things differently."

"Because those problems were attached or created by the old way of seeing it. They don't exist anymore from the new way of seeing!" said Dan as his eyes grew wide with his realization.

"But pain can't go away just by having…'new thinking,' as you put it, can it?" challenged Tali. She had watched her husband go through several transformations in his career; what was he starting on now?

"It has for many people," responded Dan. He was getting excited by the conversation and started pacing up and down. "Honey, remember when the kids were really little, how an ice cream would stop them from crying about pretty much any bump, injection or injury? And your father, well, he can forget all about his angina the minute your mother parks the car wrong or as soon as the cricket comes on the TV. The physical stuff is still there…but their thinking shifted, so they are in a new experience!"

Deborah nodded in agreement, thrilled that Dan was

getting it so quickly. "Tell me about these therapies you offer."

"Well, as I said, it's a multidisciplinary approach, so we offer a wide range of treatments, from physiotherapy, pilates, homeopathy, Feldenkrais, somatic tracking, massage, as well as various kinds of psychotherapy, DBT, CBT, NLP, EMDR, and EFT—it's new, it's sometimes called Tapping. The biological, psychological and social are all interwoven for all of us, so we use the Mind-Body connection to treat the whole person."

"Wow, you've got the whole alphabet soup of therapies on the menu! And this works?"

"Sure, we get great results, our clients always come back anyway… they love it!"

"Sure they do!" laughed Deborah.

"But…" Dan hesitated, something was bothering him again.

"But what, sweetheart?" Tali was getting a bit nervous.

"Well, I'm never actually sure why…" Dan went to the fridge for another beer.

"Why what?" Now Deborah was curious.

"Why they need to keep coming back. I mean it's good for business, but I'm not sure why it isn't permanent, and that's why I wanted to do more research...to find out why."

"I can tell you why," offered Deborah confidently.

Dan looked up. "Okay?"

"Because if you boil down all those ideas, everything from Freudian analysis to this Tapping thing, all those therapies from A to Z, what's happening is that they are helping the patients' thinking to slow down. Anxiety and stress are just speeded up thinking after all, so slowing it down calms the nervous system, right?"

"Y...e...s?" said Dan slowly, following along with Deborah's thinking. "We know that the fight-or-flight response has over-activated the nervous system and that's what messes with the blood flow and floods the body with adrenaline and cortisol—I always got that part from Dr. Sarno. But you're saying that all the treatments we are using are just slowing their thinking down and that's why the patient feels better?"

"Exactly! Your clinic is beautiful. I saw the pictures of the therapy rooms—who wouldn't feel better after a massage, the soft music, the essential oils, a kind therapist listening to your problems for a whole hour? It's a break from the hustle and bustle. That special attention is calming."

"So, what's wrong with that?" Tali was getting a little concerned.

"Nothing, but your patients keep coming back because once they leave your clinic, they eventually get all stressed out again. I bet some are stressed before they even get home! Traffic, kids, career, and mortgages can be overwhelming sometimes. Until they understand how their minds work, they will have to keep coming back for more...*calm*. Dan, you are running a very fancy gas station: your customers come and fill up on calm, and when they run out of calm, they feel low and they come back for a top-up. Great business model." Deborah smiled at them both.

"You are making me nervous." Tali got up to go finish the supper.

Dan sat quite still for a minute and then nodded his head in agreement.

"Look, I don't think there is anything wrong with massage and pilates or physio, especially if someone is recovering from surgery or a stroke for example, or is in so much pain they can't hear what you are saying," said

Deborah. "But if you have told them there is nothing wrong physically and that the pain is stress-induced, encouraging them to focus on the body is just adding to the problem by telling them that it needs fixing. If the problem is in their mind, isn't that where you should be focusing their attention?"

"But we do! We have amazing psychotherapists, they do all kinds of inner child work and get people journaling and doing expressive writing. And Tapping is…"

"But that's just more thinking!" interrupted Deborah. "You are trying to fix the content of people's thoughts, the way they think, what they think. That's a distraction, a misunderstanding. By giving them something to do, the writing, the tapping, you are confirming the lie that there is something wrong that needs fixing. It's like you are saying the shadow on the wall is a real monster and here's what they can do to fight it! I'm suggesting to go upstream a little further. The answer isn't in *what* they are thinking, but *that* they are thinking! Once people insightfully understand how the mind works, where their experience is actually coming from, they become free of the need to analyze and dig around in the past or use treatments and techniques or *do anything* to solve thinking that has already passed!"

Dan stared at her in amazement. His whole vision of what health and well-being meant was changing before his eyes. "And besides," continued Deborah, "there isn't any healing in the past; the past doesn't exist! Listen, this is my favorite quote from Syd Banks:

'If only people could learn not to be afraid of their own experience, that alone would change the world.'"

Dan sat silently for a moment as it sunk in. "Wow, that really does change everything… So many of my patients are terrified by their own experience and most of the time it's not even about anything…well, *real*."

"Ah, but it is to them," replied Deborah. "Remember, we are all living in a thought-created world, so if their thoughts are low, stressful and anxious, then they are going to feel low, stressed and anxious, and their world becomes a very scary place, it becomes constricted. When that becomes our reality, when we fall for the illusion that something is real, we *have* to do something about it, hence all the treatments and alphabet soup of therapies. That's why I was in so much pain for such a long time after my injuries healed, my muscles became constricted, and why it went away when I had the insight that I was the one innocently creating it."

Tali put out the Chinese chicken salad and Dan started to cut up some crusty homemade bread. Dan knew he had put his wife through a lot with the changes he had already made with his career. She had stood by him as he went from country doctor to researcher in the States and then back to start the new clinic. She was confident that his deep desire to help his patients was coming from an intuitive connection to healing, but were things about to change again?

"This looks delicious, thank you. I hope you aren't regretting inviting me!"

"Not at all, this is fascinating," replied Dan, but Tali wasn't so sure. They continued to talk and share experiences. It was a lively evening. The kids joined them and asked about Hollywood and all the famous people she had met.

"I think I'm getting it," reflected Dan. "When I changed from practicing as an MD to chiropractic it seemed to many people like I had lost it, but I knew I had to change the way I helped people get well. Then I saw that I was still looking in the wrong direction and that led me to setting up the new clinic. It's a journey, right?" He paused again. He couldn't put his finger on it but he could feel something forming. "So Thought, this gift of Thought as you call it, is how we experience…well, everything? Whether it's being hungry or angry?"

"Mad or bad," agreed Deborah.

"Sore or sulky, burning or…yearning?" added Dan, laughing.

"Itchy or…bitchy." Tali put her hands over her mouth when she realized the kids heard what she had said, then everyone fell around laughing.

"Exactly!" cried Deborah. "Symptoms are thought in physical form. That doesn't mean thought created them necessarily, but that it's the form they took in that moment. In the next moment, it might be an emotion or hunger or inspiration. Thought is fluid and always creating our experience…"

"I can't wait to see the look on Archie's face when you tell him about this, he is going to plotz!" announced Dan.

"Sorry, when I tell who about what?" Deborah didn't understand.

"Ah, sorry. Yes, I need to tell you what this is all about. See, we really do love your movie and it's great to see you again, but it's confession time." Dan looked at his wife and then back at Deborah. "You see, I give all new patients a full medical exam including blood work and X-rays to rule out anything organic or structural when they first come to the clinic, then I work out a comprehensive treatment plan and hand them over to the therapists and practitioners, depending on what they need. It reassures people to hear from a medical doctor that there is either nothing physically wrong with them or that their pain is not caused by their previous diagnoses. Nurturing is an important part of our treatment plan. I'm about to start a new pain research program and I thought you would be a good candidate, what with your medical history, but now I'm thinking...I'm thinking that you might be more suited as researcher rather than patient."

Deborah was stumped for a moment; she knew it sounded like an amazing opportunity but she wasn't sure what on earth she would be getting into.

"Deborah, if I can get, say, ten or 15 patients together for you to present your ideas to, would you be willing?"

Deborah was taken aback. "Uh, you mean introduce them to the Three Principles and see how it affects their pain?"

"Yes, exactly. It helped you, don't you want to see if it can help others?"

"Sure I do, that sounds amazing, but I'm only here for another few days. That would take months, no?"

"Well, a couple of weeks probably. We already have nearly everything in place, we would just change the model. Your ticket can easily be changed, that's not a problem, and I would pay your fee, etc. What do you say?"

Tali stood up suddenly and started to clear the plates away. She was nervous and turned to put her hand firmly on Dan's arm. "Honey, are you sure you don't want to slow down a little? Maybe run this past Archie and the others first? If this is a...a *thing*, it's going to mean a lot of changes at the clinic. No offense, Deborah, it all sounds fascinating, but shouldn't we take some time to look into this more?"

"No worries, my love, it's just research, nothing is changing, and Archie will come around. Besides, this is what I have been looking for! I knew there was something missing, I knew that stressful thinking was at the root of my patients' problems, I just didn't know how to help *them* see it. We have been throwing a whole bunch of mud at the wall hoping something would stick. But that was a mistake—how did you say it?" Dan was on his feet now. "I was busy trying to fix their thinking when I should have seen...I should have seen that you can't heal an illusion!"

He turned back to Deborah. "Will you? Can you stay?"

5

Killarney Country Club

Deborah drove away from Bondi Beach with her head spinning. This was an amazing opportunity, but what did it mean? Did it even matter? It was so exciting! Dan had asked her to stay for an extra two weeks. It would be intense, but it was going to give her so much experience and exposure. She knew it was going to be challenging with the other staff; most of what she was going to say would mean they could be out of a job… Yikes, she was going to be the enemy! *They're going to hate me!* Then she caught herself and stopped overthinking the whole thing. Her thoughts started up again straight away, so she laughed at her humanness and enjoyed the excitement she felt inside. Dan had suggested she give him a day or two to set things up, and in the meantime, he would send her all his relevant medical research to read up on. She lay awake for a while enjoying the serendipity and then gave in to sleep.

She woke up to the morning sun streaming through the

window and went over in her head all the things she needed to do. Change her flight, cancel clients back in L.A., tell Bob the director of the SMDC that she wasn't coming back for another few weeks, and, oh! Where was she going to stay? She couldn't stay on at the country club, could she? After breakfast, she called Lonnie the driver and asked him for advice.

"Listen, love, the Sharpes are loaded and I doubt they will even need the suite. They have a mansion that is half empty, so no harm in asking, eh? I'll give you some Aussie advice for free: '*You can ask anyone anything as long as you are prepared for the answer you don't want to hear.*'"

"Wow, Lonnie, driver *and* philosopher!"

He laughed. "I'm driving Richard over to the club later, why don't I come and get you when I've dropped him off in the lounge?"

"Perfect, thank you."

Deborah took her laptop out onto the patio and found the email from Dan.

I'm very excited about this, Deborah. I hope you are too. Here is my research, and links to some of the most interesting work being done in pain science right now. Don't worry about the medical stuff, I just thought you might find the back story interesting.
All the best.
Dan

'*Back story,*' thought Deborah, that's funny, the story of my back. The research Dan had done in Chicago was fascinating. They had discovered that when acute pain becomes chronic, it actually moves to another part of the brain, the emotional part.[5-1] This made total sense. It confirmed the theory that we are always feeling our thinking, but now she saw how we feel it in our bodies, too. The links to the work of Drs. Sarno, Moseley, and Moskowitz were equally compelling; it was like reading a history of her own journey with pain but from the point of view of science. She was familiar with the fight-or-flight response; she had studied it in London when she trained with the Islington Crisis Center. There had been a few presentations by a very feminist emergency room nurse and extensive homework on how various systems in the body, like fertility and digestion, get messed up when people are over-stressed for too long. *Of course*, thought Deborah, *it all makes total sense.*

Just after 3 p.m. Lonnie came over to say that Richard was in the lounge.

"I told him you wanted a word and he said it was okay for you to join him."

"Great, thank you." They walked together back to the main building and Deborah asked him about the Sharpe family. "Do they own a business or property, what's their story?"

"Newspapers, or it was. They have a national and a few locals, which made the family fortune, but then they got into TV and more recently the internet. He had to retire after the golfing accident and then the surgery not working. His brother runs the business now, which of course drives him crazy."

Deborah went into the lounge. Julia's father, Richard, was sitting in his wheelchair facing the golf course at the open French windows.

"Hi, Mr. Sharpe, how are you today?"

"G'day, call me Richard. Would you like a drink?"

"Yes, thank you." She ordered a lemonade and pulled up a chair next to his. Deborah had been curious as to what had happened to him. *Was it appropriate to ask?* she wondered. What kind of accident can you have playing golf, anyway? *Could Mr. Sharpe have been struck by lightning perhaps?*

"How is Julia doing now that she's home?"

"She's okay. Thanks for what you did for her."

"But I really didn't do anything."

"Ah, don't be modest, girl, she really appreciates you."

"But I'm not being modest, we hardly had even a full conversation, so I have no idea what she means. It doesn't matter, but really I just made sure she got here in one piece."

"Well, Sylvie and I appreciate that."

"And I really appreciate you letting me stay here, it's so beautiful and relaxing."

"No worries." He watched some of the members who had been in the bar get into a golf cart and drive out to the first hole.

"Actually, I have been offered some work and will be staying on in Sydney for another two weeks. I, uh…"

"Stay in the suite if you want. Might as well, it'll only be empty if you don't."

"*Really?* I didn't want to presume or take your generosity for granted…?" Richard shook his head and took a sip of his whiskey. "Thank you so much, it really is very generous of you." They sat for a few moments and Deborah wondered if she should leave him alone.

"Ah strewth, *what a drongo!*"

"Who?" Deborah was taken aback.

"That one! He just missed the hole by miles! Idiot shouldn't be allowed near a damn golf club!"

"I'm sorry, I don't know the first thing about golf. The closest I have ever come before this was visiting a friend in Palm Springs!" Richard snorted a laugh. "Is it hard for you to sit here and watch the other members playing?"

Richard Sharpe paused and took in a deep breath. He was a powerful man and not used to being denied anything, especially his favorite sport. "Yeah, it's *a fair suck of the sav*, uh, I mean it's tough at times. I used to play all the time until my back went crook on me. Can't even stand up on my own these days, let alone swing a golf club."

"Did you have an accident?"

Richard nodded. "I was on the 4th hole and I heard this pop in my back as I bent down to pick up the ball— the pain shot through me like a red hot poker! The MRI showed that I had a slipped disc and the surgeon said I needed surgery straight away. They operated and it felt better for a while, but then the pain came back and now I can barely stand without someone there to hold me up."

"That's terrible."

"Damn right!" He took another sip of his drink and blew out a long, frustrated sigh.

"But how could bending over do that?" Deborah was curious; she had been reading about discs and vertebrae and sciatica all morning.

"The surgeon said I had disc degeneration and that had weakened the spine. He said that if I didn't have the surgery it would probably happen again, and then I might never walk again, but hey, guess he was right."

"But it didn't happen again…"

Richard turned to look at her. "What do you mean, love?"

"Well, you said it was okay for a while after the surgery, right?" Richard nodded. "Did you fall or hurt yourself again in some way after that?"

"No, deary, it just started to seize up again."

"So, the surgery didn't work?"

"Yes, it did…for a while."

"For how long exactly?

"About six weeks after it healed."

"I bet it cost a lot."

"Damn right it did. What's your point?" He turned to her, trying to conceal his anger.

"Well, I'm guessing you're a pretty good businessman, and that doesn't sound like a good deal to me. Only six weeks' relief for what, thousands of dollars? What did the surgeon say?"

"He said it was one of those things."

Of course he did. "Richard, can I ask you something?" He raised an eyebrow. "The reason I'm staying on is to do some research into chronic pain relief. Would you be interested in participating in the program?"

"No, thank you!" Richard replied sternly. "I've had enough of doctors and surgeons poking and prodding me for a lifetime. They want to put a machine into my spine now, some kind of spine stimulator thing, but I've had enough. And no acupuncture or other voodoo woo-woo nonsense either!"

"No, no, it's not a medical thing, it would just mean coming to some presentations, joining in a few workshops, that kind of thing. Nothing medical, I promise." Richard grunted dismissively. Deborah suddenly realized that attending workshops probably wasn't his thing. He was used to running a massive national business with a few thousand employees.

"I don't have time to sit around with a bunch of namby-pamby winging drongos complaining about their problems." He looked out across the golf course again, trying to contain his frustration.

"Yes, you are probably right. You have so much to do…what *exactly* is it that you do?" Richard gave her a sideways look. "Look, I'm sure you have a lot of experience that would be useful to the group. I think you would make a great role model for the others and besides, it will mostly be me talking, presenting some new ideas, that's all. I'll give Lonnie a copy of the clinic brochure. No harm looking, eh?"

Richard tapped his fingers on his knee. "Nothing medical?"

"Nope."

"I'll think about it. I'll have to check my schedule, but I'm not promising anything, all right?"

Dan called at about 5 p.m. with a lot to say. "Okay, we're on! Archie blew his nut when I told him I wanted to change things last minute, but he's just the money man and I told him this could be a massive breakthrough for us, so he gave in after a few drinks at lunchtime. It's not really anything to do with the other staff and Melanie is working on getting the patients to agree to a new model, which shouldn't be too hard, people in pain are desperate, and..."

"Ooh, I think I have one for you, too! Do you know the name Richard Sharpe?"

"Sharpey, the newspaper magnate?"

"Uh yeah, I guess."

"How the blazes are you talking to Richard Sharpe? I heard he went a bit recluse-like after some early retirement thing."

"It's his suite I'm staying in at the country club. It was his daughter I had to accompany back here from L.A. Anyway, when I was asking him about staying on, I took a chance and asked about why he was in a wheelchair and he said he got a slipped disc from bending over to pick up a golf ball, had a surgery which didn't work, and is now in so much pain he can't stand up." Dan was laughing his head off. "What's so funny?"

"Sorry. I shouldn't laugh, but discs don't slip and certainly not from bending over! That surgeon saw him coming and made a nice bundle out of the surgery, I bet!"

"And it didn't even work!"

"Of course it didn't. That disc was probably damaged before he bent over, he just didn't know about it. Like you with your broken neck, old Sharpey had been walking around without pain for years, the surgeons only found it because they were looking for a cause, any cause to justify an expensive surgery. Look, it would be amazing to have him in the group. Can you get him to come in for a physical workup tomorrow?"

"Oh no, I promised him no doctors or physicals. He won't come if you make it medical, he's had enough."

"Ah, that's a shame. I need to check him first in order to be in the program and for insurance reasons. Can you try?"

"I'll try, but he's pretty stubborn and intimidating."

Dan laughed, "I bet he is! Okay, come to the clinic tomorrow and meet Archie and the others and we will set you up with an office and everything you need. I've got a really good feeling about this!"

6
Pyrmont

It always amused Deborah to see the names of very English towns so far from home. Areas of Sydney were called Liverpool, Padstow and Guildford. And then out in the country, there were fabulous local names like Wollongong and Jamberoo. As she drove to the clinic she wondered what this new chapter was going to bring. Chronic pain is so difficult, there is so much uncertainty and misunderstanding. It's exhausting, frightening and expensive. To be able to help people get free of that would be incredible. She was met by Melanie, who showed her into a small office on the upper floor. Deborah had never had an office before and felt a little out of place; even at the SMDC in Los Angeles where she did her counseling work she didn't have her own room, it was just a matter of grabbing what was available. She was used to messy, dirty workshops and movie sets, and the occasional production meeting at Universal Studios or the Beverly Wilshire Hotel, but an actual office of her own was never something she imagined for herself.

"There is coffee, etc. in the kitchen downstairs and a photocopier and printer in my office that you can use. I have nine definite patients already who have agreed to switch to this new program and am waiting to hear back from about five more. They are all filling in questionnaires—here's what I have already. I'll bring you more as they come in, and let me know if you need anything else. Dan told me a little about what you are doing; it sounds fascinating." With that, Melanie gave her a big "good luck" smile, shut the door and left her to it.

It all felt a little strange, everything was so new: the whole medical thing, the corporate office thing. What were they expecting from her? She sat for a moment and watched as her thoughts got a little fast, and then realized that actually, she was presenting something new to them so everyone was having a new experience and felt calm again. She decided to just follow what came next. This plan of letting it unfold seemed to be working so far, so she looked over the questionnaires, intrigued to see who she would be meeting next week.

The first was a woman in her 50s who had been diagnosed with frozen shoulder. Deborah looked up frozen shoulder on the internet and suddenly felt scared. She didn't know what any of these medical diagnoses were. How was she going to do this? And then she remembered Dan hadn't hired her as a medic, so no one was expecting her to be an expert overnight. The next had sciatica—*Deborah knew all about that.* The other two had neck pain and back pain. Okay, not too scary, Deborah was familiar with all of these. They had all tried the traditional approach of either surgery and medications, even multiple surgeries, and the endless rounds of chiropractors and acupuncture, plus a whole array of alternative therapies Deborah had never heard of, and had ended up here at the clinic since nothing had worked.

The phone rang. Deborah jumped; she wasn't expecting that.

"Hi, it's Melanie. Dan says can you come down to the conference room to meet Archie? It's on the ground floor at the end of the corridor."

She had faced many intimidating people when working in the movie business, from directors like Steven Spielberg and Nora Ephron, to that time she had to fix the dinosaur head for Elizabeth Taylor in front of a bunch of expert special effects guys when she had no idea what she was doing, but this was the first time she was going to have to sell her counseling work to someone and had no idea what she was going to say. She gathered up the questionnaires to have something to hold as she walked in. She felt she needed to look like an organized and professional researcher even if she didn't feel like one, and then felt a wave of calm as she remembered to stick to what she knew.

The conference room was a spacious, light, airy room and Dan and Archie were sitting at one end of a large table, drinking coffee.

"Deborah, come in, come in. Please meet my financial partner, Archimedes Alexopoulos."

Archie smiled and welcomed Deborah. He was cautious but friendly, and they discussed the plan for the research program of workshops and videos. Each person would need to schedule a private meeting with her and Dan during the week and then again to follow up in the week after. He was very clear that he had low expectations, which gave Deborah some relief.

"So, who is this joker Syd Banks, anyway?" asked Archie.

Deborah laughed, "He was a Scotsman who ended up in Vancouver in the 1970's and, like a lot of people back then, was trying all kinds of self-realization things to fix his insecurity. He had a transformational enlightenment experience, which he shared with everyone who wanted to hear about it for the next 30-something years. He passed away a few years ago, but allowed some videos to be made toward the end. I suggest you come and sit in, or at least watch the videos, and you will find out more."

"Maybe, if only to see what it is you are spending our money on. Anyway, is this room good for you to work in with your group?"

Deborah looked around, "Yes, it's beautiful, thank you. What about the other staff, what have you decided to tell them?"

Archie shrugged, "Nothing. They are all independent contractors, they don't have a say in how we run the business. Dan here is the doctor and clinical director so it's kinda up to him, I just make sure he makes us both money."

"We have a staff meeting first thing tomorrow morning and I will introduce you. I'm going to say it's an addition to our facility. I don't want to upset anyone, they are an amazing group of people."

"I don't want to upset anyone either, but we both know that if they hear what I am talking about they might feel a bit threatened."

"But didn't you show me last night that no one can make anyone feel anything, that it's only coming from their thoughts?"

"Touché, Dr. Dan! Yes, absolutely." They both laughed.

Archie shook his head as he stood up. "I guess I'm not in on the joke, but just don't go upsetting anyone too much, as we need them to keep our customers happy while you crazy kids work this out." He opened the door and then turned back, "I hear you might be getting Richard Sharpe to come, too?"

"Maybe. I think he might just be an observer though, he's very skeptical."

"Okay, that's going to be interesting."

Deborah went back to her office and was surprised to find that Melanie had left some more questionnaires and a message.

> *If you still want me to come to your little program,*
> *I might have time to stick my head round the corner, but <u>NO</u> doctors.*
> *Richard*

Deborah was excited that Richard had called. Maybe she could help him and he could get free of his anger, even if his back was totally messed up. She called him back.

"Hi Richard, I just got your message. I'm so pleased you are coming."

"I didn't say I'm coming, I'm just letting you know that I might have some time available."

"That's fine. And I promise you no doctors will poke you but that will mean you can only be an observer, not part of the actual research. Is that okay?"

Richard hesitated. "Right. Just keeping an eye on you. Call Lonnie and tell him the address and time…but I'm still not saying I'm coming, mind you, so don't count on me…"

"Sure, no worries mate, see ya Monday," said Deborah

in her best Aussie accent, trying to make him laugh.

He didn't laugh, but she could feel him smile just a little.

She looked through the other questionnaires. There were more back and neck pains, some eczema and IBS, and a woman with migraines. 'Plantar fasciitis,' read Deborah, *What's that?* she wondered. She looked it up and found out it was foot pain. Each person had been asked the same questions, things like what was the diagnosis, how long they had had the pain, and what other treatments and therapies had they tried. They also had to fill out the McGill Pain Questionnaire, a standard in the pain research world. For the foot pain, the patient had written that one doctor had told her it was because of overuse. *Overuse?!* thought Deborah. How can you overuse your feet? Another one, a woman in her 30s, had had 9 surgeries on her back—*9?! What?!*[6-1] First of all, didn't she get that it wasn't working after about five or six? And what doctor keeps operating on a clearly desperate person with no hope of success? Deborah was beginning to see the extent of the desperation of what people in pain go through. She herself had managed to avoid such interventions and only kept to chiropractors and hot water bottles. Many of these people had not only been the victims of injuries and trauma, but the added injury and trauma of the treatments they were then given, many paying highly not just in money, but in more pain and despair.

Dan had arranged a meeting with her at the end of his day, so she went down to see if he was ready. Melanie informed her that he was running late and needed another 15 minutes, so she took a look around the clinic. It was so nicely laid out, with soft music playing and that soothing smell of massage oil. Was it lavender, she wondered? She went into the small kitchen to make herself some tea. There was a young woman in a white T-shirt, white cotton trousers and white sneakers making tea, too.

"Hi, I'm Deborah."

"Oh, hi, I'm Laura, nice to meet you."

"Can you tell me what that wonderful smell is? I'm guessing it's from the massage oil they use here?"

"Oh, yes, it's lavender. I'm one of the massage therapists."

"Thank you, it's so relaxing."

"Yes, but you can probably smell eucalyptus, too. Tony, the other massage therapist, loves to use eucalyptus. It's organically grown locally. Are you here for treatment?"

"No. I'm actually an old patient from the days when Dr. Dan was out near Bowral. We are just catching up and sharing our news." Deborah wasn't quite sure how much she should say, so she kept it very general. "So nice to meet you."

"You too."

Melanie called to her that Dan was finished with his last patient, so she took her tea into his office. He was washing his hands as he welcomed her in.

"Okay, tell me how it's going."

"Well, it's been a fascinating day. I have read over about 12 questionnaires and a lot of your research. I can't believe some of the things I have read. One woman was told she had *long neck syndrome*! What on earth does that mean?"

"Well, who knows? There are a lot of theories out there and of course, most of them are trying to sell their treatments. I don't blame them and most of them really do care, they are just doing what makes sense to them from the training they have had. When I was in the U.S. I met one young doctor who got very angry with me. He was a knee surgeon who had this supposedly revolutionary new approach in that he *danced* with his patients after surgery. He claimed a very high success rate."

"Of course he did. What old granny wouldn't feel better having a dance with a young, handsome doctor!" laughed Deborah. "They felt special and cared for, their thinking improved and therefore their chances for recovery improved. That's not science, that's just…flattery!"

Dan laughed. "Now that you come to mention it, he was quite handsome. He got angry with me because he said that work like mine was going to take away his career. He asked me how he was supposed to put his kids through college if I kept telling people that his surgery doesn't work."

"He actually said that?"

"Yep. I don't know if you read it yet, but a Dr. J. B. Moseley did placebo knee surgery."[6-2]

"What?!"

"Yeah, he had 180 patients split into three groups. One group had real arthroscopic debridement surgery, another had real arthroscopic lavage, and the other group had placebo surgery."

"How do you do *placebo* surgery?"

"Well, it's all done with a local anesthetic so the patients were partially aware of what he was doing behind the surgical screen over their legs. He made two incisions on each side of everyone's knee. In the surgical groups he went in and did the actual work and on the others, he just asked the nurse for implements, sloshed around some saline and then closed up the incisions. The patients had no idea who had the real surgery until two years later! But here's the thing—they all got better! I read somewhere that people in the placebo group even got up out of wheelchairs and others were playing basketball with their grandkids. Go figure!"

"So this goes to prove that knee surgery is a waste of time? No wonder the dancing doctor didn't like you!"

"Well, yes, that kind of surgery anyway, and they do about 650,000 a year in the U.S. at about $5,000 each, so I totally get why he didn't like me. But more than that, it proves how powerful placebo really is."

"And placebo is really about thought and state of mind, right? Dan, you just proved it, the gift of thought is so powerful that it can heal a damaged knee."

"Well see, that's what my new research was going to be about. Is the knee actually healing or has the pain just gone away?"

"Does it matter?" Dan raised his eyebrows, but Deborah continued. "I mean, if I'm in pain and the pain goes away, would I care if the disc is still slipped out of place or my spine still crooked? No, I'm pain-free and I can dance or play with my grandkids."

"Ah, I'm so glad you mentioned slipped discs. Deborah, a disc can't slip! It's anatomically impossible."

"What? But we hear it all the time, slipped disc. Richard Sharpe had surgery on his slipped disc, he told me."

"I know, but discs are held in place by a strong sheath of cartilage. They just can't slip out of place unless by great force like a...a fall from six floors onto concrete." Deborah started to laugh. "What's so funny?"

"I saw a lot of chiropractors after you got my neck moving again and they would often have pictures of spines that were all deformed and out of shape on their walls and I would think, no wonder my back felt so bad. One guy even had a broken one of those spine models on his desk. One piece of the spine was lying on the table next to it and I remember thinking how painful that must be! Do you get it?" Dan shook his head. "If I see a picture or a model of a spine that is all damaged or broken, my back feels worse. I think they call it autosuggestion? If they can convince me that the pain is coming from something wrong with my back or shoulder or whatever, then I will need more of whatever treatment is being offered! The power of thought… Dan, you mentioned the Harvard psychologist William James yesterday? It's funny, but someone told me something very interesting about him recently. I believe he is regarded as the father of modern American psychology, and about 100 years ago he wrote that he believed all sciences have principles. Physics, chemistry, biology, they all have reliable principles that are true throughout the universe, like aerodynamics and photosynthesis. Gravity, for example, is a reliable principle; if I drop my pen it always goes down, it doesn't randomly go sideways. Apparently James wrote that psychology also has principles, but he didn't know what they were yet. Well, Syd Banks knew, he knew that they are Mind, Thought and Consciousness. In fact, he called them *Universal* Principles."

"Why's that?"

"Because they are the principles of, well, *everything*!"

Deborah woke up Friday morning feeling nervous about the staff meeting. Her heart was pounding fast and her thoughts were immediately speeding into the future. There was so much unknown. Was the staff going to hate her? What if no one in the research group had any improvement? What if someone gets worse and blames her? What if she messes up and Dan is disappointed? She took a deep breath as she became aware of the insecure thoughts flowing through her mind. One of the many wonderful things she had discovered since coming across the Principles was that she didn't have to be scared anymore when she got...well, scared. It was a big day with all kinds of things that would make anyone feel uneasy. New people, public speaking, lots of opportunities for vulnerability, not to mention not being in control. She felt the waves of insecurity wash over her and as she observed the ups and downs, she felt a deep sense of calm below the surface. She knew a deep reservoir of resilience and wisdom was holding her, keeping her safe. The Quiet that she had found as she recovered from her traumas in London had stayed with her and so no matter what happened today and next week, she would be okay. Besides, she hadn't promised anyone anything, so...

"Once more unto the breach?" Dan grinned at her as he opened the door to the conference room.

"Shakespeare's Henry the Fifth battle speech?" queried Deborah as they went into the conference room for the staff meeting. "Is there going to be a fight?" There were about 20 people seated around the table, all chatting, many wearing white of some description, what she now understood was the ubiquitous uniform of a health and wellness practitioner. She recognized Laura the massage therapist and Archie, and then Melanie beckoned her to come sit with her. Once the meeting started, Dan led a discussion about some of the ongoing cases—some had improvements and some had none. Archie went over some numbers and scheduling stuff; it wasn't so different from the staff meetings at the SMDC in L.A. There was a report from one of them about the new website, and then Melanie reminded everyone *again* to please not leave their food in the fridge unlabeled or it will be thrown out.

"And finally, I want to introduce a very special visitor."

Everyone looked at Deborah. "Deborah Stark is here from L.A. and was one of my patients back in the old days when I had the clinic in Mitagong. Not only did she have a full recovery from a partial paralysis due to a fracture at C1 and C2, but she is now a researcher into chronic pain relief! She will be running workshops in our new research program and case studies for us here next week with about fifteen of our new patients, and I expect you all to assist her where necessary. Please give her a very Aussie warm welcome!" Melanie led some clapping, Laura mouthed "good luck" and the others smiled. Deborah breathed a sigh of relief as she didn't have to say anything to the group. As they started to file out, Laura came over to say hello.

"Wow, how exciting! What exactly are you going to be doing?"

"Well, it's nothing hands-on, I'm not a medical person in any form. It will, hopefully, be transformational conversations."

"Okay...sounds fascinating," responded Laura, not quite understanding. "Uh, this is Tony, the other massage therapist I was telling you about, and this is Jordan, she's a psychotherapist, and that's Bernie, he does energy work. Oh, and that's Julie over there, she does EFT."

"So nice to meet you all." They slowly filed out of the conference room and Archie, Dan and Melanie turned to Deborah.

"There, that wasn't too painful, was it?"

"Not at all; in fact, it's never as bad as we think it's going to be."

"Okay then, I think we are all set to start on Monday. Will you join us for Sunday lunch? My parents are coming over and Tali wants you to feel part of the family while you are here."

"Thank you, that's so kind. Will you be slapping a few

steaks on the barby?"
    "Of course!"

7

Monday

Deborah got to the clinic at about 8 a.m., right as Melanie was opening the doors.

"Are you ready?"

"I really don't know," replied Deborah with a mischievous grin.

She went up to her office and looked over the last two questionnaires. 14 in total, and hopefully Richard Sharpe would make 15. She decided to fill one out for him just in case he showed up and called him Patient X. *The very mysterious Patient X,* thought Deborah, amusing herself. The participants had been asked to be there at 9:30 a.m. for a 10 a.m. start. Just after nine, Melanie called up to say some of them were already arriving, so, clipboard in hand, she went down to meet them.

"Hi, I'm Deborah Stark and I'm going to be presenting the program."

"Hi, I'm Mia, I'm so nervous to be here. You won't believe how much pain I'm in. It's been constant ever since

I was about 14 years old. I've had so many surgeries I don't know where to start, and I'm booked in for another after this. My doctor even sent me to a therapist—he said it was all in my head and that I should just relax! Relax?! How can I relax when I'm in so much pain?"

"Yes, I know, it's exhausting." Deborah was partly amused and partly taken aback. Mia was young and frail, like a rabbit caught in headlights. She then turned to the other woman who wanted to hand her an envelope.

"Hi, I'm Karyn. Here are my X-rays and my MRI reports; I wasn't sure if you would need them so I just brought everything."

"Oh no, I don't need anything from your medical records. Dr. Gieger told you that I'm not a medical person, right?"

"Yes, but don't you want to have a look? Everyone who sees them just cringes at how painful it all looks."

"I'm sure. Why don't you give this to Melanie and she will see that Dr. Gieger has it in your file. Would you both like to follow me into the conference room?"

Melanie was setting up with hot and cold drinks. "I'll put out snacks and fruit at the break. Is there anything else you need?"

"I don't think so, thank you."

Mia and Karyn got themselves drinks and started to compare medical war stories. Deborah looked around the room to see where she would stand. She suddenly had a weird feeling that standing was not the right thing to do. She wasn't a teacher and this wasn't a classroom. There were notepads for each person laid out on the conference table; it was all very professional-looking, but Deborah got a sinking feeling. Notepads meant writing and she didn't want them to feel like they were students or being tested.

Writing would mean they wouldn't be fully listening. Something in her gut told her that a circle of chairs would be more conducive to a transformative conversation.

"Melanie, sorry to be a nuisance but I want to move the table, is that possible?"

"I guess. Let me grab Tony, he just walked in. Oh, and I'm giving people name tags if that's okay?"

"Amazing, yes, thank you!"

Deborah started pulling all the chairs out and taking them to the window at the end of the room.

"I'd love to help," offered Karyn, "but my shoulder is in such bad shape."

"No problem at all." Melanie and Tony came in and they all pushed the conference table up to the other end, creating a nice space in the middle to put the chairs in a circle.

"That's so much better, thank you."

More people started to come in and she did her best to put together faces and names with questionnaires. Everyone was there on time. Dan came to do the introductions, but there was no sign of Richard Sharpe. Deborah was a little disappointed but soon forgot about it as the participants took their seats and she cleared her mind, wondering what she would say first. Melanie sat behind the group at the table and Dan stood in front of the window, with the fountain and tropical plants behind him.

"So, here we are! Welcome everyone, welcome. I'm very—oh!" The door flew open with a bang and everyone looked around. It was Lonnie. He was trying to help Richard get in, but Richard had almost run him over with his wheelchair. Melanie jumped up to take away the extra chair and help make room for him in the circle. He waved his hand rudely at her to stop fussing and then refused a name tag. Lonnie sat down with Melanie at the back of the room and everyone settled again. "Okay...so I'm very excited to be starting this new program," announced Dan. "I think it's going to be fascinating for all of us. As you know, it's not a clinical trial for anything medical, and everything said here is absolutely confidential."

"You can't guarantee that!" interrupted Richard sternly.

"Well, everyone else here has signed an NDA, everyone except...well, you, actually." Richard pulled a face. "But I'm sure my assistant will be happy to assist you at the break. Anyway, as I explained to all of you, well, nearly all of you, I won't be doing most of the presentations, I will be supervising, supporting, and reporting. I am passionate about pain relief and so it is with great pleasure that I introduce you to our presenter, Deborah Stark."

Deborah felt her stomach flip. It suddenly felt very real as she thanked Dan for the opportunity and honor to work with him in his clinic.

"Thank you, Dan... I think I'm going to stay seated, as I really want this to be more like a conversation than a lecture. It really is an amazing adventure we are on, the first of its kind as far as I'm aware, in a pain clinic anyway, and so we are taking this journey together." Deborah could hear the words coming out of her mouth and they sounded okay, so she kept going. "I'm going to ask you all to listen with an open mind, listen for something new. When we listen with a quiet, open mind, there is a much better possibility of hearing something new." She gave everyone a big smile and they all seemed to relax a little. "It seems right to start by telling you a little about who I am and how I came to be sitting here.

"I first met Dr. Gieger about ten years ago when I

limped into his clinic, white as a ghost. The clinic was out in Mitagong near Bowral back then, and I was here in Australia to work on a movie for six months. About two years before this, I had been mugged in London—a teenager had thrown a child's bike at my head whilst I was riding fast to get home late at night. The impact was ferocious and landed me in the gutter of a busy London street with cars whizzing past my head as he made off with my bike. I picked myself up and slowly carried on with my life. My neck was always sore and stiff and I made the best of it, but then when I was here working, I suddenly woke up one morning to find my chin stuck down on my right collarbone. I couldn't move my neck at all. I tried a hot shower to loosen it up but the pain was off the charts, so I fumbled around for a Yellow Pages and looked up the nearest chiropractor. Dr. Gieger was in the next village, but I couldn't drive as I couldn't move my head, so I walked. I can't believe I did that now that I come to think about it, but I did, and by the time I stumbled into his office, I was in agony and could barely stand. Luckily, the good doctor had an X-ray machine and promptly told me that I had a fracture in C1 and C2, the bones right at the top of the neck just below the skull. Basically, I had been walking around with a broken neck for two years and didn't know it." Everyone gasped.

"Why didn't you go to a doctor in London?" asked a man. 'Marc' was written large on his name tag.

"Actually I did, the day after the mugging, but my family doctor told me I was okay." The group made some general grumblings about doctors but Deborah continued. "Dr. Gieger was amazing. He got full movement back in my neck, treated me every day for a week and then every other day until I was able to move again. He told me that I would need to have regular treatments for the rest of my life, and so I did. I saw a chiropractor back in London and then in Los Angeles where I moved shortly after, every month for years. But I would still get these horrific back spasms due to three herniated discs which landed me in the emergency room, and several times I was completely paralyzed from the chest down. My neck was always stiff and sometimes I would wake up with my arm completely numb. I tried all kinds of treatments and some of them worked temporarily, but the pain would always come back." The group all nodded in agreement and sympathy.

"Then, about three years ago, I came across a new understanding of the mind. I had trained as a counselor back in the UK and have been counseling people for over 25 years in between movies, but this new understanding is what I want to tell you about. You see, my pain has all gone away. It's been gone since I came to understand that we are always *feeling our thinking*, that we live in a world created by thought. Understanding this leads to clarity, less struggle, and peace of mind. Moment to moment, our thoughts create our reality and at any moment we can step back and observe our thinking because we all have the innate wisdom, well-being, and resilience to do this."

There was a painful silence. The participants just sat there and looked at her, not reacting at all. She couldn't tell if they were impressed or disappointed. Melanie gave her an encouraging smile from behind the group so she kept going.

"Last night when I was thinking about ways to explain this, I came up with an analogy that I'm excited to share with you. Primo, I understand that you have a restaurant?"

"Yes, 'Primo's'—the best Italian a-restaurant in a-Sydney!"

"Wonderful, but imagine for a moment you had a

bakery. What are the basic ingredients you would need to order every week?"

"I guess a-flour…oil…eggs…and a-sugar?"

"Good. Now with those basic ingredients, you could make…cannoli, biscotti—"

"Cornetti, bombolone, sfogliatella, so many a-good Italian cakes!" added Primo with excitement.

"Exactly, and in Mexico, a Mexican baker is making tortillas, in New York, a New York baker is making…doughnuts, bagels and bear claws, and an English baker is making scones and crumpets, yes? With those same basic ingredients, each baker around the world is making an endless array of baked goods with the same basic ingredients; could you see that?" They all agreed. "So what we are going to be talking about this week are the basic ingredients of human psychology, and we are going to call these three ingredients Mind, Thought, and Consciousness. With these basic ingredients, we create all of our experience. All three need to be present for us to experience life.

"Maybe you are all thinking, how can understanding how the mind works help my pain? How can something so simple relieve you of the agony and frustration I know you all feel? Well, that's what we are going to explore together. It helped me, and the amazing thing is that I didn't even *work on my pain,* I didn't apply it to my physical problems. They just went away." Everyone continued to stare at her.

"I'm curious, how many of you here have had any of the following: IBS, allergies, dizziness, asthma, OCD, cystitis, TMJ…?"[7-1] She looked around the room. Every single person had put their hand up for one of these, in addition to what they thought they had come for. "Me too, I had nearly all of these and more, and they have all gone away. I am going to show you how they are all connected and how learning not to be afraid of our experience is going to set us free. I think before we continue, it would be good to go around the room now and we can all introduce ourselves." Richard gave an audible groan, but Deborah was getting used to his antics by now. "Please tell us where you are from, how you spend your day, and what brought you here. Would you like to start?" She turned to the person on her right, a young man called Andrew, who told them he had sciatica and taught computers in a high school. They continued around the room introducing themselves; when it got to Richard he announced, "I feel like I'm in one of those wretched sitcoms with a 12-step meeting that never ends… Hi, I'm Richard, and…*this* is how I spend my day and *this* is why I'm here." He gestured angrily at his wheelchair with both hands.

The next person continued and, as many of them had overindulged everyone's patience with their stories, Deborah suggested they take a 20-minute break.

"I'm really excited about this." The lady on her left was smiling hopefully.

"Thank you…Kate, right? Would you like some tea?" They all got up to get drinks and started to chat amongst themselves as Dan came over to see her.

"Well done! You've broken the ice, now we shall see what they make of the next part. What is the next part?"

"Thanks. Well, I thought I would go into the stress response and how it relates to pain. Please feel free to back me up with any medical info you think is relevant."

"Sure, sounds good." One of the participants was eager to talk to him, so he excused himself and Deborah went over to see Richard, who had wheeled himself to the window in an attempt to avoid the others.

"Thank you for coming, Richard."

"Well, I didn't like to think of you sitting here all on your lonesome because no one showed up for your pity party, but I should have guessed the losers and wingers would be here."

"*Aww, you are soooo sweet.*" She gave him a big grin and introduced him to a man with Costos written on his name tag.

"Costos, this is Richard and he is the kindest, the most warm-hearted bloke you will ever meet."

"G'day, mate," said Costos, putting out his hand enthusiastically but Richard just grunted, so Deborah guided Costos away to meet some of the others.

They slowly all came back to their chairs, and Melanie asked if she could make an announcement.

"Before I forget, as you all know you will need to make an appointment with Deborah and with Dr. Gieger this week and one each next week to follow up. I'll be arranging this, so please come and see me before you leave today to get the times that suit you best. There are plenty of nice restaurants in the mall next to the hospital for lunch, and if you need anything else, please let me know. We plan to be finished by about 3 p.m. each day."

"Thanks, Melanie. So I thought we would start off by talking about stress. Now, I'm sure you have all heard of the flight-or-fight response?"

"Actually there's a third!" interrupted Yohan, "Freeze."

"Thank you, yes, that's right, and we are going to talk about them all in this part of our workshop. Now, let's imagine we are in a real emergency, God forbid, let's say…the building is on fire and we are all running for our lives." Mia let out a gasp of terror. "Your body is now being pumped with adrenaline, cortisol and glucose to give you energy to escape from danger. This is all natural—it's the amazing way our bodies are made to help us survive. The adrenaline makes your heart pump faster, glucose is needed for energy, and the cortisol makes all this metabolize quicker to give you energy to move and think clearly. This is designed to happen for about 30 minutes, and in 72 hours, we are ready to face another emergency. How am I doing, doctor?"

"Great!" said Dan, nodding his head in agreement.

"Okay, please feel free to correct me if I get any medical facts wrong. Now, some other interesting things happen, like certain body systems shut down in order to conserve energy. For example, if you are running for your life, you don't need to be digesting lunch or making babies. So the intelligence of the body shuts down digestion and reproduction, which is why so many people in prolonged stress have digestive and fertility problems. What's a little more interesting is that certain parts of the brain also shut down, like for example…creativity. If you are running for your life, you don't need to be redesigning your living room, and forward planning isn't important at that moment, so you don't need to be thinking about that trip to Bali next summer. Which explains why people with depression and anxiety have trouble thinking clearly about the future or contemplating anything creative. Everyone with me?" They all nodded. "Now, let's dial it down a bit."

"Oh, thank God," said Mia. "I can't take too much of that kind of stress."

Richard threw her a look of disbelief.

"Let's say we are worried about our job or our family or…"

"Or our health?!"

"Yes, Mia, or our health. All those same stress hormones are being pumped into our bodies, only this time we aren't running anywhere. And we aren't stressed or angry or worrying for just 30 minutes, but two hours, four hours, eight to 16 hours a day sometimes, day after day!" Everyone nodded in agreement. "So with all that glucose in the system we are susceptible to diabetes, and all that adrenaline is going to mess with your heart. We get high blood pressure and inflammation, fertility and stomach issues, the list is endless. So you can see that with all this prolonged dysregulation, it's no wonder we have so many other physical problems. The other issue this brings is that when we are constantly feeling anxious and unwell, it's hard to sleep. Sleep is necessary for so many reasons—it's when our bodies really get a chance to heal and repair. This constant state of worry, pain, worry is a vicious cycle, and one we are going to learn how to get out of."

"So, you are saying it's all in our heads?" asked Andrew. "Are you saying that I am imagining my sciatica?!"

"No, not at all! Remember, I had chronic pain too. There were times when my pelvis felt like it had been hit with a baseball bat! *The pain is real*, it's excruciating!" She took a sip of water and continued. "Back in the early 1980's, a rehabilitation doctor in New York by the name of Dr. John Sarno started some pioneering research in this area of Mind-Body medicine and stated that chronic pain was some of the worst pain he had seen in his 40 years of clinical practice. He put together a fascinating body of work and taught that continued anger dysregulates the nervous system, and this causes a depletion of oxygen in the blood that flows to the muscles and *that* is what is causing the pain. He wrote several books describing how many of his patients got better as a result of his explanations."

"What treatment did he give them?" asked Parker, a young mother and doctoral student.

"He didn't." Everyone gave her a quizzical look.

"Actually, many people have gotten well just from reading his books alone and have never even met him! Others got well just from consultations with him in New York and others just from attending lectures. There have been amazing advances in pain research since then, and the theories about what actually causes chronic pain have changed, but what we want to do here with you guys is take this all further, to learn how they really got well."

"Is that what you are going to do with us, curing us with words?" asked Kate.

Deborah gave a reassuring smile. "Please remember, no one has promised anyone here a cure, but I do think that taking the mystery out of something and understanding how it works eases the mind."

"Yes, but *I'm* not angry! I don't understand where you are going with this…" Yohan blurted out impatiently. Deborah's heart went out to the young man sitting across from her, his face and arms red from eczema, his bubbling frustration bursting through his skin.

"Bear with me, everyone, it will become clearer, and remember that with an open mind we will all hear something new. Anger isn't always screaming and shouting; it can be quiet and reserved, even dignified. And as Yohan said, there is the Freeze response too, where we stop dead and the brain just shuts down any kind of obvious outside reaction, but the nervous system and body are still being dysregulated. Maybe words like 'frustration' or 'resentment' might fit better?"

Deborah continued. "Dr. Sarno noticed that most of his patients had a certain personality type, that they were perfectionists. He also coined a phrase, *'Goodists,'* to describe the people who came into his office." Everyone shifted in their seats as they laughed a little. "Would anyone like to share why they are laughing?" asked Deborah gently. She knew why, but she wanted someone to say it.

"Because that's who we are!" responded Richard sarcastically. "*We* are all perfectionists and…goodists."

"Thank you, Richard, yes, and I'm including myself in this. When I was first called a perfectionist some years ago, I took great offense. I'm quite sloppy at times, I don't mind dirty dishes in the sink and I don't get upset if I don't win. But I started to see that certain things really bothered me. I hate injustice, I hate it when people don't follow the rules, or I notice things that aren't quite right, like…like the sign for parking when you drive into this building, it's slightly off-center."

"That bothers me, too!" called out Marc. They all burst out laughing as they admitted that it bothered them, too, but knew they weren't ever going to say anything about it. Dan sat there in the middle of them, not getting the joke at all.

"Now, that is a silly example, but see how we are all bothered by something minor every time we come here? Just think of all the frustrations and, yes, anger that we swallow every day. No wonder our nervous systems get messed up and we are in pain! So, what I want to show you this week—what I want to point you all toward—is seeing that we all live in a thought-created world, that our realities are created by our thoughts, and if those thoughts are frustrated or negative, then we are going to feel frustrated and negative."

"If this is about positive thinking, then I've tried all that and it doesn't work," said Andrew.

"No, this definitely isn't about positive thinking, and yes you are right, that doesn't work."

"It works for me," said Mia.

Richard groaned and folded his arms, but before he

could say something cruel, Deborah quickly asked, "Forgive me Mia, but if it really worked, would you be here today? Yes, sometimes it can make us feel a little better the same way a beautiful sunset or a compliment can seem to make us feel better. But I have found that any kind of personal change that is dependent on my willpower to make it happen, sooner or later is doomed to failure. Think about all the exercise programs or diets or self-improvement techniques you have embarked on only to find you ran out of energy…or that you'll start tomorrow or…just one more bite. When I'm honest with myself, I know that my willpower is limited. I only have so much patience, only so much strength and at some point, it always runs out. But when change comes from insight, a *sight* from with-*in*, that kind of change is coming from the Infinite. There is no limit to the Infinite." She paused and looked around the room; everyone was trying to follow. "This is not an intellectual understanding, it only comes from insight and as I said, listen with an open mind. We want to look and see where our experience is actually coming from…

"I think we will leave it there for this morning. Lunch will be an hour and then we will come back here for a video and more discussion. Thank you!"

They all got up and moved out of the conference room, thanking her and making lunch plans together.

"Well done, just…well, I had high hopes, but that was great," said Dan.

"Yes, you had them in the palm of your hand!" said Melanie.

"Thank you, but I was a bit nervous I had lost them at times."

"I thought Richard Sharpe was going to attack Mia at

one point—I could see the veins in his head bulge every time she said something. Talk about angry!"

"Oh, me too," laughed Melanie. "So I have two patients for you to meet with this afternoon after you are finished with the group. Can I get you some lunch?"

"Thank you, but I brought my own. I think I just need a time-out, you know, some quiet by myself to reflect, if that's okay."

8
Monday Afternoon

It was nice to get away to reflect on the morning. Deborah was thrilled that Richard had shown up, but a little nervous at how his fury might boil over and spoil the group. She glanced over the schedule and saw that Jeane and Andrew were booked for the individual meetings later in the afternoon. Jeane was a migraine sufferer and Andrew had back pain.

After lunch, they all came back and watched the first of some Syd Banks videos that Deborah had been able to locate on the internet from a friend in the U.S. Syd's soft and calming Scottish voice wafted over the group as they all settled into listening. Archie and some of the therapists had come in too, to soak in the good feelings. When it ended she encouraged everyone to reflect on what they had heard. They all said it was interesting, but weren't quite sure what it had to do with pain. "It's okay, it will become clear soon. I hope you all enjoyed today. There's no homework, but I do want you to get curious about where your experience is really coming from… Is it coming from your situation and circumstances, or is it coming from your thoughts about it? I look forward to seeing you all tomorrow at 9:30."

"But I think I have an appointment with you at 8 a.m. tomorrow?" One of the ladies in the group looked very anxious that she had been forgotten about.

"Oh, yes, of course…Rose. I'm looking forward to it, I'll see you here at 8 a.m.!" Deborah looked around as they were gathering up their things and filing out, and she saw Jeane and Andrew waiting for her. "Okay, I think Andrew is first, right? So sorry Jeane, that you have to hang around."

"Oh, no worries, it's fine. I'll take a walk and stretch my legs."

"Okay, in about an hour then, I'll be upstairs in my office. Andrew, let's go up now."

He followed her up the stairs and they sat down facing each other. He was in his early thirties, dressed in chinos and a plaid shirt, and seemed quite tense. "I see that you have had a terrible time with back pain?"

Andrew nodded. "I fell about a year ago and got two herniated discs. I'm a school teacher and had to take a few weeks off, you know, lying on the floor, chiropractors, etc., but it got better. But then I would get these terrible back spasms where I just can't stand in one place for too long. The pain shoots down my right leg and I'm bent over again."

"I'm so sorry to hear that. I know that sciatica pain, it's awful. I really hope this understanding will help alleviate it… So, what did you get out of this morning, anything ring true for you? I noticed you were very curious…?"

"Uh, yeah, it was very interesting. I don't think I

understand any of it yet, I mean I get that I get frustrated sometimes, but like that guy said, I'm not an angry person. I don't think so anyway."

"I didn't think I was either, but that was part of the problem. I would get *very* frustrated by things, but I never said anything. I think I was probably afraid of what you would think of me if I spoke up or that if I did, it would unleash this tidal wave of emotions that would engulf me."

"I guess. I can get pretty frustrated at times, it's true."

"Give me an example. You said the pain often comes when you have to stand for too long?"

Andrew thought for a moment. "Yes, like in line at the bank or the supermarket, I guess. My back starts to stiffen up and I get really uncomfortable."

"Well, that makes sense. Now that they want us to do more banking with the machines and online, there are fewer tellers and so it's frustrating standing in line for a long time. Or when some idiot has 15 items in the 10-item line in the supermarket, right?"

"Oh, that drives me crazy, can't they read?! And the tellers at the bank all seem to be about 12 years old and *can't get anything right!*" Andrew suddenly sat back as he realized just how frustrated he was. "Oh, wow. I had no idea that was anger. I just always thought it was, well, they are all wrong and I shouldn't have to put up with it…"

"It's okay, take a deep breath… But I think that's where I started seeing my perfectionism in that I had an idea in my head of how it should be, and if everyone just behaved, then we'd all be better off. It never occurred to me that this was somewhat perfectionist or idealistic because, well, I was *right*." Deborah laughed at her own realization. "Have you ever noticed how other people can stand in line and not get upset?"

"Yes! They annoy me too, why am I always the one that has to complain? Why don't they see that it's wrong?"

"Because they don't. They aren't having our kinds of thoughts about it, they are living in their own reality. We are all living in a reality created by our own thoughts and if they don't think it's frustrating, they won't feel frustrated. Maybe they are thinking about the other errands they need to do, maybe they are grateful to be away from the kids or out of the office for a few moments… We are all living in separate realities created by our thoughts in the moment."

Jeane was perched anxiously on the edge of the chair outside as Deborah said goodbye to Andrew. Nervous at the invitation to come in, Jeane hurried past her and sat down, staring at the floor. She was maybe in her mid-forties, nicely dressed, but looked quite uncomfortable.

"How has the day been for you so far?" asked Deborah with a smile.

"Oh, fine, thank you. Yes, very nice."

"I see you have been having migraines for a long time?" She nodded. "Did you have one today?"

"No." She shook her head and smiled forcefully.

"My mother used to get them," said Deborah, trying to build some rapport. "I remember her having to lie in a dark room. Even daylight would make her nauseous."

"Yes, oh yes, that's me. I get the flashing lights and then *boom*, it's like a knife through my head and into my eyeballs. I have to lie perfectly still until it passes."

"Oh, that sounds awful. Did any of what we discussed today resonate with you?"

Jeane hesitated. "I, I can't say I really understood too much, but I understand we just got started… The Scottish man was very nice… I don't get angry though. I'm not a worrier. My sister worries, she is always concerned about this or that. I don't see the point in worrying. It's a waste of time, right?" Jeane looked very disapproving.

"Often, yes. They say worrying doesn't change anything, but it will change your physiology, as we saw this morning. Any prolonged stressful thoughts can upset our bodies, including bringing on a migraine."

"Yes, I see that, but as I said, I don't get angry." Deborah thought that maybe the *lady doth protest too much,* so she asked Jeane if she ever got frustrated with her sister or any other family members for wasting their time with things like worrying. "Well, yes, sometimes. It's such a waste of time to fuss over things that don't matter or might never happen."

"But maybe they matter to her. Jeane, you have just helped me decide what to start with tomorrow."

"Oh, no worries," said Jeane with a confused smile.

"You see, we are all living in our own separate reality, a reality that is made of thought. We only ever experience our thoughts about something and that's what creates our experience. The thoughts you are experiencing right now are creating your reality right now, it's that simple."

Jeane looked confused. "Sorry dear, I didn't quite follow that."

"Have you ever watched a movie with your sister and she loved it and you hated it?"

"Oh yes, many times. I really can't see the point in a lot of those silly romantic movies but my sister loves them, I don't understand why. Mind you, she'll laugh at anything!"

"Right, so could you see that it's not the movie that is giving you both the experience, otherwise you would both be laughing, or, not laughing?" Jeane looked more confused. "It can only ever be your thoughts about the movie."

"Well if you mean it's a question of taste, then yes, we have very different tastes. She has always been very silly and well…irresponsible."

And you have had to be the responsible one?"

"Well, yes."

"That must be frustrating." Jeane pulled a tissue out of her purse as she tried to hold back some tears. Deborah saw the cause of the migraines even if Jeane didn't. "I think sometimes we get caught up in thoughts about how things should be a certain way, that people should behave a certain way and when they don't, it is just so unfair, like they are getting away with it." Jeane looked out the window; she was in turmoil. "Does it feel like you are always the one who has to…be the grown-up…take care of everything?"

"Well if I don't, who will?" snapped Jeane.

"It can definitely seem that way sometimes, but what if you could see it another way?" Jeane looked at her as if she clearly didn't understand the situation. "What if it was okay to let your sister make her own mistakes and work out her own problems, and then you wouldn't have to feel so responsible for her all the time? You could watch those disapproving thoughts go by and let her come to you when she needed something." Jeane gave a look as if to say, *but that's so irresponsible.* "Does it feel like you don't care if you were to let go and let her make her own mistakes and decisions?"

"Yes. I'm the older one and I have to take care of her."

"Jeane, could you see that you have created a story that being a loving older sister means you have to do everything for her, that you *have* to worry?" Jeane nodded cautiously. "And when she doesn't appreciate it, it hurts?" Jeane sobbed into her tissues. Deborah reached out a hand to comfort her. "It's amazing how much you care and do for your sister, but maybe it's time to let go and take care of yourself." They talked for a while longer and Jeane was able to relax a little. "I think this will become clearer tomorrow. I'm excited about where this could go for you!"

They both stood up and said goodbye, and Deborah finished up writing notes in some of the files.

"Hey, Dan, just finished up with the clients for today."

"Yes, me too, got some good feedback. They are all totally confused but that's okay, I think it's a good confused. I mean they are really curious where this is going!"

Deborah laughed, "When I was a little girl my uncle who worked for BOAC, the British something Aircraft Corporation, was sent to California for six months to work with Howard Hughes. When he and my aunt came back, they invited us over for an evening to tell us all about their foreign adventures. I had no idea where or what California was, but he had us come into the kitchen to watch something. I couldn't understand why we were all crowded around the stove looking at a saucepan, but all of a sudden it started to pop! Pop, POP, POP POP POP POP!! It was popcorn! None of us had even heard of popcorn in 1968, let alone seen it in action. We all sat in the living room and watched a Super 8 Laurel and Hardy movie that he projected on the wall while eating our fresh *American* popcorn. Why am I telling you this story? Because you never know when someone is going to pop. You got it straight away, but others can take a while and some don't get it at all, or maybe I should say they don't get it yet."

Dan smiled. "I'm not worried, I think it's all fascinating. It's so clear that all these people are suffering some form of stress-related illness, I just hope they…'pop' real soon."

"Me too, but I think something popped for me today. Remember I was talking about being a perfectionist and how I never saw myself that way but I did notice everything that was *wrong*, at least to my eyes and way of thinking? Well, many of my friends have said that my personality has softened since I came across the Principles. I mean, I hope I wasn't too much of a monster before, but I know I was very certain about what I believed and thought anyone who didn't agree with me was either stupid or needed educating." Dan raised his eyebrows and gave her a look. "I know, well, I'm seeing now that as I got more clarity about the illusion of thought, it automatically relaxed my need to be right; it's very stressful having to be the responsible one all the time. As my mind relaxed, so did my body and well, that's when the pain left. Now that I know my well-being comes from inside I don't need to be so vigilant about everyone behaving the right way for me to be okay anymore."

"That actually makes a lot of sense," agreed Dan. "Now I think about it, I've noticed that many of my clients have been through some kind of trauma, whether it was abuse, violence, loss, an accident, even the surgeries, and as you know, one of the symptoms of PTSD is hypervigilance."

"Yes! But like the textbooks, I always thought the hypervigilance was about the possible dangers out there in the world, but that's a very *Outside-In* understanding."

"Outside-In?"

"Yes, thinking that things out there, on the outside, are responsible for how I feel. For about ten years after my muggings, I was so hyper and jumpy about anything or anyone that my nervous system was on edge all the time, but as I got better, my thinking still stayed all psyched up only now it was on a self-help mission, vigilantly looking inside for imperfection." Deborah paused. "Huh, see, I never saw perfectionism as a way of protecting myself from danger before. The vigilance had turned inward by religiously and meticulously checking my thoughts and motives, trying to improve myself all the time, but that was still an Outside-In understanding, do you see? I was still under the misunderstanding that I had to fix something for me to be okay, only now I had to fix *me*! Like…if only I could be better, do better, be more likable, more successful, then I'd be okay, but now I was trying to control my *thinking* in an effort to protect myself rather than my circumstances. Trying to control our internal world is still Outside-In." Dan watched as she worked it out. "But life is actually what we call an *Inside-Out* experience, and now that I know it's all made of thought, the world has become a much safer place."

Deborah was woken up by the phone ringing. She sleepily looked at the clock and saw it was 2 a.m.! Who was calling at this hour? Maybe someone back in L.A. had forgotten the time difference?

"Hello?"

"I don't know why I let you twist my arm into coming to your crackpot 'show and tell!' I'm going to sue you and that quack doctor!" It was Richard and he was raging. "I have been in agony since I left your amateur horse and pony show! I can't sleep, and every time I try to move I get a back spasm that shoots pain through the top of my head!"

"Richard, slow down. What happened?"

"What do you mean what happened? I came to your stupid workshop thing and have been in agony ever since, that's what

85

happened! I had to get the doctor out at midnight for some muscle relaxers or I was going to shoot someone. I still might if they don't kick in soon!"

"How many did you take?"

"Not enough, clearly! You've got some nerve sleeping there in my suite. You better be out tomorrow before I come over there and throw you out myself!"

"And how would you do that?" asked Deborah. She wasn't sure what possessed her. She knew she should be calming him down, not aggravating him.

"*What?!*"

"Well, it would take some miracle for a man in a wheelchair to throw a young woman and all her belongings into the street, don't you think?"

"I'm not a cripple! I'm not going to be stuck in this chair for the rest of my life!"

"That's right, you are *not* a cripple. Could it be that you are in so much pain because you are so angry at the world and that's what's causing your blood to boil, boil so hard that it can't get around your body to feed your muscles the oxygen they need? Could it be possible that you heard something yesterday that you saw to be true? So true that if you acknowledged it, it would mean letting go of this…this need to bully everyone? You don't have to be so angry to get what you want; you don't even have to shout. Your family loves you, wants to be with you, but you make it so hard. Take a deep breath and listen." Deborah took a deep breath and waited for a second to see if he was still listening. "May I continue?" There was silence so she went for it. "Richard, you have created a story in your head where you are the innocent victim and in a very twisted way, it's given you the right to shout and shame, be unable to trust anyone, always criticizing and complaining that nothing is ever good enough… No wonder you are in so much pain, but it's your broken heart that is hurting." Richard shouted some more abuse and then hung up as abruptly as he started.

Deborah lay back down; adrenaline had shot to her toes. What if he did sue? Just the publicity would be a nightmare for Dan and the clinic, it could shut them down! Oh no! She wanted to cry—the stress chemicals that she had been describing to the participants in the clinic were now racing around her own body. It was such a strange sensation, even as she lay down and observed her thinking going in and out of panic, her body needed to relax and get the message it would be okay no matter what Richard said or did. It was really going to be okay.

9

Tuesday

Melanie had arrived early and Rose was waiting for her in the main waiting area.

"Did Richard Sharpe call here by any chance, leave any messages?" Deborah had been concerned since she woke up and was hoping it had all just been a nightmare. She knew Richard was acting out of insecurity, but she was also aware of what harm he could cause.

"No, but he called Dan at home. Something about lawyers? They are in his office now."

Oh no, what does that mean? She decided that wasn't a helpful thought and watched it go by. As she turned and looked at Rose, another thought went through her head. *These pain clients are always so on time! Huh?* "Hi Rose, please come this way. Thanks Melanie, and if they want me, tell them I went to the airport or something."

Rose followed Deborah cautiously up the stairs. They sat in her office and chatted for a few minutes as Deborah looked over the questionnaire, doing her best to focus.

"Carpal tunnel?"

"Yes." Rose waved her right wrist in the air. It was wrapped in one of those black support braces. "It can get so painful at times."

"What times?" asked Deborah thoughtlessly.

"Sorry?"

Deborah caught herself. Even though she wasn't actively thinking about what Richard might be yelling at Dan, she could feel she wasn't present. She paused. She knew that just noticing she was not fully present meant that her consciousness had risen a little and looked for that quiet mind that she knew was always there, always available. "I'm so sorry, Rose." Deborah became very aware that there was only this moment, this one right here, sitting across from Rose, and nothing else existed in that moment... "I'm wondering, at what times does it get more painful for you?"

"Oh. Well, at work mostly. I'm at the computer all day, you know how it is, the stress of banging away with your hands...it's all that repetitive motion...all day."

Deborah gave a warm smile, "You know, I have never worked in an office, in fact, this is the first office I've ever had, so I'm not familiar with it. Tell me what it's like."

"Well, my boss is a monster, he demands way too much of us and it's not just me, all the other women in the office feel the same. Everyone hates it."

"That must be hard, doing a job you hate."

Rose sighed heavily. "Several of us have this Repetitive Strain Disorder now. I've looked for other jobs, but they are all more typing jobs and we need the second income for the mortgage."[9-1]

"Sure. And what do you like to do to relax? What takes your mind off it?"

"Um, well...I love going to bingo night with my friends."

"*I love bingo!*" responded Deborah. "Legs 11, number 11, two fat ladies 88, at least that's how they did it back in England, every number has a nickname, buckle my shoe 32." They laughed. "I bet that's a lot of fun. Do you place those plastic discs on the cards, or do you have the fancy slider ones?"

"Oh, we are old-fashioned, it's only at the local community center, you know, we all have a snack and a few glasses of red. We have those little plastic chips, like tiddlywinks that cover the numbers."

"I know what you mean, but aren't they very small?" Rose looked puzzled. "Must be hard to pick up with your sore hand."

She hesitated for a minute. "Yeah, they are tiny...never thought about that..." Rose trailed off into thought.

"Could it be that when you are having fun it doesn't hurt?"

Rose looked back at her cautiously. "I guess so...but how could that be? My wrist is still messed up..."

"Well, pain is only experienced when it comes into consciousness. Don't worry, I know that's a lot to get your head around. I'm going to talk about it later."

"Oh, no worries."

They wrapped up the conversation and went downstairs to find the others. To Deborah's surprise and grave concern, Richard was now holding court in the conference room. Everyone, all the participants, even some of the therapists were standing around him and she could just make out through the glass doors that he was waving his arms around. Her stomach flipped as she made her way in to see what he was saying and was now deeply regretting that she had asked him to join… He was going to spoil everything.

"And here she is!" They all turned to see her walk in. Deborah held her breath. "After I yelled at you last night, or was it this morning, you won't believe it but I slept like a baby! A deep sleep, the most relaxing sleep I have had in years. I woke up refreshed and I thought it must have been those horse tranquilizers the doc gave me, but they were still sitting there, right there on the nightstand! I hadn't taken anything! Whatever you said to me, deary, must have just calmed me right down!"

Deborah felt such a wave of relief. She had felt sick at the thought of Richard suing the clinic and Dan losing everything he had worked so hard for.

"Hope I didn't frighten you, luv? I know I can be a bit of a tiger when the pain has kept me up. No hard feelings, eh?"

"Uh, no, not at all…huh. Okay, why don't we all take our seats and gather our thoughts." She knew she was talking to herself as much as anyone else. Dan and a couple of the other staff came in and smiled at her, so she took a deep breath and started the session.

"I'm so glad you all came back! Why don't we start with some feedback? Anyone *else* want to share any thoughts about what they heard yesterday?" There was a pause and then Erin put her hand up.

"I can't say I understood much and my feet still hurt, but I felt very calm last night…"

"I felt very calm too. I haven't slept like that in ages," offered Jeane quietly. Some of the others nodded.

"Me, too," said Primo. "I don't know, I just had this a-calm feeling?"

Deborah smiled.

"As I said to the others, I was in a right old rage by the

time I got home last night, kept me up most of the night," said Richard. *And everyone else too,* thought Deborah. "I'm not even sure why. But when I woke up this morning, I had this deep calmness, it was almost…it was like…I dunno really."

"That's wonderful, everyone, thank you." The others in the group who hadn't shared were looking a bit lost, as if they had missed out on something, so Deborah started with her ideas for the day. "I find it fascinating that we could all be in the same room hearing the same things yesterday and yet all have a different experience of it. I know, I didn't quite get this the first time I heard it, so bear with me… Cast your mind back to the last time you watched a movie or TV show with someone you know well, a partner, a parent, a child, a sibling. Did any of you have a different experience from the person you were watching it with?" They all just stared and then Aliki, who had been totally quiet up to this point, blurted out:

"You mean like when my boyfriend can't take his eyes off the sports channel every Saturday *and* Sunday, but it drives me crazy?"

Everyone laughed. "Yes Aliki, exactly like that. He is in heaven and you are…"

"*In the other room!*" Everyone laughed again and Aliki blushed.

"Right. And does he ever watch anything you like?

"I tried to get him to watch a romantic movie with me once, *never again.* He was so uncomfortable that he talked all the way through it, asking when would it be over."

"Okay, so this proves to me that our feelings are like a barometer, they tell us where we are holding in our thinking. It can't be the sports channel that is making your boyfriend happy, because then it would make you and everyone else happy. Don't worry, I know you are not the only girlfriend who wants to leave the room after the third game of the day. I have been a guitar widow, a surf widow and a TV sports widow in my time." The ladies in the room laughed. "It's his thoughts about sports that are making him happy and your thoughts about it that make you want to be somewhere else, could you see that?"

"And his thoughts about romantic movies make him want to leave the room?" offered Parker.

"Yes. Here's another example: I had a client once who was about to have a treatment for IVF to help her have a baby, which consists of multiple injections. She called me in a panic, as she was terrified of needles. So I explained that it wasn't the needles that were making her panic, it was her thoughts about the needles that were creating her fear. It couldn't be coming from the needle itself, as some people don't mind injections and some people actually like needles. Junkies, for example, get very excited about them! It's the same with flying, some people love it and some people hate it."

"I hate flying!" interrupted Mia. Deborah anticipated a groan from Richard, but he was listening intently like everyone else.

"Can I ask you, Mia, when do the thoughts about flying start?"

"Oh, weeks before the flight."

"Okay, can you see then that it's not being up in the air, or even on the plane that is creating your fearful experience, it's your thoughts about it? You haven't even packed your bags yet."

"Yes, I had," said Mia, sensing she was about to be judged. "I get so nervous, I pack, and then I worry about the plane crashing so I unpack as I know there is no way I can go, and then I think about the waste of money so I pack again, and it just continues till I'm in such a state." She looked terrified just saying it out loud.

"Love, can you see that nothing is actually happening except you are all in a silly tiz about it?" offered Richard kindly.

"Well, yes," confirmed Deborah, a little amazed at Richard's compassionate insight. "**We are the authors of our own reality**, we create what we experience with the gift of thought. It's uniquely our own, no one else can get inside your mind. Remember what Syd Banks said in the video—believing that our feelings are a result of outside things is an innocent misunderstanding. The more we think something is real, the more we think about it and it just gets bigger in our heads." As she spoke, she tapped her finger on the folder she was holding, her nail hitting it first. The tap on the hard plastic popped something in her mind. "Oooh, I *just* had a cool insight! We all know from physics class that everything is made of atoms, right? And that they are whizzing around at great speed. As scientists look further and further into atoms, they see that at the center, there isn't actually anything there, just empty space, and it's just the speed of the atoms that make things appear solid. This is like thought! As our thoughts speed up—anxiety, worry, overthinking, panic—our circumstances *seem* more real. '*Look, my heart is pounding,* or *my hands are shaking, it must be real!*' When we put our attention on things like jealousy, frustration or anger, that gives us our 'feeling experience.' But really, it's just speeded-up thought. As we begin to understand this, our thoughts slow down, the problem fades and our nervous systems can calm down. All we have to do is understand that thought flows, and there is no need to do anything to fix or help it flow. When left alone, its natural state is to slow and settle, and that brings fresh, new thought, experience and insight. Thought is—*and I have no* *idea what I'm saying right now*—some kind of mystical, spiritual energy that is going through our minds, and the more we fall into the illusion that things out there are real, the more our thinking speeds up and we believe it to be true. Just like atoms that speed up and make things seem solid, but really...there is nothing there, it's just thought in the moment." The group soaked up what she was saying, some started to nod their heads, so she paused for a moment to let it land with them all.

"I think I'm getting it," said Richard. "Are you saying that I have been doing this to myself?" Deborah nodded in sympathetic agreement. "I have been torturing myself with my own thinking?"

Deborah nodded again, still not sure what had happened to him. "When I saw this to be true, I saw that because I had created my own experience with my thinking, no one else had to change for me to be okay, that I could be uncomfortable, even be in pain, and be okay. It was only ever my thoughts that were making me miserable. Now, had you said that to me back in London when I was in the depths of my PTSD, I would have said you are nuts! I had police reports and X-rays to prove the world was a dangerous place, but it was still my thoughts about it that were creating my experience. Yes, some of you have X-rays and MRIs showing physical things wrong, but if you look closely at anyone's back or neck, you will always find something wrong."

"The doc just told me this morning that everyone's spine starts to degenerate at age 20! I couldn't believe it!" announced Richard.[9-2]

"I just read that in Dr. Dan's research, and I was amazed, too! I guess it's like getting gray hair or wrinkles, it's not wrong, it's just how the human body ages. What we are going to see is that prolonged busy, anxious thinking dysregulates our nervous systems no matter what the actual circumstances of our situations are.

"Let's take a break. See you all back here in 20 minutes."

The group sat for a minute soaking up what had been shared. Deborah could sense that things were starting to pop. She was even more fascinated to hear what had happened to Richard.

"I can't believe that I have been torturing myself with my own thoughts!" cried Richard, immediately wheeling himself right up in front of her. "I've never been in for all that psychobabble therapy nonsense, but the good doc just gave me a workup so I'm officially in your little group, can't get rid of me now, luv! I think I'm supposed to meet with you. Lonnie will bring me over to the club at 8."

"Uh, sure, can't wait!"

He wheeled himself away to chat with his new friends, and she got up to look for Dan. She was feeling quite buzzy by all the ups and downs of the last few hours.

"So happy Richard isn't going to sue you!" whispered Deborah as Dan beckoned her out into the corridor.

"Uh, me too, but that wasn't what he called me about at 8 a.m. He wanted a medical evaluation so he could be included in the research. He mentioned something about getting angry with you, but I didn't realize it was that bad!"

"Oh, it was bad. He called at 2 a.m. screaming something about lawyers. I was terrified that it was the end of your clinic. So, what did he say this morning?" They moved into his office, away from the participants.

"He said he accepted that whatever the surgeon had done had permanently ruined his back, that he was never going to walk again, but he also knew that his anger was causing the continuing pain, and if being in the group meant it might help someone else, then he would appreciate being allowed to join officially. He was very insistent. I was a little shocked, so I gave him a physical. I'm going to look at his MRIs and X-rays later."

"I'm meeting him tonight. Weird, eh?"

"Yeah, pretty weird, but keep going. Something is happening in there."

They came back together after the break and settled down, ready for some more. Deborah started with a question.

"I'm sure some of you have heard of phantom limb pain?" A few nodded, so she continued. "I was doing some research last week and I found this amazing neuroscientist, I think his name is Dr. Ramachandran.[9-3] Anyway, he tells a story of a patient who comes into his clinic with excruciating pain, only the pain is in his amputated arm. The man had lost his right hand from the elbow down, but felt pain in a clenched fist that didn't exist, and because it didn't exist, he couldn't unclench it. Now, when I read this, I pictured this poor guy. If I hold a clenched fist up at you, what does it usually mean?"

"Anger?" suggested Marc.

"Exactly! The poor guy was so angry, and who could blame him? *He's lost his arm!* It doesn't matter how or why. Now, I have only been clenching my fist for about a minute here and it's already hurting! So the doctor explains that my hand is sending a message back to my brain to let go, only his patient doesn't have a hand, so no message is being sent back." Everyone shifted in their seats; they knew that constant pain intimately. "So the clever doctor built a box about the size of a small fish tank with a round hole in one end. The right-hand wall of the box is made of a mirror and the top is open so you can see in. The doctor asked his patient to clench his left hand, his real hand, and put it in through the hole. The man then looks into the box, sees his "missing hand" reflected in the mirror, releases his real hand and, guess what? The pain leaves immediately!" Everyone let out a gasp of admiration. "Do you see, the pain was never in his right hand—it couldn't be, he didn't have one! Pain is always experienced in the brain, so we can only know we are in pain when it comes into consciousness."

"Santa Maria!" gasped Primo out loud.

"So, what is consciousness?" asked Andrew.

"It's being awake?" suggested Kate.

"Well, that definitely helps. I always like to think of consciousness like an elevator, a lift, that goes up and down. Consciousness can go up and down over our lifetime. It can also go up and down throughout the day. Think about your local department store for a moment. When you walk in, I bet there's, uh…cosmetics and ladies' shoes, right? It's light and airy, maybe some fresh flowers, a guy playing the piano if it's Harrods." They all nodded. "Now, if you press the elevator button and go down a floor, you usually come to housewares, right? Now, in a posh store, you might find French LeCreuset cooking pots from Paris and silver candlesticks, but in a store in downtown Wollongong, I'm probably gonna find power tools and curtain rods, yes? Now, if I press the button and go down again, I will probably come to the basement. It's dark and cold down there and very cramped. It's dirty, there's garbage and broken mannequins and, huh, *what was that?!*" Deborah's shoulders were hunched up as she pointed her finger across the floor acting as if a mouse had scurried over her feet. Mia screamed! "Okay, you get the idea. Now, as we go back up, we go up past housewares, past cosmetics, next is ladieswear, cute dresses, next up is menswear, cute guys, and then imagine there is a café on the roof. You can see out to the beach and the sparkling turquoise water, or you can see inland to the snowy mountains. Feel the fresh air as you take in the view." Deborah lifted her arms up and spread them wide over herself with a relaxed, contented smile.

The group was entranced. "Now, imagine you and I are sitting, drinking our cappuccinos at the café on the roof."

"I'd rather have a stubbie!" laughed Costos, but Deborah didn't understand.

"A beer," explained Richard.

"Ah, sure. Hey, it's all made up, so you can have whatever drink you want!" replied Deborah, grinning. "Okay, we've got our drinks, we are hanging out and I tell a joke, but you don't laugh. Maybe you just don't get my British humour? But that's okay because I'm sitting in the sun with my cocktail and I feel good, so I can see the bigger picture. I'm relaxed. I'm not bothered that you don't find me funny, that thought just goes on by. I was going to say like the clouds, but there aren't any, it's such a fabulous day." She leaned forward. "Now, imagine we are in the basement and you don't laugh at my joke… I can't understand why you are behaving the way you are, you are an idiot, I hate you, I hate everything about you! And now I just want to leave, I want out of here. *Now!*" Deborah spoke dramatically and stared at them for a moment. They all looked concerned. "Could you see how my level of consciousness, my state of mind is affecting how I experience you not laughing at my joke? If I'm in a good place, I hardly notice, but if I'm in a low place, then I can't bear it. How I experience it completely changes my world."

"Because my world is made up of my thoughts?" asked

Mia.

"Yes, Mia, well said… Let's think about pain for a moment: if I'm in pain and I'm watching the cricket and England is beating Australia…"

"Like that's ever gonna happen!" mumbled Corey.

"Just checking you were still with us, Corey…then I might forget about the pain for a few minutes. Or let's say you are watching your grandkid graduate from university, or you get that promotion or win a game. Could you see how even if the pain left for just a few seconds, that it's because it went out of your consciousness?"

"It's funny, but I haven't felt my back hurt since you started talking today, and I usually have a terrible time sitting in chairs like these," Kate shared. "Then when I realized that, it started hurting."

"Wow, that's a great insight. Can you see the thought about the pain as just a thought and watch it go by?"

"Maybe."

"Huh," said Richard, "I just realized something. I don't feel my pain when I get angry."

"But my eczema isn't in my consciousness! Look, it's real, it's right here." Yohan pulled up his sleeve and showed everyone his sore, cracked and inflamed skin.

"Can I ask you, Yohan, does the itchy soreness ever fade, or are you always aware of it?"

"It's *all* the time."

"So if I followed you around with a video camera for the next 24 hours, we would never see you not feeling it?"

"Well, maybe when I'm asleep, but that's not my point. My point is that even if I'm not feeling it as bad, it's still there!" He pointed to Kate. "She forgot about her back pain so the problem went away, she's good to go, but I've still got red, blistering skin!"

"I'm so glad you brought that up. Doctors always told

me that my pain was a result of the fact that my right leg is longer than my left. They said that's why my pelvis is slanted, which is making my back unstable. But my body is exactly the same right now as it was then. Nothing has changed for me anatomically, and yet the pain is gone. I'm going to ask Dr. Dan to talk to us about this some more this afternoon, but my point is, no matter what is going on with my body, it depends on my level of consciousness as to how I actually experience it."

"You mean like those guys who can walk on fire coals in Bali? I saw them when I was there with my boyfriend last year," announced Aliki.

"Yes, but do you know what the amazing thing about that is? I used to think that they just weren't feeling the heat because of some voodoo thing, but the skin on their feet doesn't even burn, not a single blister! Their skin isn't reacting because of their elevated state of mind! Now, can I ask, does anyone here feel that their pain never falls below…say…a five on a scale of zero to ten?"

There was a pause and then Erin spoke up, "My foot pain never goes below a five. It's been hurting all morning. I'd love for it to be a zero, for it to just go out of my mind."

"Okay, and when things get tough, maybe some bad news or someone is behaving badly, something stressful, does it feel worse?" She nodded. "What would you say it can go up to if you are stressed?"

"Oh, it goes up to an 8 or 9 quite regularly when my kids are acting up, even a 10 sometimes, and then my husband has to carry me to the emergency room!"

"Okay, so wouldn't a 5 be better than an 8 or 9?"

Erin looked at her curiously. Deborah could tell that, for a split second, she got that it was a thought-created experience, but then she went back into the story of how her foot pain stops her from having a life. Deborah thanked her for sharing. "I think we will stop there for lunch… Thanks, everyone, that was amazing, see you all back here in an hour."

10
Tuesday Afternoon

"Okay, hope you all had a nice lunch break." Dan looked around the room to see that everyone was with him. "So, Deborah has introduced us to some amazing new ideas. Now I'm going to tell you about the research I was part of at Chicago University as a visiting fellow, and by the end of the week, I'm hoping you can help me put this all together. Our aim here really is to help you manage your own health, okay?" They all nodded in agreement. Dan pointed to the first page of a flip chart that Melanie had set up for him.

"Now, I'm sure at some point you have all either fractured a bone, sprained an ankle, or had a seriously bad burn? It's hard to get to this age without something really hurting at one time or another, and it may or may not be why you are here today. We call this acute pain. It's the pain you experience when the injury first happens, the kind that makes you want to scream." He pointed to various pictures of people with terrible looking injuries.

"We call this nociception. It's when the sensory nerves in your body send a message to your spinal cord, and then your brain decides how dangerous it is. If it's a sprain or a fracture, then your brain will have a reflex action and tell you to take the weight off. If something burns you, your brain says, pull back! Most injuries like fractures and sprains heal within four to eight weeks, and all injuries or surgeries should heal within a few months, so when the pain continues long after normal healing has occurred, it's now called chronic pain.

"We, the researchers, wanted to see how pain organizes itself in the brain; how does it actually go from acute to chronic? We had 94 participants who had lower back pain for less than two months with no previous history of pain, and 59 participants with lower back pain that had lasted for more than ten years. Using fMRIs we examined their brain activity over a period of one year. Everyone with me so far?" Dan turned pages of pictures in his flip chart to illustrate what he was saying.[10-1]

"Okay. So we made brain-mapping images and observed that brain activity in the acute back pain group was limited to regions at the front of the brain, the prefrontal cortex. This is normal." He touched his forehead to show where this was.

"Whereas in the chronic back pain group, activity is confined here, to the emotion-related circuitry, what's called the limbic system." Dan moved his hand to the back of his head. "In the group that recovered normally from their acute back pain, brain activity diminished over time. Whereas in the persistent back pain group, activity diminished here, in the front but increased here, in the emotion-related circuitry. This showed us that pain can undergo large-scale shifts in brain activity as it transitions to chronic pain."

Everyone stared for a moment; the science was a bit overwhelming. Worried he'd lost them, Dan tried to encourage some feedback. "Okay, so what does that mean for us?"

"It means that we all have pain in the back of our heads and not the front, but it's still a pain in the neck," laughed Richard.

"Well, kind of," said Dan. "What it means is that something else is causing the pain when it becomes chronic pain. If it's only showing up in the emotional part of the brain, then this ties in with what Deborah has been teaching us! As she said, '*We are always feeling our thinking…*'" Everyone was concentrating; they were all trying to get their heads around what Dr. Dan was saying.

"Now, in the first group, they had injuries like Deborah did, but some of you have been told that you have structural causes for your pain. You might have been told that you have things like bulging discs[10-2] and degenerative disc disease[10-3], pinched nerve[10-4], stenosis, bone spurs, or inflammation.[10-5] I'm not going to go through them all now, I will address yours personally when we meet, but I do want to give you a few statistics.

"MRIs show that 40% of people with bone-on-bone in their joints have no pain, and 10-15% of people with a healthy X-ray will have pain."[10-6] The group murmured in disbelief.

"Now, bone-on-bone sounds awful, right? But it doesn't automatically mean pain. In fact, surgeons often perform an operation called spine fusion, which is what bone-on-bone really is, the bone is fused together. This means that there are plenty of people walking around with a bulging disc and no pain, and we are all walking around with some degree of degeneration in our spines, and most people are okay. Ladies and gentlemen, you cannot see pain on an X-ray or an MRI.[10-7] So, when a patient comes to a surgeon in agony and the surgeon sees a 'normal abnormality,'[10-8] he operates because he has no other solution and, surprise surprise, it doesn't fix the pain, as the harmless bulging disc or normally degenerating spine was never the cause of the pain in the first place!"

"But my pain goes away after I've had my surgeries!" said Mia.

Dan took a deep breath. As a physician, it broke his heart to see someone so taken advantage of by well-meaning but misinformed surgeons. "Mia, yes, there may have been a period free from pain, but that's what is called the placebo effect." Dan continued and told them about the placebo knee surgery, how a red sugar pill is more effective than a blue one, an injection with saline solution is more effective than a sugar pill, and that surgery is the ultimate placebo. "Do you see where I'm going with this?"

"But it wasn't fake! They did stuff, I had several bone fusions! I have another one booked in a few weeks!" pleaded Mia.

"They messed my spine up big time. I won't let them near my back again," scoffed Richard.

"I'm sorry to tell you this, Mia, but every time you have a fusion, it puts extra strain on the vertebrae above and below the surgery site, causing those vertebrae to now fracture. You keep needing surgery because the previous surgery is causing the next fracture. It's like, like dominos. The only…" Dan took a deep breath, "the one and only piece of research that shows fusion surgery works was sponsored by, guess who? *The company that manufactures the metal implant material!*"[10-9]

Everyone was horrified, and Mia looked like she was going to crumble despite the metal in her back.

"For a surgeon, finding a structural source for the pain is like finding gold, it's a triumph. For them, it's like they hit the jackpot, but from a Mind-Body perspective, it's a total red herring, a distraction. If your pain is now coming from the emotional part of the brain, then nothing a surgeon can do will fix that. Surgery cannot fix your fearful thinking, or your worry about the mortgage and the kids, your need for approval, your anxiety about germs or fear of failure. Surgery will never fix your stress." His words hung in the air for a few minutes as people soaked up his meaning.

"My friends, this is why opioids don't work for chronic pain either. Opioids are designed to work in that part of the brain that is receiving the nociceptive information, i.e., you have had surgery or an acute injury. If the pain is showing up in the front part of the brain, then the opioids can do their work to dull that pain. But as it shifts to the emotional system and becomes chronic pain…"

"I get it!" shouted out Kate. "It's so obvious now!"

"What? I don't get it, my pain meds work fine," scoffed Karyn.

"If it's in the emotional part of the brain, it's the wrong kind of drug. You would need anti-anxiety drugs or pot to get rid of it now, right doc?"

"Sadly, yes, which is a whole other problem. That's why there is such a terrible opioid problem. As people up their dose of Vicodin, which isn't working anymore because the pain moved to another part of the brain, they become addicted. Opioids decrease breathing ability and tragically, as the medication isn't working, people add other drugs like Valium or alcohol to ease their discomfort. These also decrease breathing and all it takes is too much of this lethal combo, and then one tragic morning, well, they just don't wake up.''

After the session, Deborah had another two participants to meet with. Karyn, a flight attendant, was on full disability from a major airline after injuring her shoulder helping someone put their carry-on in an overhead bin. The diagnosis written on the questionnaire was Rotator Cuff Tear. She had had surgery but still had pain.

"I'm so sorry the surgery didn't relieve your pain as you had hoped for…"

"Well, the idiot doctor must have messed it up, so now I'm stuck with it. Thank God for good health insurance and pain meds." Deborah didn't know where to start; the fact that her shoulder would have healed within two months of the injury,[10-10] the fact that everyone has rotator cuff tears if you look close enough, or the fact that a surgeon can't remove anger no matter how skilled he is.

"So, how long have you been on disability now?"

"Why?"

"Oh, nothing, I was just wondering what you do with all your time. You are smart and otherwise able, so it must be a drag. Surely there are other things you would like to do with your life besides being 'disabled'?"

"Sure, but hey, I'm 45, how much longer was I going to be a flight attendant? It's a bit like early retirement, I'm not complaining."

"And what did you make of Dan's research?"

"Well, yeah, doctors say all kinds of things. Anyone can produce statistics to prove their point."

"Sure, what's Bart Simpson's line? 'Anyone can make a good argument using statistics, 80% of all people know that.'" Karyn didn't find it amusing. "But they tested people's brains for a year! I find it fascinating that the pain shifted to the emotional part of the brain after their injuries healed… It proves that we are always feeling our thinking. When I heard my colleagues and teachers say this, I had always thought of that as our moods, that our moods are a reflection of our thinking, which I still believe is true. But now I also see that for some of us, we are feeling our thinking in our backs, our shoulders and our skin."

Karyn raised her eyebrows. "If you say so."

"I do! Think about it, if the injury has healed and you are still feeling pain, then the pain can't be coming from the injury! Research is showing that things like prolonged frustration, anger, boredom and despair are messing with our nervous systems, and this sends mixed-up messages to our bodies, and that hurts like hell."

"Well, I'm not angry. I may get bored sometimes, but I'm certainly not in despair!" She crossed her legs and cocked her head to one side as if to say, *you got anything else?*

"I'm thinking it might be hard to contemplate getting well… I mean, that would mean going back to work?"

Karyn stared at her some more. "Say what you like, I have several shoulder experts who all agree that I'm disabled, and now the other one is hurting from overuse."

Deborah could see that antagonising her was not helping, so she thanked her for her time and said see you tomorrow.

Next was Kate. Kate was in her early 30s, worked at the Sydney Opera House as a stagehand, and had lower back pain. She had also written down that she suffered from bad seasonal allergies, and had had cystitis as a child.

"Oh, that sounds like such fun work, the Sydney Opera House! I used to work in Hollywood and started out in the theater in London. I know how physical it can be."

"Yes, it is, but I love it. My pain doesn't come all the

time like some of the people in the group. There's often a general ache, but then *struth*! I'm on the floor, can't move!"

"Have you ever been told that something provoked it?"

"Yes, well my chiropractor says it's the lifting of course, but last time my back went out, all I did was turn to put my seatbelt on! My back is really messed up!"

"But didn't you say earlier that your back had stopped hurting in the session until you thought about it?" She nodded. "Well then, can you see that the pain you are experiencing can't be an accurate description of what's going on structurally? If your back was that messed up, it would hurt all the time and you would never be able to turn and put your seatbelt on safely…?"

"I never thought about it like that before. I mean, all the chiropractors I've seen around the city just say my pelvis is unstable, so I imagined some days it was stable and others it wasn't…but that doesn't make much sense, does it?"

"Kate, what did you think about what we have presented so far?"

Kate scrunched up her forehead as she thought. "Well, I get that it's all thinking, but…well, it's pretty tough at work, I mean I'm the only female stage hand, and I feel I have to prove myself all the time. The guys are great, but it's tough trying to be one of the guys all the time. I heard what you said about being a perfectionist and I never thought of myself that way; I wear overalls at work and I don't pay much attention to the way I look, but I am pretty hard on myself to do everything the right way, the best way. That way, they will never find out."

"Find out what?"

"That I'm a…a fake, that I'm just winging it."

"I get it. I was the same way in Hollywood, always scared they would send in the Impostor Police and I would be found out and sent home. But it's all a story we have made up in our heads…You must be good at your job or they wouldn't have hired you and kept you on. I know how competitive these kinds of jobs are. Watch those thoughts go by, they really are just made of…fluff…like prop clouds on a stage rig made to fool the audience."

After she had packed up for the day, Deborah headed back to the country club. She needed a rest, and with Richard coming over in a couple of hours, she knew it was going to be an intense evening.

She lay on the sofa on the patio and soaked up the last of the sun as it was setting over the golf course. The program was going great and the people were starting to pop.

"Hey, sleepyhead." It was Lonnie. "Mr. Sharpe is waiting for you in the lounge."

Deborah sat up and shook her head. "Sorry, I must have dozed off after dinner. Thank you."

"No worries. So I have to ask, what did you do to old Sharpey?"

"Sorry, what do you mean?" She grabbed her purse and they walked back to the main building.

"Well, he usually greets me with a grunt if I'm lucky, and then a whole bunch of demands and a fair few insults. I heard from the house staff that he went on a rampage the other night, screaming and shouting like a crazy person. But this morning he asked how I was, and this afternoon, he remembered that it's my daughter's birthday this week! He never remembers anything about my private life even though we spend so many hours together. It's just weird, that's all."

"That is…weird. I'm not sure yet, but let's hope it

stays, eh?"

Richard was sitting in his wheelchair at a table looking out across the golf course. He turned and smiled at Deborah as she sat down.

"I ordered you a lemonade, I remembered that's what you like?"

"Yes, thank you. So Richard, what happened?"

Richard took a sip of his whiskey and spoke slowly. "I was so angry with you that night for tricking me into coming to the clinic, there was such a rage in me that I wanted to break something, anything. It really scared me, so I know that it must have scared my family and the staff. I was completely out of control, it was frightening. I have been trying to understand why, what was it in what you said that got me so worked up, and then I saw it… I saw that it wasn't you that had made me so angry, you *didn't trick me into anything*, it was my thoughts about the whole thing that made me so mad. Then I saw that if that's true, it's true *all the time!*

"I have been so angry since my first wife died, Julia's mother. And it's not that I don't love Sylvie, I do, she's a wonderful woman and has done her best with Julia and me, but when I lost my first wife I felt…abandoned, like I was robbed of my best friend." Deborah was taken aback. She had no idea and suddenly felt deep compassion for Richard and Julia. "We had so many plans and dreams and it was all taken away. Julia was just five years old and I was so angry that she would never know what an amazing woman her mother was. I took it out on my business staff, the staff at home, my brother, everyone. But it wasn't her death that was making me angry either, was it? It was my thoughts about it! About the injustice, the doctors, her leaving me alone with a small child. *I was torturing myself with my own*

112

thinking." He paused and looked across at Deborah. "I need to make so many apologies, I don't know where to begin."

Deborah's heart was so full for the man sitting opposite her. It was just like Syd Banks said, 'We are all one thought away from good mental health.' All it took was one new thought and Richard was free of all that torment.

"How is Julia doing?" asked Deborah. "You know, we never really talked, she and I never even had one conversation longer than two or three sentences and that was often mostly grunts and mumbles."

"My poor little Julia, she lost her mother to cancer and then she lost her father in an ocean of anger. So, all things considered, she is doing pretty well. I knew her suicide attempt was a cry for attention, we all know that, but she has been wanting, needing…deserving attention for the last 15 years. She left to stay with some family friends when I flipped out, but will be home on Friday. I can't wait to see her."

"Wow, this is all quite amazing. Thank you for letting me in and sharing this with me, and please know I am available to you and your family as much as you need."

"Thank you. So what happens now? Am I going to have to live on a mountain in Tibet or something?"

Deborah smiled. "Not unless you want to…! You begin to live your life from this insightful place, from a quiet mind. Life gets easier when you realize there is something deeper, something beyond the limits of our thinking. It's outside of our personal thought and all it takes is insight. I found that once I saw the truth of what Syd was saying, that there is no need to blame anyone, or fight or push. That might seem hard as a businessman, but I think this could open up whole new worlds for you, no? I think we are always going to be students of these

Principles. No one is an expert, so stay curious and you will continue to have insights and get a deeper understanding that is bound to have a ripple effect on your family and business."

They finished up their drinks and Richard wheeled himself out to the car where Lonnie was waiting. He turned and gave Deborah a grateful smile. "Thank you."

"No, thank *you*."

Deborah went back to her room. It was dark, but the sound of the crickets and the fountain were like music. She thought about the last couple of days and how different things can be with new thinking. Nothing has to change, but everything changes.

11
Wednesday

The next morning Deborah had a meeting lined up with Corey before the first session. Corey was a 20-year-old basketball player who had a promising career as a professional before his dreams were smashed by a knee injury that took him out of the game. He had been pretty quiet throughout the sessions so far, and she wondered if maybe he felt a bit different from the rest of the group.

"So, Corey, what's been going through your mind? Anything resonating with you?"

His long legs projected way over the edge of the chair and his long arms dangled by the side of his very long torso. "I get it, I guess. Like, I get that it's all thinking…"

"But? I sense there is a 'but' coming?"

"Well, yeah. I get that thought sparks like a physical reaction, we get told that by coaches, you know, think positive before a game, imagine the prize, you know, but that doesn't change the fact that my knee is blown out and

I won't be playing at championship level now. That's fact, that's reality." He moved forward, motioning his arms like a New York rapper, then leaned back and became an Australian kid again. "I've missed my chance and like, no amount of positive thinking is going to change that!"

"I could see how you might think that, but who said anything about positive thinking?"

"Well, that's what y'all have been talking about, right? It's like our thoughts that get us messed up and so positive thinking gets us straightened out. My old coach told us that all the time."

"And did it work?"

Corey hesitated. "Not really. I would think like all positive and then maybe miss a shot or we lost a game and I'd feel bad so I would tell myself to get it together and get back in the game. I would give myself a good talking to like, 'Yo, jerk, you idiot, y'all can do better, you are better, you are the *bomb*!' You know, that kind of thing, and eventually I'd pull myself out of it and do good again."

"Hmm, that sounds like a lot of hard work. I used to yell at myself to shut up when I was in a dark place." Deborah took a sip of water.

"Cool."

"No, not cool, it was brutal! I only did it because I didn't know what else to do. It was a misunderstanding of how the mind works. Corey, here's something interesting. Remember the first day when I opened up with an introduction? I said listen with an open mind, listen for something new. I haven't mentioned positive thinking once, not once. I wouldn't, because I don't believe it works." Corey shrugged his bony shoulders. "Remember how yesterday we talked about separate realities, how people can be in the same situation and have completely different experiences?"

"Yeah, like that girl who can't stand sports, pity her boyfriend…although she is cute."

"Well, you were in the same room as everyone else and heard something completely different, can you see that?" Corey shrugged again. "You heard positive thinking and yet we discussed how it wasn't that. Could you see that you were hearing your busy thinking and not what was actually being said?"

"Maybe." Corey untied and then tied his sneakers again.

"Can I ask, do you have a girlfriend?"

"Broke up."

"Because?" Deborah was aware she was asking about private stuff but had a feeling that it was important.

"She said I never listened to her." Corey shrugged his shoulders again and looked away.

"Hmm, can you see why she would say that?"

"Look, I didn't come here for some shrink session on relationships and listening. What's this got to do with my knee?"

"Everything."

"Good morning everyone. How are we today?" Deborah encouraged everyone to come and sit down. "Anyone have some insights or thoughts they would like to start us off with?" Dan and Melanie slithered in and sat down at the back at the start of the third morning session.

"Yeah, when are you going to tell us how to be pain-free?" Marc, a middle-aged businessman with neck pain leaned forward. "I'm not sure how much longer I can sit in these chairs!"

"Me too, my shoulder is killing me today," added Karyn, "I had to take extra Vicodin at just the thought of being here!" Deborah suddenly saw the morning turning into a complaint session when Rose cautiously put her strapped-up wrist in the air.

"May I say something?"

"Please!"

"Well…my wrist hasn't hurt since we had our meeting on the first day!"

"Amazing, Rose! Wow, can you tell us anything else about your experience since then?"

Rose hesitated. She was nervous to speak in front of the group, but everyone was eager to hear what she had to say. "I've had RSD, you know, carpal tunnel, for about two years. My colleague, Sharon, we share an office, she had it first. She was in such pain, and then some of the other secretaries got it. I remember saying to Sharon, I said that it looked painful and she said, 'Just wait till it goes up to your elbow,' and then a few days later, my wrist started hurting!"

"You can't catch pain!" dismissed Karyn. She sat back in her chair and rubbed her sore shoulder. "My shoulder pain comes from an actual injury. I'm a flight attendant and a lot of us get shoulder injuries helping passengers put their bags up but we don't *catch it* from each other!"

"What do *you* think happened, Rose?" asked Richard, fascinated by the whole thing.

"Well, we weren't sure. Our doctors all said we needed to rest our wrists, and so that meant disability leave. The boss was furious, but we weren't making it up! We were all in so much pain. We all thought it must be the typing, we type for eight hours a day." She looked around to see if people were understanding her. "But Monday night I went home and thought about it. Before computers, before electric typewriters, secretaries were typing on those big heavy manual typewriters for a hundred years without any problems,[11-1] so I thought about it…could it really have been our thinking? I mean, I *hate* my boss, he's such a mean, critical old bugger. He shouts at us all the time, never shows any appreciation and barks orders at us like a sergeant major, like we have no feelings at all. I often spend all day feeling like I'm nothing." Richard closed his eyes; it was painful for him to hear what an effect an angry boss can have on their staff. "I don't know what happened Monday night, but the pain just went away. I was nervous to say anything yesterday in case I jinxed it, but it felt fine all day. In fact, I don't even know why I put this stupid thing on this morning." Rose lifted her arm and undid the velcro straps on her wrist support. With a nervous grin, she threw it on the floor! The others were all stunned, and then they started to clap and cheer! Rose blushed bright red, but the relief shone through her fingers as she tried to cover her face.

"Wow! Go Rose!" cheered Deborah, amazed, and slightly relieved. Dan gave her a thumbs up from the back and Melanie was clapping in amazement with the others. "Okay, wow, that's just amazing, thank you for sharing that, Rose!" She took a deep breath of gratitude. "Okay, so what did I want to share with you today…

"I made a statement the other day that we are the *authors of our own reality*. I want to talk more about this today. Authors make up stories, they imagine characters, twist plots and tell tales that draw us in and light up our imaginations. I'm not a literary expert, but a colleague of mine once shared this great insight with me.[11-2] Some of you may be aware of the novels of Agatha Christie. Agatha Christie was an English novelist in the 1930's, very polite and very proper. She wrote over 75 murder-mystery stories. Now, when you read a novel like hers, the story is usually narrated either by the hero, as in, 'Suddenly, I turned and saw the dead body in the library,' or a neutral, third-person voice, like, 'She screamed when she saw a dagger in the dead body,' etc., etc. You get the idea. In one of her books, *The Death of Roger Ackroyd*, the story is told by the doctor of a small village where the murder takes place, but it's not till the end of the book you realize that he is the murderer! Think about it for a minute, you have just read 200 pages of his version of events! The doctor, therefore, is an *unreliable narrator*! He fooled you! You saw everything from his point of view, but he was up to something the whole time. He's a doctor, so why wouldn't you trust him? But he fooled you! Our thinking does this to us all the time, it's an unreliable narrator."

Parker spoke up first. "That's a very cute analogy, but what you are really describing is the subconscious."

Deborah didn't want to get into a discussion about concepts in the group setting, so she smiled and stuck to what she knew to be true. "I used to narrate everything in my head. When I was in the darkest parts of my PTSD I used to retell the story of what happened, the violence and the terror of it, over and over all the time as if there was an imaginary audience listening. I didn't actually think there was, but I already knew what had happened, so who was I telling it to? When I was in pain, I would have terrifying thoughts, like maybe this time the paralysis is going to be permanent, or maybe I'm going to be in a wheelchair for the rest of my life!"

"It was a coping mechanism," offered Parker again.

"Yes, it was, but a coping mechanism made of thought, and it became a habit. Maybe I had it before, I don't know, but it continued for a long time until I started to understand the way the mind works. I started to see that I create all kinds of stories in my head. For example, when I worked in Hollywood, I decided that success was having your name on the poster. It meant you had arrived, that you were one of the 'grown-ups.' Every time I worked on a movie, I would watch the credits to see where I was. On one movie, they put our names alphabetically and because I'm an S, I was below girls that I had trained. I was furious! From then on, I had my credit put into my contract so as to not have to feel that anger again! Can you see how I created a story which led to me getting upset? I wanted to blame the producer, but I made up that story, that rule, and I was the one suffering. Like Richard said the other day, we torture ourselves with our own thinking. Once I got to see that my thinking is unreliable, I was able to step back and not take it all so seriously."

"Sure, but I run a business. I have responsibilities like fulfilling customer orders and payroll, you know, *actual important things*, I can't just throw those thoughts out," scoffed Marc.

"Ah, but we are not saying to throw any thoughts out. Just watch them go by and as your thinking slows down and you get clarity, you will know which thoughts to listen to. You will intuitively know which ideas will benefit your business and which thoughts are just commentary, and then thoughts and ideas about better marketing or more efficient work practices that you never dreamed of can come through." Marc wasn't so sure, but Deborah continued.

"Before, when I had to take a flight, I would check and triple check my passport, my tickets, the time of the flight, the terminal, my passport, again. *What if I'm not in the computer, what if I miss the flight, what if there is something wrong with my ticket, what if, WHAT IF?!* It was exhausting. When I fly now, I still make sure I have my passport, I check the times and the terminal because that's a good idea, but there is no story anymore about what *might* happen and consequently, flying isn't stressful anymore.

"I also had a story about my pain. Maybe some of you do, too? I knew this story very well; in fact, I had a few versions. There was the version called, 'Why?' which had chapters about the medical problems, one leg longer than the other and the unstable pelvis, the injuries, and the diagnoses from the various doctors and chiropractors explaining the pain, all of which I had skillfully compiled into a nightmarish tale of agony. Then there was the 'Victim' story about how they beat me, how no one understood my torment, my suffering. I had others, too: the 'Heroic' one of how I have been through so much and come out the other side. My thought narrator was very creative and I relied on it for my identity. But it was just a lot of distressed thinking. Sometimes the narration shows up as rules and regulations: *Don't sit in that kind of chair, Don't let on that you don't know the answer, Don't trust happy people, they're stupid…*" Everyone laughed a little, but they were laughing because they all knew they had their own set of rules. "A dear friend of mine by the name of Shelly once said something to me, she said, 'Deborah, you have very high standards for everyone, only you can't live up to them yourself.' I see now that these stories are showing up in our headaches, our backs, our skin, and our stomachs."

"Our emotions are stored in our bodies," commented Parker, repeating what she was taught in graduate school.

"No, I disagree." Deborah had never been convinced by this theory so she continued. "I've heard that said, but stored how? Is my anger in my sciatic nerve, my jealousy in my rotator cuff? My resentment of my mother in…in my knees?"

"No, it means it's trapped, like an energy or

something…" Parker tried again to explain what she had heard.

"The thoughts you are thinking in this moment are creating the way you feel right now. It's that simple." Deborah paused. "These symptoms are the body's way of sending us signals that we are off, like distress signals. If we are awake enough, the signals can be small and subtle and we'll understand the nature of them, meaning we don't get frightened and can address the problem. If we are all caught up in our thinking, our story, then they need to get louder and louder, more and more painful, since we weren't able to hear them when they were small and subtle. The secret for me was when I realized I didn't have to have anything on those thoughts."

"What does that mean?" asked Yohan impatiently.

"It means that when these kinds of thoughts come, and they will, because we are human, what if you didn't have anything on them? What if they could travel through your mind and you didn't have any judgment or fear of them? What if you knew you didn't have to fix them?" Everyone looked at her curiously. "Let's try and understand this. Does anyone here have a person in their life that drives them nuts?"

"Oh yeah!" said Marc instantly. "My competitor, RPM Inc., is always trying to undercut me and steal my customers. I want to kill that son of a—"

"And did you?"

"Did I what?"

"Kill him?"

"Of course not."

"Hmm, that's interesting, don't you think? See how you had a thought that you wanted to kill someone, but you didn't? I'm guessing that you didn't have a huge struggle to hold yourself back from running at him with a knife or hiring a hitman to take him out?" Everyone laughed and Marc raised his eyebrows as if to say, *don't tempt me*. "What I mean is that thought just went through your mind and you didn't need to judge, control or analyze it. Could you see that thoughts are constantly going through our minds, chitty, chatty, boring, creative, even criminal thoughts, thousands of them a day, and most of them we don't even notice, so all of you are actually already doing this. All of you are already having thoughts without anything on them. So now this is becoming clearer to you, get curious and watch those sticky thoughts like frustrations, anger, even pain go by just like all the rest." Everyone nodded in agreement and they took a break to relax.

Melanie beckoned Deborah over to the side of the room, away from the participants. "I want to do this," she whispered under her breath.

"What?" asked Deborah curiously. She had no idea what Melanie meant.

"What you do! I just know this is going to take off and unless you are planning to move to Sydney, Dan is going to need someone here to carry on this work with his clients...*me!* I love what you are saying, I get it!" She squeezed Deborah's arm in excitement. "I totally get that it's our thinking. I get that even if the pain doesn't go away, even if it's cancer or, I don't know, something the doctors can't cure, we are still only ever experiencing it in our thoughts." She turned Deborah away from the group. "I used to have agonizing IBS. I had been in a terrible, violent marriage, he cheated on me and raped me, and I was doubled over in stomach pain all the time. I was fired from my last job because too many times I couldn't show up.

Then I got this job as Dan's assistant and just loved the supportive atmosphere here. As I settled in and finally relaxed, my pain faded away. Don't you see, I didn't have any treatment, so it could only have been my thinking that changed, right? But I couldn't tell anyone that the 'atmosphere' cured me, they would think I'm nuts! And I didn't want to suggest that people don't actually need the therapies done here, but now I see why I got well. My thinking changed and so my stomach calmed down!"

Deborah grabbed Melanie by the arms and gave her a huge hug. "I'm so sorry you went through such a terrible ordeal. Your recovery is amazing, though! Yes, everything you say is exactly right!"

After the break, Deborah was keen to continue. Learning that you could have thoughts and not have anything on them was crucial to understanding how this would calm their nervous systems.

"So I want to carry on with where we left off. I really think we are onto something here."

"I don't get it," said Costos. "Are you saying we should ignore our thoughts?"

"Actually, no. I did that for years and I see now how that was a kind of denial. We are not going for denial here. We want honesty, we want to be in the moment, right here, right now. One of my favorite stories about Sydney Banks is that back in the early days when people were coming to Vancouver to hear him speak, some of the early visitors to the island were curious about what techniques he must be using to help so many people. The story goes that one of them asked him what he does about anger, and apparently, Syd couldn't understand the question. Now, Syd wasn't an educated man, but he wasn't stupid either, so why couldn't he understand the question? They kept asking and Syd kept not understanding. Eventually, someone rephrased the question: 'Syd, do you ever get angry?' 'Of course I do!' he replied. 'Okay, so what do you do about it?' 'Why would I do anything?'" Deborah paused and then laughed at her own comments, but most of the others just stared at her. "Don't you see, Syd didn't see anything wrong with being angry! He had nothing on it!"

"May I?"

"Yes Melanie, please share with us what you are hearing."

"Well, I think it's because he didn't see it as a problem. I mean, he was somehow separate from his thoughts, like they were just passing through his head and he didn't judge them."

"Exactly, yes, well done." Melanie glowed with her secret excitement.

"Okay, so we have to control our thoughts, work on not judging them," observed Andrew.

"No, see that would be doing something. Like Melanie said, we want to see that you are separate from your thoughts, observing them if you like. You are not your thoughts, they are just…energy flowing through your mind. Any kind of working on or controlling them is like messing with the system. Syd was teaching us that there is actually nothing to do."

12
Wednesday Afternoon

Deborah's afternoon clients were Aliki and Primo. Primo needed to go first, as he had to get back to the restaurant to set up for the evening shift, so Aliki kindly went to sit downstairs with Melanie; she was in too much pain to go walking around the mall.

"Come in, Primo, I'm so excited to finally get to talk to you."

"Oh, me too, Miss Deborah, this is all so a-very interesting! But my back, it is strong, it's a-good, strong Italian back, see?" He stood up and did a middle-aged man's version of a Mr. Universe pose, then plopped back down again.

Deborah laughed. She loved his energy and openness. "But you have migraines?"

"Ah, yes a-terrible pain in the head. My head, it is bursting like a-the pressure cooker, you know in the kitchen, I feel always like a-the lobster about to be boiled alive!"

"Oh my, that's not good. So, how long have you had these headaches?"

"Since a-1995."

"And what happened in 1995?"

"Australia."

Deborah tried not to laugh. Australia was one of the most laid-back, chilled countries she had ever been to! America and England were busy, the Middle East was crazy, but Australia was chilled right out and even when things got tense, they always seemed to calm down over a beer and a barby. "So, how did coming to Australia give you migraines?"

"No, not a-the country. Australia it's a-very nice, very nice people, very nice a-harbor bridge. No, it was my mama." *Ah*, thought Deborah, *mama*. "We couldn't leave her behind so she had to come with us and ever since she is driving my wife a-crazy with the nudging and the criticizing. The pasta is too thin, the pizza crust it is a-too thick, the sauce it is too salty. Nothing is ever right and they fight a-real bad, sometimes I'm afraid for the kitchen knives. I try to keep them apart and happy, but it is how you say, a bloody seasickness."

"Nightmare?" suggested Deborah.

"Yes, this. Sometimes I get my languages a-mixed up, *mal d'mare* is French for the seasickness and I was thinking it was *mare* something. Anyway, you see, my problem, it is a-the family and they are making me a migraine. I have to lie on the bed, none of the daylight even or I am a-throwing up."

Deborah sat back in her seat. It was obvious that the stress of trying to keep his wife and his mother happy for over 20 years was making him sick. He was a sweet man and she could see how not wanting to upset anyone was making his life miserable.

"They, how you say, are a-shooting me? No, a-triggering. My wife and my mother are a-triggering me, no?"

Deborah couldn't help but adore this man. "Well, yes, *they* say things can 'trigger' us, it's a common phrase used in therapy circles, but I never use it. Let me see if I can explain. If I believe that my feelings are created by other people or situations, then yes, they would have the power to 'trigger' me. But that's not really how it works. Remember we talked about the fear of flying and injections, that our experience is only ever coming from our thoughts about our circumstances, not the actual circumstances." Primo nodded. "So with this understanding, nothing on the outside can trigger me because there is only ever my thoughts about the outside. To say that something triggered me is like saying it's their fault I feel this way, but that can never be. That's what we call Outside-In thinking and it's a misunderstanding of how it all works."

"Ah, like the a-Twinkie! '*The Twinkie made me do it!*'" They both fell about laughing. "So I shouldn't a-blame them anymore?"

"Well, yes, but it's not really about not blaming. Don't get me wrong, it's good not to blame and to take responsibility for our feelings and actions, but that would be what we call behavior modification. This is much deeper than that, Primo. This is about seeing that even deciding not to blame is also a thought, and that's what has produced your experience, not deciding to let go of blaming your wife and mother."

"Ah, yes, they are innocent of the crimes."

Deborah laughed. "We are all innocent when we misunderstand. When we see that the world is actually an

Inside-Out experience, meaning we always experience it from our thoughts, then yes, we can see people are innocent of making us feel bad, and as our thinking settles, we can make much better judgments and decisions for them and us."

When they had finished, Aliki was sitting in the chair outside Deborah's office. She moved slowly and came and sat down. Deborah hadn't noticed how pretty she was, as she was always hiding behind her long, dark hair, even when she spoke in the group.

"Thank you so much for waiting, Aliki. Please, come and sit down." Deborah looked at her questionnaire. "I think I've had most of the aches and pains that the others have at some point so I can relate, but I don't know what it's like to have fibromyalgia. Could you share a little with me?"

Aliki took a moment and then said, "It feels like sunburn, but with fiberglass under my skin…sometimes it's like an elephant just stomped on me and all my nerves are screaming, and sometimes, sometimes it's as if someone is sparking electricity through my whole body."

Deborah wasn't expecting this. She took a deep breath. "That sounds awful."

"Actually, you are one of the first people to believe me without saying or hinting I must be exaggerating. My family thinks I'm lazy because I find it so hard to work, and I'm sure my boyfriend thinks that I'm exaggerating. No one believes me, which just adds to the misery."

"I believe you. Pain is always real, whether there is a structural reason for it or not. Has anyone ever given you an explanation that makes sense?"

"No, they say they don't really know what causes it, which makes it even more scary, as there isn't a cure."

"And when did it start?"

"About three years ago… I get what you have been telling us. I get that it's my thinking. But I just can't stop it. I'm exhausted from the pain, so I get stressed, then I can't sleep because I can't switch my brain off so I'm more tired, and it's a vicious cycle. I've been trying so hard. I've tried so many things, I'm desperate. I haven't slept all this week. I'm trying to do this, I want it to work so badly."

"Okay, okay. But maybe the trying so hard is part of the problem. Remember the discussion we had about perfectionists? Could you maybe be trying to do your pain perfectly? Remember what we talked about this morning, how Syd didn't have anything on being angry? By not having anything on it, I bet his body didn't have much of a reaction to it… Think of the sky. Clouds, birds, and planes all move through the sky, but the sky doesn't have anything on it. Your mind is big like the sky, and thoughts are like a flock of birds flying through."

"That's nice. I mean it's more kind and loving than what I was doing. I have been told to talk to my brain and tell it to stop with the pain, but I end up telling myself off when I forget. I have been told to journal and record my thoughts, but it just gets my mind all mixed up again. I wrote and I wrote and then when I didn't have anything left to write, I used to write, *I have nothing left to write* over and over just to make them happy. If I can just find the right treatment, or as you say the right understanding, then I know I will get better."

"Oops, do you see what just happened? You went back into needing to do it right again. Syd Banks taught that all this busywork is a misunderstanding. He said that love was the answer."

"Like the Beatles?"

"Yes, *all you need is love!* He said that pure love and pure understanding are the same thing. That under these conditions of love and positivity, the mind would open up and evolve into great heights to assist you through life.[12-1] Doesn't that sound better than yelling at yourself?"

Aliki nodded, "So, you mean I really don't have to do *anything*? That thoughts will just go by?"

"Yes. I asked a psychologist once if thoughts can die of neglect and she said yes. What I understand now…no, what I *know* to be true now is that it always passes, whatever it is, and the less you have on it, the less the scary thoughts come and the less they stick around. And as your thoughts slow down, your nervous system will heal and your innate wisdom will guide you what to do next."

As Deborah was leaving her little office, she saw a middle-aged man who wasn't wearing white but looked like he worked there come out of the next room. They started toward the stairs, then he turned and introduced himself.

"Hi, I'm Paul. You're Deborah, right?"

"Yes, I'm doing the research program with Dan. Nice to meet you."

"You too, I'm the resident psychotherapist here. Would love to hear about your work. I heard you are working with the ideas of Dr. Sarno, I'm a big fan. I actually had the honor of meeting him in New York a few years ago."

"Wow, I really want to hear about that, but I should warn you, I'm exploring the work of several pain scientists and I actually don't agree with everything he said. Don't get me wrong, I fully appreciate and respect his medical explanations. I'm very grateful for that, saves me having to go to medical school."

Paul immediately stopped on the landing, turned, and

raised his eyebrows. "But it's so obvious. All his patients were *Perfectionists* and *Goodists*, their rage was pushed down into their unconscious and that's what caused the pain. It's a distraction technique; I see it over and over in all my patients."

Deborah couldn't help thinking of the analogy, *if you only have a hammer, everything starts looking like a nail.* "Okay, but I don't buy it, that's all." She smiled as they walked down the stairs.

"You don't have to *buy it,* it's fact!"

Deborah followed him out to the reception area. She knew better than to challenge someone about a concept they saw to be 'fact.' It always leads to a battle of egos, which isn't good for anyone.

"Are you free for a drink tonight?" asked Paul suddenly.

Deborah raised her eyebrows.

"I'm meeting my girlfriend for a drink and I thought maybe you'd like to join us?"

"Oh, sure…thank you."

They met in a café in Kings Cross and took their drinks to a quiet area out back with tables and chairs under trees, with fairy lights strung around the walls. It was very trendy; some soft samba jazz played in the background as they settled for the corner table. Paul informed her that his girlfriend was also a psychologist who worked at the hospital and that she would be joining them soon.

"So I was reading that before Dr. Sarno got into this idea that subconscious repressed anger is causing the pain, he originally believed that it was caused by stress dysregulating the oxygen levels in the blood flow to the muscles, is that right?" inquired Deborah.

133

"Yes, that was true for about the first fifteen years of his work. Then he met Stanley Cohen, a Freudian psychoanalyst[12-2], who suggested that physical symptoms were not a physical expression of anxiety but were, in fact, the result of what we call a defense mechanism. This explained why someone could read his books and get well without ever meeting him. It was such a breakthrough."

"How?" Deborah was curious about what Paul saw to be true.

"Well, once they understood that their brain was diverting their attention to their body so that they could avoid the awareness of, or confrontation with, subconscious anger and repressed feelings, they saw through the brain's strategy, and the mystery was solved. Our bodies are strong and are able to heal once the hidden emotions and repressed rage are discovered and released. This was an amazing scientific breakthrough!"

"How is that scientific?"

"It's the basis of psychoanalysis."

"Uh, I think you'll find it well documented that Freud considered his self-reported 'therapeutic success' to be his proof, which, let's admit it, isn't at all scientific and was often wrong and biased. All he did, in fact, was repackage the act of confession and pathologized his patients' resistance by labeling it as neurosis. I've been reading up on him this week. I hadn't realized that he actually started his career by treating the physical symptoms of neurotic patients... Did you know that he was turned down multiple times for a professorship because his theories were so bizarre and unprovable and he only became elevated to the title of professor because he asked one of his wealthy patients to bribe someone in the Viennese Ministry of Education?" Deborah couldn't help laughing at this revelation. "She donated a painting to a gallery and then suddenly he got accepted! He admitted it in a letter to a friend!" Paul raised his eyebrows.

"The really funny thing was that he deemed everyone to be carrying around this idea of neurosis and repressed rage and therefore mental illness, but he himself was incredibly neurotic, ambitious and vengeful. Look at how he treated Adler and Jung when they disagreed with him. He spread slander, threatened them and threw them out of his secret little club—no repression there! The whole Id, Ego, Super Ego thing was just another way of saying that man is governed by his environment and instincts, which is a massive misunderstanding of how the human experience works! So it baffles me how Sarno, who was so brilliant, could have had his head turned by, well, nonsense… I read that Sarno admitted that he screened his patients before treating them, which I don't actually have a problem with, but I would say it's all a lot of subjective observation and definitely not science." Paul sat back and gave her a patronizing grin as Deborah continued.

"Okay, here's the thing: many people got well from reading or working with Sarno before all that Freudian stuff came into the picture by understanding that it was their dysregulated nervous system that was causing the pain, right? So these new subconscious, unconscious ideas didn't stop that from being true, did it…but the bit I really don't get is…how you can believe that the brain has independently and deviously decided that agonizing pain is better than experiencing fear and emotions? That makes no sense! Who would choose crippling, unrelenting pain that itself never fails to produce fear and terror, over 'unacceptable' emotions, as you call them?"

"But it's their subconscious that is choosing."

"See, that's what I mean, you make it sound like they

are possessed by an alien being that's out to get them! Can't you see that it's just fearful thinking? It's just more thought!"

"But that's the power of the unconscious: it doesn't *want* you to know. Physical symptoms come as the result of the underlying conflicts, the uh, the desire to retaliate that is battling with the taboo of impolite conduct, for example. That convergence is what causes the distress," insisted Paul.

Deborah laughed again. "Did you know that George Orwell's response to Freud's dream theory was something like, if I'm not frightened about thinking about such things when I'm awake, why do they need to be disguised when I'm asleep?[12-3] Paul, what's the point of a disguise if when you look at it, you can see right through it?"

Paul shook his head. "In my experience, people would rather be in pain than face uncomfortable feelings or admit they are angry. You'd be surprised."

Deborah leaned forward, "I am. In fact, I am so surprised, I don't believe it. Have you ever asked anyone?" Paul looked at her like she was crazy. The waitress had just brought out some drinks for the table next to them, and Deborah called her over. "Excuse me, can I ask you a personal question?"

"Sure, no worries, whatcha got?"

"Can I ask, do you ever get any physical pain? Sorry, I don't mean to pry, but we are having a disagreement and I was hoping you could help us."

"Uh, yeah. My feet kill me by the time I finish my shift each night. I work in another place before this so being on my feet all day is a real pain, ha ha, not funny. I'll be soaking them in hot water and Epsom salts when I get home tonight, that's for sure."

"So sorry to hear that. Please don't take this the wrong

way, but which would you rather have, throbbing, painful feet or deep frustration?"

"*I have both! Struth, have you ever waited tables for a living?*"

"Right, but if you had to choose?"

The waitress looked confused but didn't hesitate. "I would take the frustration, of course."

She left and went inside to take an order from some new, unsuspecting customers.

"See?" said Deborah triumphantly. "A. The pain hasn't distracted her *at all*, she is still frustrated, and B. she would swap the pain for having uncomfortable emotions!"

"Okay, very clever. But it's repressed. She needs psychotherapy to help her get in touch with her emotions."

Deborah almost fell off her chair laughing. "You are too funny, Paul. Look, can't you see that the people who got well from reading Dr. Sarno's books clearly had a new thought, an insight? Understanding that there was nothing physically wrong with them was great news and *that's* what solved the mystery of what Sarno called TMS, i.e., Too Much Stress. Digging around in the past only stirs things up more. How can that help an already over stimulated nervous system? The past is only a memory brought alive in the present moment by a new thought, which isn't even physical, it's…it's spiritual. And here's something else I don't get: How can you say that our bodies are so strong and then say that the mind isn't? How could one system be so brilliant at self-healing, able to fight infections and heal fractures, but the mind be so weak and easily duped? It doesn't make sense…?"[12-4]

"But the mind doesn't come with a *'user's manual.'*" Deborah had heard this lament many times, so she jumped right back in.

"Paul, the mind is *strong*. It's full of so much more

137

resilience and wisdom than you are giving it credit for. It's capable of unbelievable depths of love and joy, insight and creativity, but it just gets covered up sometimes by stinky thinking, stress and old ideas, and even that is just an illusion now that I come to think of it… When my clients see this, when they get that we are Divinely engineered, body *and* soul, they fall into a quiet mind, that place before thought where they find peace, they feel that connection, they see that we are life itself! No work needed and nowhere to get to because it's who we really are… When they see that, they know they have come home."

Deborah suddenly felt a wonderful, humbling feeling inside, as if she had just brushed up against the Essence of Life and then fell into the pause that naturally filled the conversation. Paul suddenly smiled. His new girlfriend had just walked in and as they caught each other's eye, they grinned that private, knowing grin. He blushed a little as he introduced her to Deborah and asked what she would like to drink.

"Cappuccino, thanks. I love this place, but they really need to get new staff. I just walked past a waitress yelling at some customers by the door. *She clearly doesn't need help getting in touch with her emotions!*"

13
Thursday

Mia was waiting outside Deborah's office as she walked up the stairs for their early morning session. She had been very curious about Mia since they first met. Deborah had originally seen her as weak and fragile, constantly at the mercy of her emotions, but the more she understood her, the more she saw her incredible courage to keep showing up despite her terrified view of the world. As they talked, it became clear that Mia had faced frightening abandonment, neglect and rejection all through her childhood. Her fear of being alone was palpable. Could this be why she kept opting for so many surgeries, wondered Deborah? To feel noticed, connected?

"Mia, I heard someone say something that had a very profound effect on me a few years ago. He said, 'We are always looking in the wrong direction for happiness.'"

"Oh, I know, I have done that. Family hurts you, boyfriends cheat on you, friends abandon you. I know I have to stop looking to others for happiness, that's why I came here to find a new treatment…but you…don't mean that…do you?"

"No."

"You mean stop all that… You mean stop looking outside myself for the answers, for comfort, for approval…don't you?"

"Yes, Mia."

"I know it's true, it's not like no one has ever suggested it to me before, but I just couldn't stop thinking maybe this new doctor or this treatment would fix it, but a doctor can't fix me…can they?"

"No, because Mia, you aren't broken. There is nothing wrong with you. You have everything you need, all the innate courage and well-being to be the perfect you and you really are amazing. Look how you have shown up over and over, you have never given up. You were just looking in the wrong direction."

"Good morning, everyone." Deborah looked around the group, thrilled that everyone was still showing up. "Now, we have talked a lot about Thought and a bit about Consciousness, but this morning I want to talk to you about what Syd Banks called *Mind*." She took a sip of water and collected her thoughts. Deborah loved to talk about spiritual things, but with such a mixed crowd, she wondered where to start.

"When I worked in Hollywood I was once asked to make an animatronic puppet tiger for a movie with Eddy Murphy. Jake, the real tiger, lived on a ranch in the mountains north of L.A. He had retired, but you may have seen him jumping through the snow in Exxon and Esso commercials?"

"Oh, I love that tiger!" called out Erin.

"I had to go visit Jake several times, to take photos and

check color samples, etc. and in the process, I learned that tigers have unique faces like humans and no two tigers' markings are exactly alike. Tigers are very majestic animals and even though Jake was old and tired, he still had 'it' just like a real movie star. It took at least 20 of us—engineers, fabricators and computer guys—to recreate an animatronic tiger, and although it's the proudest, most amazing creature I ever worked on, it's nothing next to the real Jake. The real Jake had innate majesty, cunning and wisdom. When you look closely at something like a tiger, you can see that Intelligence in action. *Mind* was Syd's way of describing this, that there is an Infinite Loving Intelligence, a Divine Mind, a Source of Everything behind life."

"Oh, yes," agreed Jeane nodding her head. "I love seeing the majesty of God's work in nature."

"Ha! You don't think that the bottle of soda you are holding is also the '*majesty of God's creation*?'" challenged Marc. "You can't just say only pretty or 'natural' things are God. If God is your Source of *everything*, as she keeps saying, then He's also that plastic bottle holding your chemical-filled soda! He's war and babies dying and yes, He created *your* pain!" Jean blushed bright red and Deborah's stomach took a flip at the depths of Marc's anger.

"Hey!" said Richard, coming to Jeanne's defence. "You're right. There are a lot of things in this world that don't make any sense, things that hurt and maybe we will never understand. I don't understand why God took my first wife or why my little girl had to grow up without her mother, but I know now that I can either drown in a pool of misery and anger or I can pick myself up and take care of what I can and stop fighting what I don't understand."

There was silence as Deborah let things settle for a moment, then she continued. "I think Syd was very smart not to use the word God when he named the Three Principles. God brings up such a lot of issues for many of us and we all have a different concept of who and what God is, so please, please don't get hung up on the words. When I was at my lowest point after my third mugging, if you had used the word 'God,' I would have told you where to stick it. But I gradually came to see that for me, God wasn't so much a being, more a 'state of being'... I have no idea what that really means other than a state of pure love, but I can tell you from all my work with people suffering from abuse, addictions, chronic pain, or many of the other tragedies that life brings, the people that get better, the ones that transcended their circumstances, they all found comfort in some kind of understanding that there was a Loving Intelligence behind life and whatever word they found to describe it, they only found it, truly found it, when they looked within."[13-1]

Mia had started crying. She reached in her purse for some tissues but found it too much and headed for the door. Melanie met her with a kind hug and they left for some privacy.

"I have had many experiences in my life where I should have either died or been in a wheelchair, or at least in a hospital for the rest of my life. But I'm not. Now this is just my belief, and as we now know, belief is made up of thought, but I believe something was taking care of me—the same Intelligent something that brings the sun up in the morning and gives us air to breathe." She surveyed the room to see if anyone else was about to bolt. "When Syd Banks talks about Mind, he doesn't mean our personal thinking mind, he means the Intelligent Mind behind life. He was referring to that always reliable Infinite Source of Everything."

"I'm okay with that," said Costos casually. "I mean,

when my kids were born it blew me away, miracle upon miracle. It was incredible, I don't know how my wife did it."

"Can I ask you, Costos, did your wife take a course in how to make babies?" Everyone laughed.

"We didn't even do any birthing classes," laughed Costos.

"Okay, so how did she know how to make a baby and how did the baby know how and when to appear? How does a caterpillar know to make a chrysalis or an acorn become an oak tree? It's a reliable system. Think about it for a moment: if this reliable, Infinite Intelligent Source of everything is doing all that, why wouldn't it take care of healing our pain, too?"

"Yeah, but if everything is made of thought, if we really are living in a thought-created world, then God is also just a thought, so it can't be real, can it, whatever word you choose?" challenged Marc again.

His words hung in the air as everyone looked to Deborah for an answer. "You could say that…but I know I feel a lot better when I follow the thought that God is."

She looked around the room again and suggested they take a break.

Melanie and Mia joined them again for the next session and it occurred to Deborah that it was time to pull all these ideas together.

"We only experience pain when it comes into consciousness and the special effects department of Consciousness makes it feel real in the body. I know some of you have struggled with friends, family and coworkers not believing you, but whether pain comes from an acute injury or a structural fault, a disease or stressful thinking, it's always happening in the brain. It can be excruciating, needing serious painkillers sometimes, but it's always happening up here. As we saw from the phantom limb pain story and Dan's research, chronic pain is experienced in the emotional part of the brain. Research also shows that depending on the environment, pain is experienced differently; for example, if you are in a cold room, you will feel the same pain worse than if you are in a warm room.[13-2] Patients with a window in their hospital room get better quicker than ones without. Rose, do you mind if I share the tiddlywinks story?" Rose nodded that it was okay. "Thank you. Rose shared with me that she forgot about her wrist pain when she played bingo with her friends even though she was picking up tiny discs, which must have been a strain on her hand. Why did she forget? Because she was having fun, her thoughts were occupied with something else and, as we can only experience thought in the moment, she had forgotten all about it. Several of you have mentioned that you have forgotten about your pain at different times during our sessions. And the fact that some of you have felt worse at times was because you were caught up in your thinking."

Primo called out, "My mama, she a-picked a fight with my wife last night because she fired a-no good waitress, and I didn't, as you say, have nothing on it!"

"Yes, Primo! In fact, you have just reminded me of a conversation I heard between two of my beloved teachers.[13-3] Elsie was telling Linda that when her husband had been dangerously ill in the hospital, she had gone in and out of panic. Linda said, "See, Elsie, this is why I love you so much. You could have panic but the panic didn't have you." Elsie replied, "Yes, I could have the experience without the experience having me." And I thought, *I can have pain without the pain having me.* Do you see?"

"Yes!" agreed Richard. "My back still hurts, maybe it will always hurt, but the raging frustration is falling away and I just don't feel the pain in the same agonizing way anymore. I see now how there is the pain and then there's my thoughts about the pain. It's like they are two separate things. There's me, whatever that is, and then there is what my body is doing, which I can only know by thought and thought always moves! It's like you said, we haven't even worked on it. It's a bit trippy, guys, but hey, it's working."

"Amazing, Richard, we will make a hippie out of you yet! So from this we can see that pain is not an accurate indicator of the state of your body. For example, you could have a paper cut that kills and a fracture and not even know about it. If pain can increase or disappear depending on your state of mind or what colour room you are in, then it's not a reliable indicator. Think about a soldier in battle. He needs to get to safety, and he isn't feeling anything from that bullet in his leg because it wouldn't help, he just needs to get back to base. Then he can cry like a baby if he wants."

Erin let out a sound that indicated she had just understood something. "Oh, oh, my husband ran a 10k with a broken bone in his foot and didn't know until it was over! I always just thought he was a complete drongo! I could never understand how the idiot could do that, but now I see it didn't help him to feel it till the race was over! And my feet always hurt worse whenever I think about it!" She burst out laughing, as her insight made the whole thing seem ridiculous.

"Exactly! So what is pain for? Pain is to protect us. You may have heard that there are people who don't have any pain sensors, and you might be thinking that sounds like heaven right now, but these people tend not to last long.

They get cuts and burns and because they can't feel it, they get seriously infected, and you know how we were always told that lepers lose their feet or hands because of the leprosy? It's not, it's because rats come and eat their limbs when they are asleep and they can't feel it!" Everyone pulled disgusted faces and told her to stop![13-4]

"Sorry. So, chronic pain is like the opposite of that. It's as if our brain is being too protective, it's screaming for us to stop doing anything that might damage us more. Chronic pain is like having your 'pain meter' turned way up high, like turning up the amplifier in the movie *Spinal Tap*."[13-5] Those who got the reference laughed in acknowledgement. "Remember the story about Agatha Christie and her unreliable narrator? Well, here is an unreliable indicator! Pain is an unreliable indicator of the state of your body…[13-6] So, *what can we trust?* You can absolutely trust your innate wisdom. When you see past your busy personal thinking to your quiet mind that is always there, always reliable, then you can trust that you will know what to do in every situation. That's Mind, the Intelligent Source of everything in action."

"Like in the Matrix," said Corey.

"Yes, like in the Matrix."

They took a lunch break and Deborah went to see if Mia was okay. She was shaky, but she looked different somehow—maybe more relaxed? Jeane and Rose said they would look after her and they all left to get something to eat.

"Thanks for taking care of Mia, was it okay?"

"Sure," said Melanie, "I'm glad I was there to be helpful. I don't know if I said the right things, but I think she just needed someone to be with her. I think she is seeing some really important things that will change a lot

146

for her and maybe that's scary?"

"See, that was your innate wisdom guiding you to do the right thing. We all have innate compassion, *and* the ability to doubt it." Deborah gave her a big hug. "You are going to be really good at this."

After lunch, they all came back and sat in their usual seats. Then, for something different, Dan brought in four guests: Tali, Dan's wife; Laura, the massage therapist; Archie; and a young friend of Dan's from the hospital that Deborah hadn't met yet.

"Okay, now you will have noticed we have been joined by some other volunteers." Dan waved them to come forward. "Please welcome Tali, Archie, Laura and Matthew. Melanie is now going to give you a piece of paper with some job titles on it, and our friends here are going to hold up a number. I want you to match their number with the job you think they do." Everyone looked at the four guests carefully. Tali was wearing a white doctor's coat, Laura was in her regular street clothes and Archie and Matthew wore suits and ties. The choices were these:

Stay-at-home parent

Doctor

Administrator

Massage Therapist

When they were done, Dan asked who they thought was the stay-at-home parent. There was a mixture of answers, but only two out of the 15 people guessed Tali.

"Ah, so who is the doctor then?" They all paused and then shouted out various names. "Will the real doctor please step forward?" Waiting for dramatic effect, they all paused and then Archie stepped forward!

"I knew it!" announced Marc proudly, "See, I had it here on my paper!"

"Okay, Marc, how did you know it was Archie?"

"Well, because…well, I knew it was too obvious to be the lady in the white coat, that was clearly a trick, and the others, well, no offense, but they just don't look old enough."

"Archie, please tell the group what you are a doctor of."

"I have a Ph.D. in Business Administration." Everyone burst out laughing.

"So, Marc, I wouldn't be too quick to ask Archie about your neck pain, although he is very skilled at sending bills!" There was more laughter as Tali handed her husband his white coat and sat down with Laura and Melanie. Archie thanked Matthew and accompanied him out the door.

"Okay, thank you for indulging us in that little charade, but I do think it's very important to understand who and where we get our information from, and how it can affect our thinking. There is a time and place for my white coat; patients in pain often need a strong image to help them trust what is being said, but I want to talk to you this afternoon as a fellow traveler. I have been studying pain for two decades now and have looked into many different treatments, from surgery to talk therapy. I'm seeing something new here. I'm seeing just how much the mind and thinking plays a part in all of these experiences, as much for the doctor as for the patient.

"When I was in med school, the clinic supervisor would say things like, 'You have a shoulder in cubicle 4 and a meniscus tear in 5.' People are more than just their body parts, but as doctors, we forget that sometimes. I always knew that the state of someone's mind was important, but I didn't see just how much it contributed to their whole experience of pain… I can see that some people will be able to hear about these Three Principles, have a life-changing insight and their pain could be gone, and others might need more time and more help. So I want to talk about some of the things that I have learned about that I think would help to put this all together." Dan took a seat and continued.

"Some of you have told me that when your doctor gave you a diagnosis or they showed you your MRI, you felt more pain, even when the doctor said don't worry. That's because your brain is constantly assessing danger, and when hearing scary information, your brain decides you need protecting, so it stops you from moving by making it more painful; it's a very clever illusion. I had a patient recently who had terrible knee pain and she told me that it always hurt when she stood up. She told me that just before standing up, she would wonder if or how bad it was going to hurt. I realized that her anticipation of pain was contributing to her experience of the pain because she was priming her brain that something dangerous was coming and that she needed to protect herself. But ironically, or should I say innocently, she had trained her brain to produce the pain. So I tried to work with her to do the opposite. Coaches use this method with athletes, they imagine crossing the finish line as they ready themselves at the start, and piano players who practice in their heads can actually improve their technique without even sitting at the piano!"

Deborah was so excited hearing Dan talk. "When I was

in Israel," she interjected, "I met Natan Sharansky. He was a Russian dissident who was put in solitary confinement for months and months in the Gulag, and he kept himself sane by playing chess in his head. After he was finally released, he moved to Israel where he became a member of parliament and when Gary Kasperoff came to visit, Sharansky beat him!"[13-7]

"Wow, great story," acknowledged Dan. "Yes, see how the brain is always learning how to do things with the gift of thought? You may have heard the phrase, *Neurons that wire together, fire together.*[13-8] It's how we learned to ride a bike or write our names—repetition helps us retain what we learn. This is a good thing for habits like riding a bike or learning a language, but it can happen with pain, too. So, like a chess player can improve their game without even having a board, you can do the same with your pain. My patient was imagining her knee hurting before she stood up! So I taught her to retrain her brain, to imagine no pain."

"Did it help?" asked Parker.

"Yes, eventually, but I now realize that although it was an improvement, it was kind of like positive thinking, it was just more thinking... Maybe you have heard of Pavlov's dogs[13-9], how they were trained to salivate at the sound of a bell? We are always given this as the prime example of what's called conditioning, but does anyone know what happened to them after?"

"Oh, I know this one!" called out Corey, his long, limp limbs jumping into action as if a puppeteer had just picked up his strings.

"Really?" asked Dan, slightly bemused.

"Yeah, yeah, they were like eaten. There was a siege or something and the people were like starving so they got eaten. I learned it in history class, it was called the a...the Siege of Leningrad!" Now everyone was bemused.

"Uh, well, yeah. That's fascinating and slightly disturbing, but not quite where I was going… Something I learned was that after the experiment was over, they went back to behaving like regular dogs and only salivating when food came. Once the guy with the bell went away, that conditioning was gradually lost, forgotten about. Think about when you have put effort into a diet or exercise regime and then the holidays come and you start to forget that sugar is not allowed or that you still need to walk your 10,000 steps a day… What Deborah has been teaching us is that we don't have to condition or control or *think* about our thinking. Once you see that thought is…an energy that is continuously flowing through our minds, and step back and observe it, you can have confidence that a new, healthy thought will always come."

They were all a bit surprised to be hearing a doctor talk like this and fell silent for a minute.

"No, I get it," said Corey. "When I like think about my knee hurting it hurts more, and then I think about how I'll never play professional basketball and my knee hurts more, and then I think I'll be in a wheelchair by the time I'm old, like 40 or something, and that I might as well give up now, I mean like *now*. But my thinking just took me on some gnarly ride and none of it's like even true, right? I mean, Scottie Pippen got a migraine in a crucial 1990 playoff. I bet that was stress. The doc here told me yesterday that my knee has healed already, so maybe it is my stupid head that is making my knee still hurt."

"I think the only thing stopping you from doing whatever you want is…well, your thinking," offered Dan. "Like they say, if you think you can or you think you can't, then you are right."

Corey shrugged his broad boney shoulders in

agreement.

"Whilst we are on basketball," said Dan, "The thing about Michael Jordan was that he was the best of all time not because of how high he could jump, how well he could shoot, how fast he was on the court, none of that. Michael Jordan was the best of all time because he was always present. He was always in the moment."

Corey nodded and gave a rapper's gesture of agreement.

"When we really see this to be true," added Deborah, "we see that there is a space behind thought and it's where all our knowledge to navigate life really comes from. The less interested we become in our thinking, the quieter things are in here and the more room there is for us to experience kindness and compassion especially for ourselves."

"I'm really beginning to see that," agreed Dan. "It's only human to believe that the man in the white coat can heal us because we *want* to believe it. I've heard of Lab experiments where the animals that are held and loved do better than the ones that don't. But the healing isn't coming from the white coat or even the loving touch, it's coming from our belief. So when it comes to pain, when we become less interested in our thinking about it, there is less and less to do and more and more love to experience. And that is healing."

When Deborah got back to the suite she saw Lucia sweeping the patio, but she was crying again.

"What's happened now, honey?"

Lucia gave her the saddest look. "My cousin, he got fired and now everyone here, they hate me!"

"Why, what happened?"

"It was him who stole the money and he got me this

job so now I am under the suspicion from everyone. They don't trust me, they hate me, I'm going to lose my job too, and I will have to go back to Italy!" She started to cry again and swept with such frenzy that Deborah thought she might break something.

"Okay, okay, slow down. Come and sit for a moment. Have you ever done anything that might make them suspicious of you? Have you ever stolen any money?"

"Oh, no, no!" She wiped away some tears. "And he's not even my real cousin, he's my cousin's cousin's brother-in-law, and he's a really bad man. We just said cousin so I could get a job here."

"Have you ever been in any trouble?" She shook her head. "Have you ever waited tables?"

"Yes, at my cousin's restaurant in Milano, why?"

"I think I have a solution. Dry your eyes and get your things… *This was a real cousin, right?*"

The two women got in Deborah's car. She remembered that Primo's restaurant was in Bondi Beach, as that's how he had met Dan. There couldn't be too many Italian restaurants in Bondi, so the one called Primo's seemed a good bet. As they walked in, Primo let out a loud welcome and insisted Deborah come and try everything on the menu.

"No, no, that's not why I'm here. I want you to meet Lucia. Lucia is a very, very good waitress and needs a job!"

"Uh? Where you are a-from?"

"Montenapoleone, Milano."

"Perfecto! You save a-my life, Miss Deborah!"

14
Friday

It was Friday morning. Deborah woke up and realized it was the last day of the program. She took a deep breath. The weekly staff meeting would be taking place that morning, and as Dan and Melanie needed to be there, they had decided to tell the participants to come a little later. She still had to get in and meet with Parker before that, so after she got it all straight in her head, she got up and got moving.

"Hi, Parker, can't believe it's the last day!"

"I know!" She smiled as they took their seats.

Parker, a young mother of three, was in a doctoral program at the university. She had insomnia, chronic fatigue and very painful IBS. Her questionnaire was completely filled out and then some. She had written on the back of each page with more intense details. The paper, overflowing with the story of her life, crinkled with the deep impression of the words she had forced into every inch of the page.

Deborah smiled as she put down the papers. "Don't tell me you will miss hanging out with us?"

"Sort of, but that's not what I meant." She paused for a moment. "When I filled out that questionnaire, I was so stuck in the story of my life. I needed you to know everything I had been through, what I had sacrificed and how nothing ever seemed to be good enough. I love my kids, I really do, but now that I'm back in grad school and I'm trying to do *everything*, be supermum, I see now how terrified I've always been of failing. You hear about other mums who do it all, become CEOs and get PhDs, but it's really hard! Then this week, listening to you talk, I saw how I had made this all up! No one told me I had to go back to school, that I had to get a PhD. I put all that on myself! I see now how needing another piece of paper is just another attempt at getting approval." Parker started to cry.

Deborah reached out her hand. "I get it. I have felt that need for approval all my life, never being sure if I was good enough and needing to be better, louder, always more, so that I would be liked or loved, even just noticed. Parker, I really get it. But you are right, we make this stuff up and then beat ourselves up because we have failed this imaginary standard that we ourselves decided we had to live by. We are often meaner to ourselves than anyone else ever is."

"We learn all kinds of techniques and methods, theories and modalities in school to deal with people's diagnoses, but really… I see now that it's all just distressed thinking. That all those diagnoses are just the different ways people cope with their thoughts." Deborah nodded in agreement. "Some cope by hurting themselves, some by drinking, some by talking to themselves and some by trying to control everything and be perfect. I'm wondering…is pain my coping mechanism?"

Deborah reflected for a few moments; this was a fascinating insight. "I know that in the traditional approach to this, they would say it's either for secondary benefit, like attention and sympathy, or that it's a distraction. They say it's the subconscious's way of distracting you from unacceptable emotions. But that doesn't sit well with me. I mean, if I asked you or any of our fine friends in the group, would they rather have chronic, unrelenting pain or deal with their emotions, what would they say?"

"We would all yell, *take this pain away*!"

"Exactly. So I don't buy the 'repressed rage, dig around in the past to fix it, journal it to death or the boogeyman subconscious is going to get you' argument. After all, we can only ever think one thought at a time, and if you are thinking it, then it's not suppressed, is it? But that's not important right now; debating concepts gets us nowhere. What is important is that you are seeing that distressed thinking is dysregulating your nervous system, and that's messing with your stomach, keeping you up at night, so no wonder you are exhausted. Can you see now that you don't actually have to do anything about your thinking with any of those techniques and modalities? That it will flow, move on all by itself once you see the truth of how it works?"

"I do…but how come they don't teach us this in school? How come they only teach us about illness and don't teach us anything about wellness and well-being?"

"Great question! I meet psychologists and psychiatrists all the time who don't have a clue how the mind really works. They all have sophisticated ways to solve the content of people's thinking, when really, they just need to step back and see—it's *that* they are thinking, not what they are thinking that's the issue." Deborah reached down into her purse and pulled out a piece of paper. "This one of my many favorite quotes from Syd Banks."

"You must look within.
And if you look in the personal mind and all the past problems,
you are looking at the mistake.
You are looking at the mess.
You are looking at the illusion..."

"When I was recovering from PTSD, the shrink at my local hospital just kept asking me to talk about what had happened in the past. I wanted to scream at her that I was already doing that all day and all night very well at home. She had nothing more to offer me other than dragging up the memories, the 'mess,' as Syd called it, again and again. I needed help to *not* do that! Anyway, I digress. It's coming, this new understanding is becoming more recognized and it will get there.[14-1] As Emily Dickenson said, '*Truth must dazzle gradually, or every man be blind*.'[14-2]"

Parker pondered for a moment. "But what does this mean for my PhD now? Am I wasting my time?"

"I really don't know...but I do know that you have all the wisdom and innate well-being to answer that question for yourself."

Deborah slipped into the back of the staff meeting. Melanie gave her a knowing smile and pointed to an empty seat. They were just finishing up. Archie was going over some old business and then asked for any new business.

Laura, the massage therapist, asked how the research group was going.

"Pretty good, as far as I know," replied Archie, looking at Dan.

"Great! I know some of you have looked in and seen what's going on. We are very pleased with the feedback so far."

"So, what will it mean for the clinic? Are you planning any changes?" Paul had become suspicious.

Dan didn't hesitate; he had been anticipating this. "Nothing is changing. It's going to be a while before we have finished analyzing the data. You are all doing a great job and we appreciate every one of you on our amazing team."

In the conference room, everyone was buzzing around the conference table. Primo had brought in a delicious array of very extravagant Italian pastries.

"See, the best Italiano pastries and all a-made with Miss Deborah's Three a-Principles ingredients."

"Yes!" agreed Dan. "Thank you so much, Primo!"

Richard was waving, trying to get everyone's attention as they made their way to their seats with their Italian goodies. "Uh, g'day everyone. Before we start, I just want to make an announcement, if I may. I want to invite all you good people to a party at my place next Saturday night. Not tomorrow but, you know, next week at the end of the follow-ups and before Deborah goes home!" Everyone let out an *ooh*, as they had all caught on that Richard was very wealthy, even if they didn't know exactly who he was. The fact that he came to the clinic in a limo every day and lived in Bellevue Hill, Sydney's wealthiest neighborhood, was a bit of a giveaway. "I'll send out invitations with the address and everything, but save the date, 8 p.m, next Saturday!"

Deborah was amazed by Richard's transformation since the beginning of the week. What was he going to be like by the end of next week, she wondered.

"Thank you, Richard, that's wonderful… Okay, this is our last day, so I want to put aside this afternoon for questions. I'm sure you all have some, so please bring them along after lunch. This morning I wanted to talk to you about resilience. We all have it, it's what brought you here today, it's what keeps us showing up every day, and it gives us our ability to bounce back.

"You know how, if you put a cork in water you would have to force it to stay down, but when you let go it naturally comes back to the surface? That's resilience. Our old ideas and stinky thinking, our negative self-talk and constant monitoring of our pain are what make us feel like we are low. Once we see through this, the illusion of thought, and we remember that we are whole and healthy, we bounce back like the cork. You don't have to create it, it was always there…

"Does anyone here suffer with seasonal allergies?" Parker, Jeane and Marc raised their hands. "Me too, or at least, I used to. When I was a kid growing up in England, I had chronic hay fever. Couldn't stop sneezing; red, sore, scratchy eyes that were often so swollen there was no liquid left; constant sinus infections—it was miserable. My school bag was like a pharmacy, with inhalers, pills, injections in the winter, even a surgery inside my nose when I was 17 that did no good, but was excruciating. Something I have always found fascinating about allergies is that not everyone gets them. Which means that it can't be the cat hair or the peanuts that are creating the allergy, but our bodies' reaction to them. My brain, for example, believed that grass pollen was dangerous and put its best defenses into action to expel it from my body…

"I read some research last week that amazed me. I'm sure you have all heard of multiple personality disorder. Don't get me started on the diagnosis thing, that's another conversation, but I read this report about a lady who in one personality was allergic to cats, and in the other, she wasn't! How could that be? When they brought in a cat when she was in one personality, i.e., one set of thinking, she was sneezing and her eyes got all itchy and swollen, and in the other set of thinking she didn't! Another one was about a boy who was terribly allergic to orange juice in one personality and not at all in another!"[14-3]

"Are you saying my eczema could go away if I had a different personality?!" challenged Yohan.

"Well, what is a personality? I would say it's how a person thinks, right? Multi-personality must be about…about different states of mind. For example, a 'depressed' personality or a…a 'manic' personality is just a shift in thinking, a shift strong enough to change how your body reacts to life." Yohan's whole face changed as he saw the possibility of something new. The group reflected for a moment as they all contemplated what this could mean.

"Remember I told you about phantom limb pain and the amazing doctor who helped his patient with the mirror box? What happened there?"

"But that was his brain," challenged Marc. "His brain sent the messages to his arm, no?"

"Yes, but that brain activity is thought; there isn't anything that isn't thought… The pain had no substance; it wasn't physical because the man didn't have an arm. In fact, Dr. Ramachandran says that pain is just an opinion! But Marc, could you see that that's true for all of us all the time? It's always an illusion that pain is in the body. The special effects department of our brains makes it feel like pain is in the body, but it isn't, it's in our minds. Syd Banks taught, '*There has to be a power behind the brain to make it function…the brain is biological…the mind is spiritual. The brain acts like a computer: whatever you put into it is all you get out. This is logic.*'[14-4] The clever doctor followed his logic and the mirror put information into the patient's brain; what he did with it was up to him. But what it proved was that pain is only experienced in the personal mind… We really see this with little kids, how one minute they are screaming because they didn't get a treat or their sibling got the toy, and then two minutes later, they are totally fine, as if nothing happened."

Jeane tentatively put her hand up. "Yes, Jeane?"

"I once saw my sister when she was in a terrible state, all tears and misery, driving me crazy, she was—and then the phone rang. She picked it up and answered it with a cheerful, 'Hello?' I watched her mood switch instantly from one to the other in a split second, in case the caller was someone she didn't want to know that she was upset. It's always bothered me that she could just snap out of it when *she* wanted to."

"Yes, Jeane. For whatever reason, she had a new thought and acted on it, thank you for that example. Do you see that it was her resilience that enabled her to do that? We all have it. I know this is a lot to take in, but remember the first thing Syd said in that quote? '*There has to be a power behind the brain to make it function.*' Don't forget that Mind, that Loving Source of everything, is always reliable and always there to give us everything we need. A quiet mind is available to all of us, if we just remember it's there."

"Thank you, Deborah. Let's take a break for lunch, and don't forget those questions, everyone!" Dan stood up and stretched as they all made their way out to get something to eat.

After lunch they came back and sat in their usual chairs for the last time.

"Okay, here we are at our last session. I'm sure someone must have something. Anyone wanna start?" asked Deborah.

"I've got a question."

"Yes, Marc."

"Well, I don't think I get any of it. I mean, my back still hurts, I don't feel this…*calm* that everyone is talking about, and reality is still…well, reality. I guess I'm one of the ones who just doesn't get it?"

Just as Deborah was about to answer, Kate spoke up.

"It's pretty simple as far as I see it. I was on a plane once and I was so completely absorbed by the movie on my little screen that I forgot I was on the plane. So where was I? I was still physically on the plane, but my consciousness wasn't. So I was somewhere else, kind of. I don't know what I'm saying exactly, but I think we have all had times when, for whatever reasons, we drift off or forget where we are… I had this…insight last night that what we think is reality probably isn't, so what's the point in getting all upset about stuff? As Deborah said, we all make up stories all the time in our heads about what we think reality is and then how we should react to it, but really we just made it up."

"You are a smart guy, maybe you do get it, or maybe you just like to be frustrated and you don't wanna give that up? I know I didn't," added Richard. "I see now how I made up so much of the stuff that I thought was reality. And what blows my mind is that I didn't feel the pain when I was having one of my tirades, so where did it go? My back was still messed up, but my experience of it changed, so if it can change with rage, then that proves that my experience of it *can* change. So now, rather than going into a rampage, I can just…have nothing on those thoughts and watch them go by, like Kate said, like watching a movie. I'm so taken by this idea I almost want something to annoy me so that I can test it out."

Everyone laughed, but Deborah remembered how ferocious Richard's anger could be. "Please, don't anyone annoy Richard till you are at least out of the building and in the parking lot!" They all laughed. Deborah turned to Marc. "Does that help you?"

Marc still looked confused. Deborah had noticed over the years as a counselor that some people seemed to like being confused; it was almost like a technique that people used to prevent themselves from facing up to things. A client would say, 'I'm so confused,' so she would explain whatever it was clearly, and they would still say, 'But I'm so confused.' These people weren't stupid, Marc wasn't stupid, but by staying confused, it stopped him moving forward, changing, and that's the big thing: change. *What if there was something they got out of hanging on to the confusion,* wondered Deborah, *what if it were easier—safer?—to stay in the confusion than letting go and trying something new?*

"Okay, so something I don't understand is why do some people get back pain and some people get knee pain? Why do some get headaches and some stomach problems?" asked Parker.

"Great question," replied Dan. "The honest answer is, we just don't know. I wish I could give you a better answer, and maybe one day I'll be able to."

There was a pause, then Erin asked, "This morning you said pain isn't physical, right? I was with you up to that point, but then you lost me because that makes no sense. How can you say that pain is real but isn't physical?"

"I know this is very challenging, and my heart goes out to anyone living with chronic pain. But pain really has no substance. We only feel it when it comes into consciousness, and consciousness is an experience in the mind. Now, that experience may be constant if you are constantly thinking about it, assessing it, judging it, monitoring it, and treating it, but the experience of it will fade the less you have on it, the more you see it as thought and not as physical."

"Like a mirage?" asked Erin.

"Yes," laughed Deborah, "but as my teacher George Pransky says, *it's a real mirage*."[14-5]

"I see it already," Aliki was keen to share her progress. "My body usually burns all over, especially in new, stressful situations like here, where I didn't know anyone, but I'm seeing that I don't have to listen to those thoughts, I don't even have to notice them, and already it's getting easier."

"I love it, Aliki." Deborah was so excited that some of them were getting it.

Paul, the resident psychologist, had slid into the conference room for this last session along with some of the other staff, and he put his hand up to ask a question. "I still think that everyone with chronic pain is experiencing repressed rage."

The group looked around to see who was speaking.

"Sure you do, because that makes sense to you." Deborah felt a surge of confidence. "As you know, I have only just started learning about Freud and his ideas, but I think he believed that we are all dark, untamed beasts riddled with conflict, would you agree? Now, think about that for a minute… Whenever I have heard people recount near-death experiences, about what it's like on the other side, they *never* talk about meeting dark beasts. Instead, they talk about luminous light and love, clarity and a sense of pure joy and bliss. They talk about being free of their bodies, of being in a magnificent, fluid feeling of infinite, loving energy.[14-6] They don't describe conflict; in fact, they are describing the opposite, something magnificent, the true essence of who we really are. Paul, can I suggest you let your intellect have a rest and listen for something new because…" Deborah paused for a moment as she remembered something she had read. "Because if you hold your hand up too close to your face, you can cover up the highest mountain from sight. Sometimes we do this with our intellect; we cover up what's right in front of us, and miss the beauty of what's really here right now…"

Karyn had been quiet up to this point, but Deborah had noticed her agitated expression. She was getting more and more uncomfortable, shifting in her seat and rolling her eyes. Suddenly, she spoke up. "Well, I'm not setting aside my intellect! If you need me to act stupid so I can 'get' this, then sorry, but I don't see the point in that." She bent down and picked up her things. "I think I've heard all I want." She was already out of her seat and heading for the door. Deborah's heart sank a little as she watched Melanie follow her, since it was probably too late. She paused and then addressed the group.

"Okay, um…I think we have time for one more question?"

Nobody responded at first; they were all a bit stunned.

"Yes, I want to go back to this thing about the pain being real, that some say it's coming from a lack of oxygen to the muscles." began Parker. "But if pain isn't coming from the herniated disc or the drop foot or whatever our doctors said it was, but is actually coming from the brain or I don't know, the mind, then the pain can't be coming from the lack of oxygen either… You can't have it both ways. Either pain is physical or it's not, right?"

Dan and Deborah looked at each other and then grinned.

"Brilliant, Parker!" cried Dan. "You have just answered something that has been bothering me for years! Whatever the physical sensation is from—a fracture, even hunger, or the result of mental stress or hormones—it comes to this: it's always a thought-created experience. These physical things are definitely happening as our amazing bodies repair, digest and miraculously conduct all kinds of processes, but we can only ever know about them through the gift of thought."

Deborah sat back with a glorious smile. It had popped! The Principles of Mind, Thought and Consciousness had landed in the world of chronic pain. "And that's why we don't have to do anything with our thinking!" she added. "The 'special effects department' of Consciousness is creating the illusion of pain 100% of the time, no matter what the seeming cause. That's why my pain went away without my having to do any work on it. I know this is going to be so hard to hear for anyone in excruciating pain, like with cancer, and I don't mean to be unkind or dismiss their suffering; in fact, I doubt this conversation would even be very helpful. But all pain is a phenomenon, and chronic pain is the biggest phenomenon of them all."

Deborah felt it was time to bring things to a close. "When I was driving home last night, I was thinking about how I'm going home next week and I suddenly thought of another analogy. If I were to ask you how I get to the airport from here, would you suggest that I walk?" They all laughed, as it was about fifteen miles away. "Now, it might take a while, it might be uncomfortable, I may even get lost

166

on the way, but even walking, I would eventually get there. Or, you could suggest I take a taxi. All those other therapies and techniques we have all tried are like walking to the airport. It might take a while, it might be uncomfortable, I may even get lost on the way, but I would eventually, *maybe*, get there. Understanding the Three Principles is like taking a taxi."

It was the end of an amazing week and time for Dan to wrap it up.

"Wow. I can't believe it's over! Guys, you have been amazing. We want to thank you so much for your participation, we really appreciate it! And what can I say? Deborah, thank you for sharing your insights and experience with us, thank you!" They all agreed and gave a clap of appreciation. "I also want to thank Melanie for helping with the admin and the extra hours it's taken from her normal workload. Thank you, Melanie. And thank you again to all of you! Your willingness to show up and engage has been invaluable to us, and with all the feedback we are getting, I think we are really going to help a lot more people who are currently suffering from chronic pain. I look forward to meeting with each of you next week to get some final responses."

"See you all at my place next week," reminded Richard, "and Primo, *don't forget the cannoli!*" Dan and the rest of the guys laughed at the *Godfather* reference, "Yes! See you all at the party!"

After everyone had said their goodbyes and thank yous, Dan and Deborah went to his office for a chat. "Deborah, that was much better than I expected. I learned a lot, so I'm sure they did, too."

"Thanks, but is it enough?"

"What do you mean?" Dan put his feet up on his desk and loosened his tie.

"Is it enough to build a clinic on, a practice?"

"I don't know yet and it's very early days. I'm not planning on throwing the baby out with the bathwater just yet, but I think we have a clear road ahead. More research, more case studies, it's got so much potential. I'm sure you see that, no?"

"Yes, I do, which is why I need to tell you something. *I don't live here.* You are going to need a Principles practitioner here to carry on the work."

"Yeah, I have been thinking about that, too. I really want to do it, but I'll need another practitioner to help. I think we are going to be busy."

"I've got the perfect person."

Dan looked at her curiously.

She picked up the phone and asked someone to come in. Dan raised his eyebrows. He really had no idea what she was up to, and to his surprise, a minute later Melanie walked in. "Tell Dan what you told me." Melanie told Dan about her violent marriage, how she had lost her job due to the agonizing pain and how just working here, being in the clinic, had restored her health and well-being.

Dan sat up straight; he was amazed. He suddenly felt embarrassed and concerned that someone so close to him had been suffering so much and he didn't know. "But, you never said anything…"

"How could I? I couldn't tell you that I didn't need any of the techniques you offer here, the very place that had helped me, and besides, until I heard Deborah explain it all, I didn't understand myself what had happened. I just thought it was time that had healed me and being in a safe place, but now I see it couldn't be; that's an Outside-In explanation and it just doesn't make sense anymore. It was my thoughts about being here that helped me! That's Inside-Out, right, Deborah? I really want to train to help other people see this. Dan, you need me as your practitioner!"

"I see I'm gonna need a new assistant is what I need!" laughed Dan. "Okay, okay. Why don't you two keep talking? No changes yet, no promises and no telling *anyone*. We are in such early days with this. I'm excited, but we have to do this right."

15
Kings Cross

Deborah's tasks in the last week were clear: she needed to meet with each of the participants for a follow-up session, keep working with Melanie and keep diving into the latest pain science research. The hard part seemed to be over for her; presenting all the ideas was great, but it had taken a lot of digging deep into her well-being and wisdom to pull all these different ideas together. The participants had had various reactions, but no one was suffering more, which came as a big relief.

Kate was the first meeting on Monday, as she needed to be at the Opera House later for a performance of La Traviata. She felt great and was full of energy, fresh ideas, and hope. Deborah encouraged her to keep going and to stay in touch. Just as she was leaving, she handed Deborah an envelope. It was a complimentary ticket, to express her thanks. Deborah told her she needn't have, but was thrilled beyond words. She loved the opera, even just the going and the spectacle of the whole thing was so exciting, and to see

La Traviata at the Sydney Opera House was beyond her wildest dreams.

Andrew was a little less enthusiastic. He had had some insights and said he got it, but wanted to wait until he got back to school to see if it really worked for him.

Costos said his neck pain was better, and Erin reported that since she now understood how her husband could run on a broken foot, she really could see that less pain was possible if your thoughts were calmer. Consequently, she and her husband were now walking regularly and planning a family hiking holiday.

Primo was extremely grateful, not only for the fact that his migraines had almost gone, but the fact that his mother and his wife seemed to be getting on much better, too, so go figure. Lucia was working out to be such a good waitress, he had promoted her to manager—which was a big help with the family dynamics—so all in all, he was very happy.

Yohan was still anxious, but at least now he was aware of where it was coming from. He was beginning to make friends with his nervous thinking and catch himself when he was becoming too controlling. He said he was grateful to be able to notice when he saw his moods take a dive and that he could ride the wave and watch it pass. His skin was less itchy and he could see the soreness fading.

Mia was still scheduled for another surgery, but she felt a lot better and, like Yohan, was beginning to be able to catch herself when she felt like her moods were going downhill. She was still quite overwhelmed by life and thought it best to at least talk to the surgeon.

Karyn wasn't returning any calls, and Marc was still very skeptical and still in some pain. He insisted that there was something called an 'ultimate reality,' even if we all did have different experiences of it. Deborah told him that was okay and suggested if he stayed open to the possibility, he could have just as much relief as the others.

Aliki was shining. She was still in a lot of discomfort, but she didn't have anything on it, it was amazing. She fully admitted that some days were harder than others and that getting up was hard and getting in the car hurt, but she just didn't have much thinking about it anymore. She wasn't even trying to not think about it, it just didn't seem to matter. The knowledge that it was her pain 'amplifier' that was turned up too high and that there wasn't anything wrong with her was such a relief. She had decided that if she was going to be in pain, it would be better to be strong and in pain than weak, so she was going about her day as best she could. They both laughed as they looked forward to more of the pains and discomfort going away.

Rose still wasn't wearing her wrist protector and was looking for a new job, and she and Jeane were going to sign up for a dance class together. They both were reveling in their newfound freedoms and a graceful life without pain and restrictions.

Corey came in with a basketball under his arm, excited that his coach was letting him start practicing again, and Parker had decided to continue with her PhD. She realized a qualification would help open doors if she wanted to pursue this understanding as a practice in her new career. "I had an attack of the highest pain as we took my kids to see a puppet show yesterday," said Parker, "but it was beautiful. I could feel the pain, I could actually see the painful thinking, and I could *feel* that I was 100% okay behind it all. I could feel…essence, and the fact that my thinking was separate, it just 'was'… I sat in that puppet show and cried with joy because it was all okay, it was all completely safe… I cried with joy and then danced and laughed with my beautiful family!"[15-1]

And Richard. Lonnie brought him to the clinic for his appointment and he wheeled himself quietly into the conference room, as he couldn't get up the stairs to her office. He was calm and polite, reflective and grateful. Basically, he was a transformed human being.

Deborah had begun to notice two things about nearly all the participants, something they all seemed to have in common. Hope and creativity. They all had hope that they, too, could get better, and each of them seemed to have come up with a new project to work on:

Corey was going to play basketball again, and long-term, wanted to work with inner-city kids.

Rose and Jeane were learning to dance.

Aliki and her boyfriend were going to open a toy store.

Andrew was looking into using his computer graphics skills to make programs to help his students with literacy.

Parker was going to finish her PhD and become a Three Principles Practitioner.

Mia was going to start dating.

Erin was embarking on writing a mystery novel.

Primo had always wanted to open an Italian cooking school and was looking for space now that he had Lucia to run the restaurant.

Kate had always wanted to be an art director in the theater and was looking at what she needed to do to get into art school.

Costos was going to design computer games, but Yohan was the most surprising of all. Yohan had always wanted to be a hairdresser, but his skin condition always held him back. Now that he could see it disappearing, he felt confident that he was ready to do this.

173

It was amazing to see that as their busy minds slowed down, they had energy and interest in creativity of all kinds. Their innate resilience was shining through even just after a week of learning about the Principles.[15-2]

Deborah met with Dan a few times during the week, and they talked about the results they were seeing and how to proceed.

"One of the things that struck me," started Dan, "was that every single person said in their own way that they knew, that *you* knew they could get well. They all said that they had spent, well, years, some of them, going from doctor to doctor being treated as a case, as just a physical condition, but here, they all knew you believed in them, that they already had well-being and everything they needed to take care of their own health. That's the best recommendation I can think of for a new treatment, well done!"

"It was there all the time, in all of them, it had just gotten covered up by some stinking thinking."

"As we turn this into a program, a couple of things I see as crucial are getting people to sleep better and getting them active." Dan started to think about the next phase of his research. "To say 'exercise' to some people who are in constant pain would just push them over the edge, so I usually say something like 'activity,' and now that I'm understanding thought better, I can see that even having people just *think* about an activity like walking or even sitting up will be helpful. And sleep is so important. All of the participants reported they weren't getting enough sleep before, but as the week went on, they all said they saw an improvement. This is good stuff, Deborah!"

Deborah was really excited that Dan was so pleased with the results. She had only had to put in her time, which was paid for, but he had put in money, resources, and his reputation, so she was very grateful the whole experience had gone so well. But it was meeting up with Julia again that really interested her in those last few days. Richard had called and said that she was willing to meet, so they arranged to have a coffee in a trendy café in the Kings Cross neighborhood.

"Just like old times," remarked Deborah, not sure what to expect.

"*What have you done to my dad?*" Julia didn't waste any time.

"Why? I don't know what you mean?"

"You know exactly what I mean! He's calm, he's nice, *he's happy!*"

"Shame, do you want him back the way he was?"

"Of course not!" Julia shook her head. "I always knew he had a soft side, but he would get so angry and I would just want to hide from him. He says you helped him see things differently."

"Kind of. What I really did was point him back in the right direction, inside." Deborah pointed to her heart and Julia nodded. "And what about you? How are you doing?"

Julia shrugged her shoulders. "It's still vacation, so I guess I'm gonna chill with my friends. I hope to go back to L.A. to carry on with school in September if they'll have me."

"And the…" Deborah didn't know what to call it.

"The suicide attempt? Don't worry, I'm in a much better place now. I was feeling hopeless, my boyfriend was breaking up with me, it was all, you know, on again off again, and I just felt lost and far from home."

"Well, I hope we can meet up in L.A... I want to stay

in touch, you know, be there for you? You never told me what you are studying."

"I didn't tell you much of anything, did I?" They laughed. "I'm studying biology. And the boy's name is Mike, by the way. I'm sorry I was such a… I was just so frustrated with everyone, I didn't need another nose sticking in my business."

"That's okay, I get it. I'm just glad you are doing okay now and that your family is doing so much better."

"My mum, Sylvie that is, can't believe it. She is a little nervous this whole transformation thing with my dad isn't going to last, but she's very excited about the party on Saturday night. She'll be in her element as the gracious hostess."

16
Bellevue Hill

The party at Richard's had finally arrived. Deborah was delighted to end her stay with something fun. As she drove up the long driveway, she realized she had never been inside the big house in all the time she had been in Sydney. It didn't disappoint; the inside was magnificent. The grand entrance hall had an imposing staircase that wound around to the upper floors and marble columns that led through to the dining room, where French windows were open to the garden. They were all invited out to the back of the house where the pool was lit up with floating candles and tiki torches. It was very festive and everyone had come with their partners, friends and kids. Sylvie was standing proudly near Richard, who sat in his wheelchair near the bar, holding court as usual. Julia looked on from the sides where she took charge of the music, secretly enjoying the scene but not wanting to quite join in. The food was delicious. Primo had supplied the best Italian cuisine from his restaurant, and it was all just perfecto.

"This is so nice, thank you, Sylvie!" The two women hugged and Deborah took a drink from a passing waitress.

"It's the least we can do! You have saved my marriage, my family, and probably a life or two. We are so grateful." She started to tear up. "Now look what you made me do! My mascara is going to run." She gave Deborah another flamboyant hug and ran inside to fix her face.

Deborah noticed later that Karyn hadn't come, but she wasn't surprised. Karyn hadn't returned any of her calls since she had walked out of the last session. Marc showed up even though he was still insisting it had all been a waste of his time. Archie brought his wife and kids, and Lonnie had come with his family; it was so rewarding to watch everyone having fun. Rose and Jeane took the plunge and danced, aided by Melanie's encouragement, and then, toward the end of the evening, Dan clinked his glass and asked for everyone's attention.

"First of all, I'd like to thank Richard and Sylvie for hosting such a ripper party, good on ya, mate!" Everyone cheered and raised their glasses. "And Deborah, where's Deborah?" Deborah tried to hide. She hated this kind of thing, but knew she had to step up. "Come over here… On behalf of these lovely people, I want to thank you for agreeing to change your ticket!" Everyone cheered. "I think I speak on behalf of everyone here when I thank you so much for what you have shared and the gracious way you have shown up for each of us. Thank you." Dan led everyone in a toast. Deborah blushed and made a little curtsy. "And now I think Mia wants to say some final words. Mia?"

Mia stepped forward. She was wearing a black velvet dress and looked radiant. "First of all, I want to thank you on behalf of all of us. We are very grateful. I know I speak for everyone when I say you have given us hope, and that is priceless. I also just wanted to tell everyone that…that I have canceled my surgery!" Everyone gasped in amazement. "I have been pain-free for a week now, so I called the doctor's office and canceled. Two minutes later, the surgeon himself called me back to say I was making a big mistake, that I could fall and a bone spur could go into my spinal cord and paralyze me! I knew he was preying on me, trying to get me to change my mind by getting me all frightened. So I told him that he had helped me squash any doubts, that now I knew I was making the right decision, that there was nothing wrong with me and nothing that needed fixing. He got so angry, he actually shouted, *Don't blame me! I warned you, and if you want my advice: never go skiing!* Deborah, you showed me I had the courage to do it! I knew right there I was doing the right thing, but I was shaking— it was like breaking up with a lover! But I did it, it's over."

Everyone cheered as Deborah stepped up and gave her a gentle hug. "I'm so proud of you."

"And now for the finale," announced Dan. Everyone looked around. What was it? What could be coming next?

"Over here, you knuckleheads!" shouted Richard. Dan walked over to Richard, who had wheeled himself to the middle of the patio. Richard had both feet on the ground. He put both his hands on the arms of his wheelchair and very slowly lifted himself up. Lonnie had moved the foot supports out of the way when no one was looking and Richard was standing up straight, on his own!

"Where's my darling wife? I can't dance on my own!" Sylvie, trembling with disbelief, rushed to his side and took his arm.

"Music, maestro!" demanded Richard, and Julia pressed play. First, one shaky step, and then another, Richard walked forward, leaning on Sylvie for support.

Everyone had their mouths open.

"It's a miracle, Mr. Richard!" shouted Primo. Everyone laughed, clapped and cheered. They twirled slowly a few times to the smooth sounds of Frank Sinatra before Lonnie helped Richard back to his chair.

"That's enough for one night, my love," whispered Sylvie. "We have the rest of our lives to dance under the moonlight."

"Did you know about this?" asked Deborah in amazement.

Dan gave a sneaky smile. "Yes, but we wanted it to be a surprise. As soon as I looked at Richard's MRIs, I knew there wasn't anything that could be causing that kind of pain. I checked with a spine surgeon friend of mine, and he agreed that the paralysis was from muscle spasms. After Richard had calmed down, we talked and I told him it was just fear and stiffness that was holding him back, and as he listened to you explain these ideas, he got it. As he relaxed more and more, so did his body. He is going to need some physio help to get strength back after being inactive for so long, but it shouldn't be a problem. He's determined to play golf again, and that's half the battle. But that's not even the best part. He wants to come in as a partner in the clinic! He wants to invest in the business and fund more research!"

"Yeah! Oh wow, I wondered what Richard's thing was going to be."

"Thing? What do you mean?" asked Tali, holding Dan's arm with pride.

"Well, every one of our participants has discovered some kind of project or creative endeavour that they want to pursue now that they have more energy and space in their minds. Some are dancing or writing, others are pursuing careers. Hope is putting their dreams into action.

Looks like Richard's thing is going to be helping build up the clinic!"

"I can't tell you what this means for the clinic and our work." Dan was beaming with excitement. "We can do more trials, real well-documented research that can be peer-reviewed and published!"

"I'm sorry I was so skeptical," confessed Tali.

Deborah shrugged. "Don't worry, I was too!"

Lonnie tapped on the door of Deborah's suite.

"Ready to go?"

Deborah took a last look around the rooms that had been her home for the last three weeks and nodded. She felt excited about going home, but sad to be leaving what had been such a great experience. Lonnie put her bags onto the luggage cart and wheeled them out to the limo.

He paused for a moment. "If I haven't said it already, I just want to say thank you again."

"Why?"

"Well, you saw what he was like before. When a man that powerful is out of control, it makes everyone's lives miserable. I almost quit this job several times, only my wife wouldn't let me. And now, well, he treats me like a human being, a friend almost."

"He's very lucky to have you… You were in on it, weren't you? The walking, I mean."

"Yep." They got in the car and Lonnie continued to explain as he drove to the airport. "I was helping him out of the car one afternoon after we came back from the clinic and he said he felt a bit stronger. He always could move his legs a little, but he would have these back spasms that made him scream with pain. The paralysis was always temporary, but it was frightening. His body would seize up and have no strength to support his weight, so he got scared and angry and refused to try. So, with your insights, Dr. Dan's encouragement that he couldn't hurt himself, and me supporting him, he started to take a few steps every day, and at this rate, he'll be playing golf before you know it."

Deborah thanked Lonnie for his kindness and checked in for her 13-hour flight back to L.A. She had reserved a window seat, as she always liked to see where she was going, but when she boarded the plane she discovered her seat was next to a wall! Of all the window seats there were on the massive plane, hers was by the bathroom and no window. The thought of sitting all that time and not being able to see out made her sad.

"Can I help you?" asked a passing flight attendant.

"Someone stole my window!" Deborah put on a very fake sad face but she really was disappointed.

"I'm sorry, ma'am, this is the seat on your ticket."

"If I find someone who wants to change is that okay?"

"Sure."

She looked around. People were still boarding, putting their carry-ons away and finding their seats. Directly in front of her, she noticed the man sitting by the window had already pulled down his window shade and was getting comfortable for a long nap. She tapped him on the shoulder.

"So sorry to bother you, but I was so looking forward to looking out of the window, only I don't have one. Would you be interested in swapping?"

The man looked around and was already unbuckling his belt. He said something to the lady next to him and Deborah suddenly realized they were together.

"Oh, I'm sorry, I didn't realize you were together! There's just one seat available back here." But the man was already climbing over her and the next empty seat to get out. He obviously was quite happy to change! Deborah moved her stuff and climbed in over the lady, who still wasn't making any attempt to move, and into the window seat with an actual window. Good, now she could look out and see the sky, the ocean, and maybe even Hawaii. She always thought flying to be such a strange thing, you get in this tin box, and then you get out and you are somewhere else! Looking out the window gave her a sense of distance and actually travelling. The rest of the passengers settled in and the flight attendants scurried up and down to finish a few last checks. The seat on the end was still empty as two young men came on board looking for their seats. They stopped at Deborah's row.

"You're in my seat," said one of them sternly.

"Oh, no, this gentleman behind me offered to swap as I wanted a real window. I like to see out when I travel, you see," explained Deborah innocently.

"No. These are *our* seats! Look, it says so on our boarding cards!"

Deborah suddenly realized she had swapped seats with someone who had been sitting in the wrong seat and now she was sitting in this guy's seat and he really wasn't happy about it!

"No problem, I can move." Deborah apologized and started pushing the lady next to her—who still hadn't made any movement at all—to move, so they could all get out.

"Can I help?" asked a sweet, young flight attendant.

"They are sitting in our seats! Look, it says so here!"

Deborah and the other lady were now standing in the aisle, and the angry young man was still explaining to everyone who would listen that they had dared to sit in their seats.

"It's okay, we've moved. Please, have your seat!" offered Deborah, motioning them to go in.

The two young men started talking to each other and the flight attendant helped the other lady to another seat, but not next to the guy behind her, which Deborah found curious.

"Okay, you can have the window seat," said the not-so-angry young man, and so they all sat down.

Deborah looked out of her cherished window and watched Sydney disappear below as they took off into the big, blue sky. *What an amazing trip. How amazing it is when you just show up and let life unfold.* The plane leveled out and the seatbelt signs were switched off. As the flight attendants came with the first round of drinks, the very angry young man who was sitting on the outside seat beckoned one of them over.

"I want to speak to the supervisor of this section."

Deborah's stomach jumped. *What is he up to now?*

"Certainly, that's me. How can I help you?" The flight attendant beamed a huge smile and braced herself for what was coming next. He explained that there had been someone sitting in his seat when he arrived, that the flight attendant who was nearby failed to deal with the situation professionally, and that he wanted to make a formal complaint. *What?!?* thought Deborah. She had offered him back his seat, he had chosen not to take it, and he was still going to cause trouble. His voice was firm and determined.

"Oh, I'm so sorry about this, sir, is there anything I can do for you? Can I get you another seat?" She was clearly taken aback and knew she needed to do whatever she could to not have this go on her colleague's work record. He continued to complain and she continued to try and placate him. "Would an apology suffice, sir? I can get the attendant and I'm sure this can all be resolved." He agreed and she came back a few minutes later with the young attendant. They both knelt down next to his seat, their training in how to deal with difficult customers going into action.

"I'm so sorry you were inconvenienced, sir, I do apologize," said the young woman. The angry young man then went into a tirade about her unprofessionalism and demanded her employee number. "This is a taxi! People can't just sit wherever they want, and if you had been doing your job, this wouldn't have happened!" The flight attendant started to cry and Deborah couldn't contain herself.

"Look, I offered you back your seat. It wasn't her fault, and frankly, you are embarrassing yourself!"

Everyone was looking around at this point. The supervisor gave Deborah a look as if to say, it's okay, we can handle this.

"You ignored me when I showed you my boarding pass and you failed to get people in their right seats. People can't just sit anywhere!" He got out his phone. "What is your number? This is going to be reported!" At that point, several other people jumped up and offered him their seats; it was chaos. One flight attendant was crying, the other trying to calm everyone down.

"Let it go," urged the friend sitting in the middle of the row.

"Okay, but I want you to know this is not good enough!"

The flight attendants thanked him and apologized again and left. *What a jerk,* thought Deborah. Had he really been stewing in that thought all that time to the point that he wanted to ruin someone else's career? Or did he see it as a way to get some compensation? What an idiot!

Just before landing Deborah got up to use the

bathroom, but walked all the way to the back of the plane to find the young woman. As she poked her head around the area at the back of the plane, she was confronted by at least five identical-looking flight attendants, all with their hair in tight, blonde updos. Which one was she?

"Uh, I just wanted to say that I thought you handled that really well." One girl smiled and said thank you. She had recovered and was with her friends now. "He is an idiot and if you need me to say anything, I'm on your side, okay?"

"Thank you, but it's not necessary." She smiled again and they all said thank you.

As Deborah pushed her luggage cart through customs at LAX, she saw the two angry young men ahead of her.

"Over here, sir!" instructed a customs officer, indicating that they needed to stop for an inspection.

Ha! thought Deborah. *Serves you right…*

17
Santa Barbara

Once Deborah had settled back home in L.A. and had caught up with her friends, she returned to her routine with clients and her voluntary work at the SMDC. Bob had been very supportive about her extended trip but was happy to have her back.

"Well, it really was your fault for getting me the job in the first place, but I'm very glad you did. I feel like I have a whole new purpose in my work."

Bob laughed. "You're welcome. It sounds fascinating…in fact, the colleague that gave me that student referral might have some contacts for you. He lectures in biology, but I know he collaborates with people in the UCLA medical school. Let me see what I can find out."

A few days later, Bob called with a name and number for her to call. Wayne Alvarado, a neuroscientist working in the pain research lab, was willing to meet her. Deborah was excited to speak to him but sadly, he really wasn't that interested in what she had to say and preferred to tell her what work he was doing. They talked briefly about how the outdated Cartesian model[17-1] of how pain is experienced had lasted for almost 300 years, helped by the pharmaceutical giants who just want to sell drugs. He did agree that there is a 'psycho-social' element needed in pain management, but was stuck in the belief that Outside-In solutions were the answer. It was her Hollywood background that had spiked his attention. "Did you really meet Julia Roberts? What was Brad Pitt like?" He was far more interested in asking about movie stars than he was hearing about the work she had just done with Dan.

As she listened to him talk about his latest experiments, she had an insight, one of those aha! moments that shift your thinking, moving your whole experience to another level… All these scientists were desperately trying to fix the wrong problem! They were either trying to fix the body with surgery, medications or physical treatments, or, if they understood that it was the Mind-Body connection causing the pain, they were trying to *fix* people's thinking. They had all missed it! The problem with chronic pain isn't with the body or the brain or even the mind, the problem was with the fact that they all saw pain as physical! But as Syd had said, the body is a metaphor.[17-2] Pain is not physical, thought Deborah, it has no 'substance'—it is pure brain activity…brain activity is thought…*the pain itself is just thought!*

She thanked Wayne for the meeting and drove home with a buzz. She realized that she already had the answer, and her insight gave her confidence that she had to stick to her own experience and her own understanding. All the pain science was fascinating, and learning about it enabled her to hold her own in these kinds of discussions about glucocorticoids and the HPA Axis, but she had become pain-free without 'doing' anything, and this was going to be her message.

Dan continued to keep in regular contact with her, sharing new insights and feedback from the participants. Karyn had completely dropped out of the program, but Richard had played his first round of golf and was proving a wise and valuable new partner in the clinic. She had encouraged the other participants to stay in touch and occasionally got email updates from some of them. An amazing message came from Andrew. One of his colleagues had tragically overdosed and, understandably, the staff at his school were all in shock. He wrote to say that they all had questioned how appropriate or intrusive it was for them to go to the funeral, considering the way she died. Andrew wrote that he could see how they were overthinking the whole thing and paralyzing themselves with their anxious thoughts. He decided not to listen, to just show up anyway, and as a result had a beautiful, healing conversation with the parents, who just needed to know people cared.

As soon as I noticed my thinking, it moved on and made room for compassion and love. I think that was the Principles in action, as I didn't do anything or work on it, it just changed the moment I saw it for what it was.

Parker also sent some great emails. Her whole life was changing and she was excited to share her insights:

I realized something this week. Without really being aware of it, I still believed that when I'm a little upset or a little annoyed, I'm only 'a little bit' away from peace. Like, it's relatively easy to find my way back to peace. But when I'm upset because of an issue that seems very big and serious and complicated and the feeling of worry or fear or upset is very intense, I believe I'm *faaaar* away from peace and it will take a longer time and more steps to find my way back. Yesterday, when I was busy with one of those 'big' issues, I suddenly saw that's not true. It really doesn't matter how complicated the emotional issue or the situation looks – peace is still just 'one new thought' away. It really only ever is the difference between 'being in the now' or 'being in my thinking.' That's it. To me this feels so calming, like all the 'big issues' don't look so scary anymore. And I don't have to be careful to not get caught up in one of them. Because I can always find my way back in a heartbeat.

In another she wrote this:

Since the program at the clinic with you, I've been feeling much much better. Not just on a physical level, but in so many other areas. I'm seeing so much new stuff, and a lot of stressful issues have changed or fallen away. And some 'difficult' circumstances just aren't much of a problem anymore. However, during the last 2 or 3 weeks, I experienced a curious phenomenon: It seems that I sometimes get random pain flare-ups out of nowhere. Or sometimes even following a few days full of joy with new insights and feeling very free and content. Since I'm still a bit conditioned from the classic therapy approach and everything I was taught in grad school, every time this happens I immediately come up with some ideas of what I might 'have done wrong.' Like being 'too excited' or maybe having overlooked something that's been troubling me. At the same time, I could watch myself every time this was happening, getting less and less likely to get caught up in this kind of thinking. Maybe because my grounding in the 3P is deepening or something like that. With my last flare-up a few days ago, on the first day it truly felt like I was watching these thoughts come and go—they didn't affect my emotional state at all.

On the second day, it changed. I got annoyed and more 'why??' thinking came up. I remembered some of our conversations and suddenly I realized that I'm still holding on to some belief that experiencing pain is not okay. That it means I have done something wrong.

And then it suddenly shifted and for a few minutes, I got a glimpse of feeling completely innocent and completely safe in this life. That was created by something far bigger than me.

I guess what I want to say is: It's okay. All of it.

I still can't tell you why the flare-ups happen, but now I know I don't need to figure it out.[17-3]

Deborah and Melanie were meeting weekly face-to-face on the computer to continue her training. She was doing great. She had profound questions and was having amazing insights, too. Melanie was excited to tell her about a new patient that Dan had encouraged her to talk to: Miriam, a courageous young woman who had been confined to a wheelchair her whole life, had a permanent breathing tube and very limited movement in her whole body. She was completely dependent on 24-hour nursing care, and at 26, had beaten the odds of survival multiple times.

"Deborah, you won't believe what Miriam told me! She said that everyone always presumes that her problems are physical; she said, *It's not, it's my thinking just like everyone else*.'[17-4] Deborah, I cried. I was so touched by her courage and wisdom!"

Encouraged by these messages and this type of feedback, Deborah started to think about how she could advertise locally for more pain clients. She didn't want to present her work as if it was just another one of those spa treatments with pictures of bamboo shoots, pebbles and running water. She wanted something different, something that would pop and stand out. As she was eating lunch in Santa Monica with Sara, one of the other counselors at the SMDC, she looked up to see a gigantic mural filling the whole side wall of the building opposite.

"Look!" shouted Deborah, "it's Frida!"

"What, who's Frida?"

"Frida Kahlo, just one of the most inspirational women of my life! I read her amazing biography when I was in college—it reads like a thriller novel. I think she was the first woman to have an exhibition at the Museum of Modern Art in New York, but that's not it. Listen, when she was about 14 in the 1950s she was on a tram in Mexico City, where she grew up." Deborah grabbed Sara's arm. "The tram collided with another one and in the force of the accident, a metal bar pierced Frida between her legs and came out through her back! She was skewered!"

"What?!?"

"Get this, on the tram was an artist who was on his way to decorate a cathedral or something, and the gold dust he was carrying flew up into the air in the impact and covered her bleeding body!"

"Oh my gosh!"

"She spent most of the rest of her life in chronic pain and on her back, as she needed endless surgeries to fix all her injuries. That's why all her paintings are self-portraits."

Deborah pulled out her phone and showed Sara pictures of the real Frida in her native Mexican dress.

"Wow, she's beautiful! She looks amazing, but look, look up at this mural, the flowers up there in her hair are real! That's so clever, look, they have put real flowers and lights on the wall."

"Don't you get it, Sara? Frida was in constant pain, but she transcended it, she turned it into art!"

"Okay, so go take a picture and use it for your flyers."

Deborah jumped up in excitement. "You know, she also managed to have an affair with Trotsky…"

Clients with an interesting array of ailments and physical issues started to come her way. To Deborah, they were all just different ways the body was sending signals to these people to slow them down and get them to look inside. Her next challenge was to get in front of some health professionals. She wrote to all the pain clinics, osteopaths and chiropractors she could find, made fabulous flyers and brochures that she dropped off, but no one was biting. They weren't even interested in the research that Dan was putting together. She wasn't so surprised; it would mean she would probably be stealing their clients, and not everyone was as generous and open as Dan. But Deborah knew something would shift, something would show up, she could smell it; it was so close, but where and how? She knew not to overthink it, that the Universe would maneuver whatever it wanted in her direction. The Quiet that had become part of her life was always there to fall back into, so she kept looking, putting her name out there and working with the people that showed up.

"Have you seen this Pain Summit seminar thing in Santa Barbara?" Her friend Abby handed her a flyer over lunch. "I think it's all kinds of alternative stuff like meditation, yoga, and something new called *Bio-Body Bliss?*[17-5] Maybe you could get in there?"

"Nice, thank you! Where did you see this?"

"At my gym, they have all kinds of stuff advertised there. Give them a call, can't hurt, right?"

"Your work sounds fascinating," offered Greg, one of the organizers, "but I'm so sorry, we are all filled up with speakers for this year's summit. If you want to send in your info, we would be happy to keep it on file for next year."

He was very apologetic, but there was no room. Deborah decided to go anyway just to see what was being offered and how they presented their ideas. If the traditional medical world was going to drag its feet about listening, then maybe the alternative crowd would be more open. She persuaded Abby to go with her, so the next weekend they drove up Pacific Coast Highway to beautiful Santa Barbara for a girls' day out.

The seminar started at 10 a.m. in a conference room at the hospital. It was more clinical than she expected for a southern Californian alternative health event, but maybe that was good. Deborah and Abby took their seats and listened to a very fierce woman with masses of henna-red hair introduce the speakers. The first person up was a chiropractor by training, but had become a Chinese herbalist and acupuncturist and was now offering EMDR. *So much searching*, thought Deborah. She knew she had done it, too; she was remembering back to the time she and Abby and their friend Carol had gone to Pasadena to hear the Trappist monk speak: '*We are always looking in the wrong direction for happiness.*' As the speakers continued, she saw the same common theme; they all had great insights into the amazing intelligence of the body, but they were still offering an 'Outside-In' solution.

"What do you mean?" Abby was curious about what she meant. She followed Deborah out of the hall as they all got up for the lunch break.

"Well, it's great that they see that the body has innate intelligence to heal itself, but they always want to fix the content of the thinking that they see as the cause of the dysregulation with things like journaling, meditation, etc. There is nothing wrong with a nice, relaxing massage, but the other stuff has too much focus on fixing the thoughts, and it's usually a placebo, so the clients have to keep coming back for more."

"But I thought you said that it was stressful thinking that got the body out of whack, no?"

"Yes, but fixing the content of people's thinking isn't the answer; they've missed the point. The stress is coming from the misunderstanding that thought is real and therefore needs fixing. 'Outside-In' treatments are like, like believing a cast actually mended a broken leg."

"It didn't?"

"No! A cast doesn't have any healing properties, it just keeps the bone still and protected while the body does the actual mending, all by its incredible self. See, the healing is happening 'Inside-Out,' it's innate health in action."

They wandered out to the lobby and looked for somewhere they could have lunch. A man with a clipboard was flamboyantly directing 'traffic.'

"Hey, Greg? I'm Deborah Stark, we spoke on the phone a few weeks ago about me being a possible speaker; I work with people with chronic pain. Great show so far, well done."

Greg spun around, all in a whirl. "Oh yes, yes, I'm so glad you came, you *are* special." He stroked her arm. "How did you enjoy this morning? Wasn't it fabulous?"

"Very interesting. There is such a…a warmth and kindness in the room." Deborah did her best to sidestep what she really thought.

"Yes, doesn't it just *glow*?"

Abby stifled a giggle, so they soon moved away and went to eat lunch somewhere quiet. When they came back, they saw that there was a table with merchandise for sale—meditation music, prayer mats, and all kinds of equipment to relieve pain. Everything from magnets to some bizarre-smelling ointments, and even shoe lifts and massage machines.

"Look at this." Abby held up a box, "This meditation CD won a Grammy! *Only in California!*"

"I'm so glad I found you!" blurted out Greg as he came rushing through the crowd in a flamboyant panic. "Shalamis the Body Talk practitioner just got called away on a…a body emergency. Can you step in, I mean, right now?"

Deborah smiled, graciously accepted and before she knew it, she was being asked up onto the stage to talk about her work. She shared her own personal story with chronic pain and how it had all gone since coming across this new understanding of the mind. She explained how pain is only experienced when it comes into consciousness, that chronic pain—in fact, all pain—is not physical, it has no 'substance.' It is pure brain activity and we can only perceive brain activity with the gift of thought. From there she segued into an introduction of the Principles and the work of Sydney Banks. She could tell by the looks on people's faces that some were kind of getting it, but not others, which was about right. There was no time for questions, but on the spot, Greg invited her to come back for the Q&A panel at the end of the day.

"What do you mean, do nothing?" asked a lady from the audience as the Question and Answer session began to heat up. Deborah did her best to answer—starting to describe how doing anything to fix thinking only mixes it up more, putting the body back into fight-or-flight, but when you leave it alone, your personal mind quiets down and your own innate wisdom will guide you in your particular situation, whether it's health, finances, romance or, well, anything really.

"Are you saying that trying to fix the body is wrong?" asked another. Deborah explained that moving the body, getting the blood moving was excellent, that she walked every day and did water aerobics once a week, but it wasn't to fix her back or strengthen her core, because there was nothing wrong with her back. It was for enjoyment and for the general good health of her body. Greg thanked the panelists, the fierce red-headed woman came and handed him a huge bunch of flowers as a thank you for all his hard work, and the seminar ended with a standing ovation for everyone.

"Wow, that was a bit of a rush!"

"You loved it!" laughed Abby as they drove home, heading south along the coast, the sun spreading lavender and orange over the sky as it dropped behind the horizon of the Pacific Ocean.

"Deborah, I have an incredible assignment for you! It's a big one!"

"Hi, Dan. What's up?" Deborah could hear the excitement in his voice.

"Okay, ready for this? I got a new client at the clinic just after you left. Craig Kramer!" He paused for Deborah to react, but the name meant nothing to her. *"He's Australia's number one tennis player!"*

"Oh, wow! That's amazing! How?"

"His father knows Richard, blah blah blah. Anyway, he came to me for a back spasm issue he gets about once a year, and all the things he's tried haven't worked. Even once a year isn't acceptable for a top international athlete. I gave him a full workup and he's really in amazing shape, nothing wrong physically. I told him a little about the Principles and he liked it but then he had to leave for

London, he's in with a big chance of winning Wimbledon! *Don't you watch the news?* Anyway, he just finished the first week of matches beating everyone in straight sets, but his coach just called to say something happened and his back is playing up. Deborah, you have to go and straighten him out!"

"*What?!?*" shouted Deborah.

"He has big sponsors, they will pay for everything. Start packing your bag, they want you to leave now!"

Deborah's head was spinning. She couldn't…could she? "I guess, but I won't get there till tomorrow at the earliest."

"Well, you can try! You know what this could do for us and our work. His manager will be calling you very soon with details. Start packing and grab your passport!"

Deborah put down the phone and stared at it for a moment. It was like that time the Director of Operations at Universal Studios had called her in a panic and asked her to come and fix the animatronic dinosaurs at Jurassic Park, only this time it was a real person that needed help. Two minutes later, the phone rang again. An American man was calling.

"Hi, this is Jared. Dr. Dan Gieger in Australia gave me your number?" They sorted out flights and fees, and then Deborah paused to make something very clear. "I can't guarantee anything, you know that, right?"

"Dan said you were good, and Craig is willing, so we are up for trying any kind of hocus pocus thing at this point. Craig is doubled over in pain and his next match is in eight hours. They are giving him all kinds of meds and injections but honestly, I'd call Elvis right now if I thought it might help! I'm sending a car to pick you up in two hours for the next flight to London." He hung up.

Deborah didn't have time to think. She canceled all her

appointments for the next two weeks, packed a bag, and jumped in the limo to LAX.

18

London

It was raining as the plane landed at Heathrow. The gray skies warmed Deborah's heart; she could feel the excitement of seeing London again. It had been a while since she had been back and the energy of this new adventure was beginning to bubble up as the plane pulled up to the gate. She had no idea what to say to Craig. She knew nothing about him or much about tennis for that matter, and wondered if she would get to see a match at Wimbledon. She wasn't scared, well, not much, as it wasn't quite happening yet. So far all she had to do was get on a plane and she had done that. Deborah was desperate to know how Craig's match had gone while she was in the air. Maybe it was all over and she was too late? There was a Towncar driver waiting for her at arrivals, so she asked him if he had a paper.

"Sure luv, here you go. Welcome back to Blighty."

He passed her a newspaper as she got into the back seat. '*Wizard of Oz but only just,*' announced the headline of the sports page. "How corny that they call him the Wizard of Oz just because he's Australian," observed Deborah out loud.

"Yeah, well usually he is, but something is up with him," declared the driver, "an injury I think. He only just scraped through against some South American bloke! It's all over the news."

"Did you happen to see the match?"

"Sure, everyone was watching. He limped onto the court and you could see he was in pain. Everyone was on tenterhooks expecting him to miss the ball, but he just made it each time. His serve was not the magic it usually is."

"Oh, is that why they call him the Wizard of Oz? Because he plays like a wizard, because he's magic?" inquired Deborah, confused.

"No, luv. It's 'cause he's from Oz."

The driver pulled up outside a large Edwardian mansion house overlooking Wimbledon Park, the famous suburb in London, SW19. There were some press outside who shouted out some questions: "How did Craig injure his back?" "Was he pulling out of the championship?" She kept her head down and walked past the cameras as a man opened the front door of the house to let her in.

"Hi, I'm Jared." A man in super-new sports clothes stood in the doorway introducing himself. He was clearly a businessman, not an athlete. "Flight okay?"

"Yes, and thanks for the car. I'm used to slumming it on the Tube."

"Oh right, you're English. Anyway, if you are ready, put your stuff down in the front room and come and meet Craig now."

"Sure, how long is it till his next match?"

"Tomorrow, he's the number 4 Seed and will be playing for a place in the semi-finals, so you better work fast."

Deborah knew that was impressive but wasn't exactly sure what it all meant and chose to ignore the pressure Jared seemed to be experiencing. She knew all it takes is one new thought, but had no idea what Craig's state of mind was. She followed Jared up the stairs. He knocked and then opened the door of the master bedroom and showed her in. Craig was lying on a massage table while a very intimidating male masseuse finished up working on his back. Craig motioned to Deborah to have a seat and make herself at home. Jared left to take care of some business and soon the masseuse had washed up and left. Craig got dressed in the ensuite bathroom and then hobbled over to lie on the bed. It was all very new to her. Craig let out a groan as he closed his eyes for a moment.

"Can I get you anything?" Deborah asked softly.

"Yeah, there's a hot water bottle over there, could you fill it up?"

"Sure, no problemo…I used to love heat on my back when it was acting up like this. My pelvis used to feel as though someone had hit it with a baseball bat!" She prepared the hot water bottle, gave it to him and pulled up a chair. "Dr. Dan said he had mentioned to you something about the work I do?"

"Yeah. I mean, I didn't really get it, but at this point, I'm willing to try anything… I barely got through the match yesterday and when I got on the court this morning to practice, it was all I could do to keep from screaming every time I tried to serve. They've injected me and massaged me so it's a bit better now, but I'm not in the best shape and my next match is tomorrow."

"I get it. Have you had it this bad before?"

"Yeah, once…when my parents divorced. I was about 16 and my back used to kill me. They said it was growing pains."

"What did you think it was?"

Craig hesitated. "…Is this going to be like a therapy session? I really don't need that right now."

"No, it's not. I want to show you that it's not what you are thinking but *that* you are thinking."

"I can't *not think*, I have to focus my thoughts 100% on playing!"

Remembering what Dan had taught them about how the brain struggles to think clearly when it's being hijacked by chronic pain, it made sense that he was struggling to focus.

"Sure you do. It's amazing what you guys can do on the court, but I'm talking about here, right now. I'm guessing you are under a lot of pressure from coaches, management…sponsors, fans?"

"Tell me about it." He groaned as he turned on his side a little to face her. "But that's not it. I'm used to that, I kinda tune it out. My coaches and trainers have always had me doing mindfulness meditations to stay in the moment." He hesitated, "…I got some nasty news a couple of days ago and it kinda blew my mind." Deborah waited for him to continue. "My parents divorced, like I said, when I was a kid and I never knew why. Like most kids, I thought maybe it was my fault, maybe having to take me to tennis camp all those years, the early morning practices before school and the endless tournaments and training. But I just found out that…that my mother was having an affair with my old coach! I still can't believe it." He closed his eyes again.

"Wow, that must have been very hard to hear."

Craig screwed up his eyes tight; he was in pain inside and out. "For the last ten years I have been thinking it was all my fault. I remember that my dad, who was my manager until I turned pro, fired him, and there was loads of fighting in the house, but I always thought it was somehow my fault."

"You must be very angry."

"I'm…I can feel this rage in my belly. I've been visiting the bathroom a lot too, come to think of it." He let out a long breath and tried to relax.

"Okay. Look what I picked up at the airport in L.A." Deborah pulled a tiny snowglobe out of her purse. Inside was a tiny grizzly bear and California was written on the side in red. She shook it up. The glittery snow swirled around and she sat it down on the table next to the bed. Craig turned his head to stare at it, watching it swirl and then settle. "Does the inside of your head feel like this right now?" She shook it up again.

"Yeah, the thoughts are going round and round like a bloody tornado and I can't get it to stop!"

"Right, because every time you try, it's like shaking up the snowglobe again. Look, it's not surprising that it's affecting you, this is major stuff… Do you know anything about the fight-or-flight response?"

"Yeah, a little, why?"

"Well, when we are in danger, like, say this grizzly bear is coming at you, our brains send all these stress chemicals into our bodies, adrenaline, cortisol, glucose, even histamines, right? They give us the energy to run from danger, to escape when we are trapped and…"

Craig interrupted. She was about to continue explaining the stress response, but he had cut her off. "That's it, I feel *trapped*! That's why I can't move on the court like I usually do!"

"What does it usually feel like?"

"I dunno, I guess I usually feel, like, fluid, in the zone. It's so cheesy to say, but when I'm really playing my best, like last week, I almost don't feel my body, but since I got this news I feel…heavy, I feel…like a massive weight is holding me down."

"Craig, you are feeling your thoughts. It's your thoughts that 'feel' heavy, do you see? That's what's weighing you down."

"You mean, my thoughts about my mum and that **$%#* are affecting my game?"

"Yes."

"Well, of course they are! I want to smash that guy's head through the wall. He ruined my family and now he's ruining the biggest chance of my career. *I'm about to lose Wimbledon because of that jerk!*"

"Okay, I know it seems like it's all going south because of him, but could you see that really it's your thoughts about him that are creating the way you feel right now? Our bodies only know this moment right now; they don't have any sense of time, of past or future, they can only feel and react to how you are thinking right now. Your thinking is trapped in this story of judgment about them, and so your body is reacting to that."

Craig thought for a moment, "Okay, so why isn't it giving me energy to move? If it thinks I'm trapped, why isn't it helping me to move faster and escape?"

Deborah thought for a moment. "Because it's not true. Thought is a spiritual, spooky energy that flows through the mind. I have no idea what I'm saying right now, but you aren't stupid; you know you are not actually trapped, but you're believing your thinking and that's making you feel like you are. Look, I didn't come here to analyze you, far from it. That just shakes up the snowglobe again and again, which isn't helpful. The secret is that we don't have to do anything to get it to settle, we just have to leave our thinking alone. That's how our brains work if we just have enough patience, or better still, insight to see it, that all those thoughts can go by and we don't have to have anything on them."

"What does *that* mean?"

"Last summer I went to a dinner party at my friend Malka's. There were about ten of us sitting around her beautiful table outside in her garden enjoying the amazing food and great company. When I got home, about midnight, I noticed that my feet were covered in mosquito bites! I had about 15 on each foot! I'm a little allergic to mozzie bites, so they were big and angry – *arghh!* I tried to fall asleep, but I kept waking up scratching and wishing we had eaten inside. By 2 a.m., half-asleep, half-awake, I suddenly became aware that I was screaming at my dear friend Malka inside my head, *"WHY DID YOU HAVE TO HAVE DINNER OUTSIDE? YOU HAVE A STUNNING DINING ROOM, DON'T YOU KNOW I GET BITTEN?!?* I had turned into a crazy person, but the moment I became conscious enough to hear myself, I stopped. I stopped mid-sentence and suddenly there was dead silence. In that silence, I was left with just the physical sensation of the bites. By this time I felt like my legs were on fire! I don't know why, but I stayed with the feeling. I really focused on it without any fear; it was kinda like it was happening to my body but not to me. It had no substance, no dimension, just pure sensation. The next thing I knew, I woke up and it was 8 a.m."

Craig lay there taking it in. "So you are saying that if I could separate from the thoughts, this damn ache in my back will just go away?"

Deborah hesitated; she only knew what she saw to be true. "Look, what I do know is that if you don't care about it, the pain will die of neglect, but if you keep focusing on your body, treating it, wondering how it is now, then it will hang around longer. Craig, all you are up against is the low mood you have created by believing your low thinking… Okay, now get up." Craig opened his eyes and gave her a look. "Come on, you big baby. Dr. Dan told me there is nothing wrong, so you can't hurt yourself, can you? Besides, aren't you supposed to be some top athlete in world-class shape? Come on, *Motion is lotion*."[18-1] She motioned to him to move. Craig took a deep breath and turned on his side and slowly brought his legs up to his chest. Gradually he lowered his feet down to the ground to sit up. "Amazing! I see now why they call you the *Wizard of Oz*, you are a magician! Look, you went from lying to sitting, amazing! Let's see if you can stand up." Craig winced and pulled a face as he brought himself up to his full six feet two. "Remember, we don't care that it hurts. You are *sore but safe*."[18-2] Craig took a few steps forward. He was slightly bent over, but moving. "That's good, keep going."

He walked around the room a couple of times and then over to the other chair to sit down. "I can't help thinking about them, all the lies and all the hell they must have put my father through."

"Sure, you are human, it's totally understandable. But before you say it, this isn't about positive thinking. Positive thinking might get you through the next few days, but this is part of your story now, and if you can see that you are only experiencing your thinking about it, then you will see it go by, it will pass, and then your nervous system will calm and you can think straight."

"*Sore but safe*, I like that. I really need to feel safe right now."

"You are safe, and safe is a state of mind... I live in L.A. and we have earthquakes and wildfires. My mother calls me from England sometimes all nervous and asks me if I'm okay. Sure, Mum, why? Then she tells me that she saw on the BBC news that there was an earthquake in L.A. and did my house fall down? I tell her no, that I'm fine, that it was 40 miles away and I hardly felt it. She is all upset and she's 1000s of miles away, while I'm near it and didn't even notice! It's a state of mind. My mind isn't focused on the danger, so I feel safe. Her mind is overthinking it, so she feels unsafe even though she's nowhere near it."

"Sure, but we are talking about actual pain here, I'm not imagining it!"

"For sure you're not." Deborah explained the theories of how stress reduces the blood flow to the muscles, causing pain. They talked more about the physiology of what was happening in the body to cause both his back and his stomach to act up, but that it was created by brain activity, so it has no real substance, it's a phenomenon. "State of mind is powerful, but you already knew that, right? That's why you have all kinds of shrinks and sports therapists teaching you sports psychology tips and tricks, like the meditations." She motioned him to stand up and walk around again.

"Yep."

"Right, so we are going to look upstream a little more. Craig, you don't actually have to do anything to improve your state of mind. You *are* well-being, you *are* courage, you don't have to do anything to get those. They are your birthright, your default factory setting. You are as strong and fit as you think you are. When you see that you are what you think 100% of the time, you see how your state of mind is always affecting you and your body. So when those thoughts come, because they will, you watch them go by…*thanks for sharing, not listening.* They are only ever made of some spooky spiritual energy, and they only have meaning if you say they do."

At that moment there was a tap on the door and it opened without waiting for a response. A tall, handsome man came in and headed for the side table to pick up some things. He was wearing a baseball cap and was ruggedly unshaven. He confidently threw Craig his cap.

"Okay, time for practice, I managed to get us another court. How are you feeling?" He turned around, "Oh sorry, I didn't realize you had company, *I thought you were resting.*" He had a soft American accent and soft proud eyes.

"Dad, this is…Deborah."

"Hi, Mr. Kramer, I'm Deborah Stark. Dr. Dan Gieger in Sydney sent me over to talk to Craig about his back."

"Oh yeah, right. Well, I'm Joe, nice to meet you and we've gotta go."

The Kramer men left and Deborah looked for Jared to see where she would be staying.

"I managed to get you into a hotel in Kingston upon Thames. Wimbledon is totally full and it's just a few stops on the train. Hope that's okay."

"Sure, no problem, thank you. Kingston is really nice."

"Oh yeah, I keep forgetting you are from here. The driver will take you there when he comes back from dropping Craig and Joe off. So I guess, get checked in and then come back here and hang out till they get back, should be in about two hours."

He left her alone and she sat down on the sofa in the grand living room to soak it all in. What a whirlwind. She thought of all the things she should have said to Craig. Was she too rough with him? Maybe she should have listened more...but most of all, she wondered...had Joe Kramer ever remarried?

19
Kingston upon Thames

Deborah got checked in and made it back to the house in Wimbledon a few minutes after they had all got back from the tennis courts. There was a lot of press outside now and she had to push her way through the boisterous crowd.

"Where were you?!" Jared slammed the door shut behind her.

"Hey!" Deborah was at a loss—why was he shouting at her? "You told me to go check into the hotel and I came straight back! What's the problem?"

"Craig wants to see you, *now!*"

"Okay, no need to shout. Uh, are Joe and his wife staying here, too?" She hoped her question was subtle enough as to go undetected.

"Joe is, but he's divorced." Jared indicated that she should hurry up, pointing toward the back of the house. She followed his directions and found Craig and his father sitting at the large, wooden table in a stunningly remodeled kitchen. It was an elegant mixture of Edwardian class and modern convenience, overlooking a beautifully landscaped English suburban garden.

"Sore but safe!" announced Craig as she walked in. She put her purse down and pulled up a chair, sensing everything had gone okay.

"Yes, you are."

"But isn't that positive thinking?" questioned Joe while pouring himself a cup of fresh coffee.

"No, it's not," replied Craig, even though Joe was asking Deborah. "Positive thinking always has that feeling like, well, that you are trying to convince yourself of something, like, you know, 'act as if.' When Deborah said *sore but safe* this morning, I felt it, I *felt* safe. I can't explain it."

"You had an insight," explained Deborah on Craig's behalf. "That's how transformation happens—your reality changed because you had a shift in perception. When I was a little girl, I remember seeing my dad get into the neighbor's car and move it. Can't remember why now, but I remember thinking, WOW, my dad can drive someone else's car?!? He must be sooo clever! I had thought you could only know how to drive your own car, but then in my five-year-old head, I realized cars must be very similar. It was an insight!" The Kramer men laughed at her girlishness and she poured herself some orange juice. "So, how was practice?"

"Good. I was moving around the court much better. I don't know what you said to me, but I felt calm. Like, I still have a sore back, and I even felt like it could go out on me again, but I sorta didn't care."

"Backs can't go out, especially yours. Everybody's back is much stronger that we give them credit for, as everything is held in place, and yours must be like solid muscle. That language is not helpful, so let's not go there."

"Well, whatever it was that you said to him this morning, say some more," encouraged Joe as he stood up. "We need him back in tip-top shape, but you only have an hour as we have to do some interviews to fix some of the bad press." He picked up his keys and left them to chat.

Deborah's heart fluttered a little like a schoolgirl as Joe shut the kitchen door behind him. She caught herself and paused to focus on Craig. "This morning you said several times that you thought the divorce was your fault?"

"Yeah, I guess most kids do when their parents get divorced. But that's what made me so angry, that I had been blaming myself all this time, but really it was *Darren the SOB coach* that had split up our family! I have a younger sister, too, and our mum, she just abandoned us!"

"That's so rough, I'm really sorry you had to go through that… Craig, I'm sure you've heard the phrase, *they are doing the best they can*?"

Craig almost flipped out. "If you are suggesting that they were…were doing the best they could, then you are out of your mind!"

"Craig, listen to me. Remember we talked about state of mind and how we are always living in a thought-created world? Well, if I'm in a low state of mind, then I'm going to have low thinking, right?"

"So? That doesn't excuse what they did! *I want to kill him!*"

"Slow down, take a deep breath. We are not looking for excuses here, we are looking for insight. Last year I visited a men's high-security prison with one of my colleagues who teaches these ideas to prisoners.[19-1] These guys were murderers, gang bangers, and armed robbers—serious stuff. Some of them were never getting out. They were so clear that the reason they were sitting there in jail was because they had had a thought and felt they had no choice but to act on it. It was incredible. You just said that you want to kill him, but I'm guessing you aren't planning to hire a hitman. That thought went through your head, but you are not acting on it." Craig raised his eyebrows. "Well, these guys didn't know that they didn't have to act on those thoughts, and so they caused terrible harm."

Deborah continued as Craig started to slow down. "Craig, there was so much love in that room in the jail, they had so much love and respect for each other, it was unbelievable. Yes, they had deep remorse for what they had done, but they didn't have any blame anymore because they saw they had innocently misunderstood how their minds work. They saw that they had done the best they could with the really crappy thinking they had in that moment. It definitely wasn't good, but they were so clear that had they known better, they would have done better. Can you see that?" Craig had his head in his hands, tears were falling onto the table. "You were just a kid, you innocently thought it was your fault and that created a story that fueled your career with furious passion. But your mum was also doing the best she could with the low thinking she had. Craig, forgiveness might be a long way off, or it might be just as close as a new thought…"

They sat in silence for a while, then Craig mumbled as he wiped his face, "It's weird…I don't know if it's what you'd call forgiveness because I still think, like, what they did was dead wrong, very, very wrong, but…I don't feel that…like that venom, that bitterness in my stomach right now…"

"Wow, that's pretty huge. We can go with that for now." Deborah sighed in relief. She had taken a chance, a risky one, but she didn't have much time. "When you can see that *all* experience is made of thought, that it always passes like…like one of those sushi restaurants that has a conveyor belt that goes round and round, you don't have to take everything that comes at you. You have choices. You'll start to see you don't have to be a victim of this."

"Dad will be back in a minute." Craig shook his head, trying to compose himself. "I can't let him down, he has worked so hard to get me here." He let out a huge sigh, "But it's weird, I can feel the weight of this nightmare coming off, like a bubble just popped or something."

"Follow that feeling and remember, you *are* well-being, courage, and wisdom. You don't have to go anywhere to find those things, you don't have to meditate or imagine it, it's who you are, it just got covered up for a few days and now it's coming back to the surface."

Right on cue, Joe Kramer came back and Craig went upstairs to get his stuff.

"Drinks tonight?" asked Joe.

"Uh, yes, sure."

"Pick you up at your hotel, 8 p.m.?"

"Great."

Deborah had only brought one special outfit; she wasn't expecting to be going on any dates. She dressed and did her hair and went down to the lobby of her hotel just before 8. Was it a date? She wasn't sure. She suddenly felt insecure and foolish. What if it was just business or he was just being polite? He probably had a girlfriend anyway. Her thinking started to dart back and forth, and she felt insecure all of a sudden. She caught herself and decided that she was going to have a nice evening with this very nice, successful, handsome man and enjoy it, whatever it was.

Joe suggested a wine bar nearby that had an enchanting

terrace overlooking the River Thames. Hampton Court Palace, home of Henry the Eighth, sat majestically on the other side. They got their drinks and sat, watching the small boats as they slowly made their way past. The twinkle of the lights on the water made it feel very not business-like. Joe asked about her life and she told him about her Hollywood career, about the movie stars and the adventures she had had. They shared stories and laughed and Joe told her how he had grown up in New York but moved to Sydney after meeting Craig's mother. When Craig had turned professional, he had realized that he needed a business that would allow him to travel and support his son and yet be home for his daughter, too. He had started a management agency, first with athletes, and then actors.

"I oversee everything they need—press agents, coaches, merchandising, etc. I have an office in L.A., too."

"Really? Where?" Deborah suddenly got excited again.

"In Century City, and an apartment in Santa Monica."

"I live in the Venice Canals."

"I know," admitted Joe as Deborah raised her eyebrows. "Do you really think I would let someone in to see my son in the middle of a major tournament in such a vulnerable state without checking them out first? Sharpey, I mean Richard Sharpe, said you were the real deal, but I still had to do some digging. Craig is my most valuable client."

"Okay." Deborah felt a little invaded, but nodded her head in agreement.

"If this works out, we should talk about offering your services to my other clients. It would be a great service to add to my business. I think several of them could do with calming down, quite honestly!"

They laughed, but Deborah had a slight sinking feeling.

Maybe this wasn't a date after all, maybe it was just business. It would be *amazing* business, but she felt a drop in her spirits. She was disappointed. This man was kind and genuine and she felt a little crushed to think he just saw her as a business asset. They shared more stories and laughed some more, and then Joe walked her back to her hotel. He paused in the moonlight. "Have you ever been to Wimbledon?"

"Me? No. My mother used to watch it on TV. I thought about taking her as a treat, but I know she would have hated it."

"Why?"

"Too much fuss, too much money. She was quite happy sitting at home watching Bjorn Borg and Macenroe with her tea and her knitting." Deborah wondered if he was going to produce a ticket for her. Maybe he was being sneaky and was about to produce the perfect romantic surprise!

"How very English," dismissed Joe with his hands in his pockets. "Sorry that I can't get you a ticket for the match tomorrow, it's always sold out months ahead."

"Oh. Uh, no problem." She shrugged her shoulders and faked a nonchalant smile. "Don't worry, I can watch the match here in the bar."

Deborah arrived at the big house for breakfast to meet Craig before his last practice session prior to the semi-finals. The house was quiet. She sat waiting in the kitchen. Craig and Joe came in, and Joe announced he would be back in an hour.

As soon as Joe had closed the kitchen door, Craig blurted out, "Okay, I wanna preface this by saying no weed was involved in this."

"You smoke pot?!" Deborah could hardly hide her surprise.

"No! I just mean it's kinda trippy… So, my revelation is…drumroll…life is absolutely, totally, 100% neutral. And then…we add onto the absolute blank canvas of life our own projections and our own assumptions, we create our own reality. And I don't know if I can say that I fully understand what you have been talking about right now, but I definitely understand it more than I did like ten minutes ago or you know…yesterday. And seriously, it kinda scares me how powerful that ability is and that it's like misunderstood or underestimated. We could be sooo wrong and have no idea. And be so caught in it and have no idea. And live our whole lives like that and have no idea…like a chronic sickness or something. Like you just live with it and you don't ever get it fixed. Anyways, I just had this realization last night and I really, really, like, *feel* it for the first time. I've heard these things before, but now I really am getting it!"

"Wow." Deborah sat back in her chair. She wasn't expecting that. "Tell me more!"

Craig got himself some breakfast and sat down. "See, I always thought that if a thought comes into my head it must be real, right, like those prisoners you talked about? And if it was a bad one, then I better hit it out of the court. Wham, don't need that one, wham, get rid of that one, you know? But last night I saw that all thinking is…is neutral until you put a spin on it, like you said. Ha! I just realized, I have been training for years to put topspin on my serve, but my mind does that to my thinking automatically!" Deborah nodded at the insightful analogy. "But it scares me that my mum doesn't. Like, how she could be so caught up in her own thinking and have no idea. She has no idea of the pain and hurt she caused us. I could never understand how that was even possible, I mean she's not stupid, just…she just doesn't get it. And as for the SOB coach, well he is just…sick."

Deborah was thrilled that he was so engaged. "Craig, if a puppy pees on the carpet or a little kid breaks a plate, they aren't sick, they just don't know any better. When you were a kid, did you ever break your arm or your leg?"

Craig got up to get some juice. "My little sister fell off her bike when dad let go and broke her arm."

"Right, she didn't understand gravity quite yet, but she wasn't sick. It's an innocent misunderstanding, could you see that? As soon as she understood how to peddle forward she was able to stay upright."

"Are you saying they are *innocent*?!" Craig almost choked on his juice.

"Only in their misunderstanding of how experience works. Nobody is excusing their behavior. I have no idea what the circumstances were but I do know that we all do better when we have better thinking, that's how it works. We are all doing the best we can with the thinking we have in that moment, in this moment right now."

"But that's the really cool thing I got last night. It doesn't matter. It doesn't matter what she is doing or not doing, what my sister or my dad does or believes, the press, the other players—it's my thinking, right? See, I always knew that I have no control over them. I used to have a sports therapist who taught me all that stuff, but then he taught me anger management, meditations and reframing techniques to deal with it. But I just now saw that is a massive misunderstanding of how it works! Trying to fix it is just more thinking, right? Like the snowglobe you showed me, it just needs to settle."

Craig stood up straight and stretched, the tips of his

fingers almost touching the original Edwardian lamp hanging from the high kitchen ceiling. He moved his powerful shoulders back and around and then took a last swig of juice. Deborah hadn't really noticed his strength until this moment; he was solid power in motion even just standing there.

"Good luck, remember—look within!"

"Hey, I just gotta beat the guy on the other side of the net, right?" He moved towards the door. "By the way, my dad likes you."

Deborah was taken aback, "Oh. Thanks." She was even more confused now.

Deborah took a taxi straight to the Kingston shopping mall. Whether this was romance or business, she needed more fancy clothes. As she walked up and down past shoe shops and boutiques she wondered about both scenarios. Did Craig mean his dad liked her as in 'you are doing a good job' or like as in *like*? Maybe she should get her nails done? *No, stop it!* She never liked getting her nails done, what was she thinking? Deborah laughed at herself for being so girly and texted her friend Abby back in Los Angeles. Abby suggested she calm down and enjoy the ride.

After some clothes shopping and lunch, she went back to her hotel. She caught up on some emails and then went down to the lounge to watch the match. There was a small crowd gathered around the large TV and so she pulled up a chair. Craig was about to play England's number one Seed, so it was a bit uncomfortable. If Craig won then he was knocking her own country out of the tournament, in her own country. And if Craig won then she was working with one of the finalists for Wimbledon. She laughed to herself; *Craig better win!* The locals in the lounge were all rooting for the English player, John Aitken, who was apparently the best hope they had had in years, so she felt outnumbered until a couple of Aussies came in and ordered drinks. She beckoned them over and they chatted while the match got started. There was talk of Craig's injuries but she kept quiet about knowing him and that there was never anything wrong.

John Aitken walked onto the court in his crisp white shorts and shirt like a young commanding officer in the military. He waved to the crowd and the camera panned around to the player's box. She caught a glimpse of Joe who was sitting next to a very attractive suntanned woman in designer sunglasses. Deborah's heart resolved to let the whole dating thing go and concentrate on the game. Craig followed right behind; he looked serious but then waved to the crowd and then to his father who gave him an encouraging fist in the air. The match started and she watched, enthralled by the speed and the agility of the two men. Every time Craig served he let out a loud groan, and Deborah prayed it wasn't from pain. The English player wasn't as good but kept up as best he could. The commentators kept saying that if Craig was at his best he would have beaten Aitken in straight sets by now but because of his lack of fitness, he was kept on his toes till match point. Craig served, letting out another loud groan that rebounded around the hushed court. He hit the ball right into the corner of Aitkens's side. Game over and Craig was through to the men's final of Wimbledon! Deborah had tears in her eyes.

"It wasn't that sad, dear!" offered one of the locals. "England always gets knocked out of everything, the football, the cricket. Every year we think this time it will be different but it never is."

221

Deborah laughed, "No it's not that. I know Craig and I'm just so happy for him, that's all."

Jared had left a message at the hotel asking her to join them for an early dinner. It would be a private catered event at the house as Craig needed to conserve his energy and get an early night. She picked out one of her new dresses and leisurely dressed for dinner. She really didn't know what her role was anymore. Craig seemed back on his feet, literally, and she wondered where this adventure would go next.

It was a nice celebration, the pride and excitement of getting to the final was everywhere. Craig's sister Melissa had flown in. It was so nice to see them all together for this special time. The attractive woman was there too and Deborah was very happy to find out that she was the rep from Nike, Craig's sponsors.

After dinner, she managed to talk to Craig alone for a few minutes.

"I'm so proud of you. I was so nervous when you let out those loud grunts when you served!"

He shrugged his shoulders. "*Sore but safe*, that's what you taught me and it's true. It does still hurt a bit but when I'm playing, when my mind is on the ball, I don't feel it. I can see the pain shrinking and leaving my body. It's getting less and less and so by the final on Sunday, I'll be fine, I know it." He paused and then asked, "Can I share something with you?"

"Please." Deborah was intrigued.

"Well, you know you said to me that I should look within?" Deborah nodded with an admiring smile. "On the court today I realized that within doesn't mean inside the body, does it? Within has nothing to do with, like, the physical…it's like a reality that's before that, before the thoughts…" He paused.

"It's okay, it's hard to put into words," confirmed Deborah. "But I know what you mean. Within is a metaphor. It's the place where wisdom tells your body how to move on the court, it's where an artist forms his creations, and it's where your father's pride and joy is bubbling up from as he watches you win."

Craig gave a knowing grin.

"Syd Banks, the guy I was telling you about, he said, 'You are not just a physical being, you are something far greater. Go beyond the physical to the spiritual. There you will find more power than you have ever realized in your life.'"[19-2]

"I get it," said Craig. "…It's where the physical meets the spiritual."

20
SW19

Deborah woke up excited, her stomach all bubbles. It took a moment to remember why… Oh, yes! It was men's finals day at Wimbledon and her client was playing! *Not too shabby*, thought Deborah, getting dressed to go down to breakfast.

"Excuse me? This arrived for you this morning."

She took an envelope from the hotel manager and went to sit in the dining room. There was a handwritten message on the outside.

You didn't really think we would leave you out, did you?

Inside was a ticket for the player's box at Centre Court with an invite to the player's lounge! *What?!* She gasped. A few of the other guests looked around as she waved the ticket in the air excitedly. *"I've got a seat at Centre Court!"* They gave her some 'happy for you' smiles as she wondered, was it from Craig, from Jared or…from Joe? She jumped up to get some eggs and smoked salmon. As she ate, she decided it didn't matter. She was going to Wimbledon and she needed to get ready.

Walking nervously into the players' lounge, she noticed a familiar face. It was Richard Sharpe from Sydney!

"How did you get here?!"

"Australia's number one is going to beat some European bloke! Couldn't miss this, could I?" Richard was loud and proud, standing up straight and strong holding a beer.

"How are you feeling? Were you okay on that long flight?"

"I'm chipper, the pain has gone, no worries. I'm playing golf nearly every day and Dr. Dan has got me doing *pilates*! Can you imagine it? Me on the floor in my undershorts with those Sheilas who wear lycra!" Deborah laughed out loud at the thought of Richard doing pilates but was so happy for him. "Sylvie gave me permission to come. Joe Kramer and I go way back, he introduced me to my first wife, and now with you here, well, I wasn't going to miss this for all the tea in China!"

"So *you* sent me the ticket!"

"No, deary…"

They got some drinks and schmoozed with Craig's sister for a bit until it was time to go to their seats. The sun was shining and the white, puffy English clouds rolled away right on cue. Centre Court was overflowing with that magical mixture of tradition and anticipation of a new champion. Joe had been talking to the press and took his seat in front of them, next to his daughter, soon after they were settled.

"G'day, mate! Your boy's gonna nail this!" Richard slapped his old friend on his back.

"Darn right! He's in top form, right, Deborah?" Joe turned and gave her a glorious smile.

She smiled back, trying not to blush; was that a flirt, or was he just beaming at everyone? They sat back to enjoy the pre-match introductions. There were royalty and superstars all around them. As the ball boys and girls and umpire came on the court, the atmosphere became electric. Finally, it was time for the players. Craig came first this time, striding with head high, full of power and resilience. He waved to them and then to the applauding crowd. His opponent, Antonio Peña, came next. He was the favourite, a little older than Craig, and much more experienced. He waved to his fans and family confidently and they took to the court to warm up.

Deborah had never been so excited to watch a sports event. The whole of Centre Court suddenly hushed in anticipation as Craig served for the first point. The first set went to Peña, then the second and third to Craig. He was spiritual power in motion, gliding from one side of the court to the other, his athletic elegance thrilling the crowd. Antonio fumbled but came back to win the fourth, so Craig had to win the last set to win. The score was 5-6 to Peña in the final set, but as he readied himself for the championship point a cell phone rang from the crowd!

Peña went ballistic. "*You need to keep this crowd under control, you amateur! You're a disgrace!*" The umpire kept her composure and gave a warning of unsportsmanlike conduct for his insulting outburst.

"Advantage: Mr. Kramer."

"See, that's the Mediterranean temperament for you," whispered Richard.

The crowd grumbled their disapproval at his bad sportsmanship. Peña was completely thrown off his game now. He was flustered, sweating profusely, jumping from one foot to the other. Was it a tactic to throw Craig off, or was he actually losing it? Craig won the next two games. He had found that place within and was rising above the drama and the tension. Peña, struggling to keep pace as his thinking descended into chaos, had another outburst, and another warning.

The umpire called for play and the crowd fell silent.

"Championship point."

Craig paused to center himself. He threw the ball way up, reached his racket high in the air, and with majestic force slammed the winning shot into the far corner!

"Game, set, and match Mr. Kramer."

Craig had won Wimbledon!

Joe and Melissa were crying, and the whole of Centre Court was on their feet applauding! Craig was on his knees.

A few days later, Deborah was preparing to leave for the airport when Joe and Craig came to say thank you and goodbye. The guests soon heard he was there, so Craig, beaming with joy, went outside to sign autographs and enjoy the attention.

"Was it you? Did you send me the ticket?"

"I did," replied Joe with a sneaky smile. "I thought you should be there."

Deborah's heart took a leap; maybe he did *like* her.

"We're leaving for Sydney tomorrow, but I'm going to be in L.A. in a few weeks' time. I have some business to take care of. Can we meet up for lunch maybe?" asked Joe.

Deborah smiled. "I look forward to it."

21
New York

"What am I going to do?" whined Deborah.

"Just ask him!" Abby was shopping for new sneakers in the Beverly Center shopping mall. "What do you think about these?"

It had been a few weeks and Deborah hadn't heard from Joe.

"Uh, yeah, nice. But what if he's not interested, what if he doesn't think about me that way? I'm going to be so embarrassed."

"This isn't like you! You really like him, don't you? Show me that picture again." Deborah held up a Sunday supplement of Craig arriving home in Sydney, triumphant, his father standing proudly next to him. "He is handsome, and the father is kinda cute, too!"

"Oh, stop it! What I can't stand is the not knowing. If he's not interested in me that way, then that's it, I'm done, I'll get over it, maybe. But every time we meet, it's like a rollercoaster—one minute I'm all excited because he seems to be flirting with me, and then he says something business-like and I'm disappointed. Next minute he's sending me tickets to *Centre Court at Wimbledon* saying he can't leave me out, and then he's all business again. Ughh!" Deborah threw a pair of sneakers on the floor and a sales assistant gave her a very disapproving look. Abby bought herself a pair and they went for a coffee.

"It's funny, I see my clients going up and down like this and I tell them to ride the wave or look for a quiet mind, and now I get to go up and down, too!"

"And what would your precious Sydney Banks say about it?"

"He'd probably say…so what! It's only a big deal if you make it a big deal. He would say there is no need to be frightened by it and to look for a quiet mind."

"Okay, there you are then. When is he arriving?"

"Tomorrow, but his assistant called me to make the plans. What's that about?"

"He's a busy man, Deborah! His son and top client just won Wimbledon! You need to relax. Did you think that maybe he's nervous, too? He's been single a long time and has two kids to think about."

"I guess. He just seems so confident, I can't imagine him getting insecure."

"Everyone gets insecure at some point. You always look like you have it together, but everyone has something that gets to them, right?" Deborah agreed. "So when are you going out?"

"Monday night, drinks at Shutters on the Beach."

"Ooh, very nice, I love that place and just a short walk for you."

Deborah walked over to Shutters, a glamourous hotel

situated right on the Santa Monica boardwalk, overlooking the beach. She felt excited to see him again and just a little nervous. The sun was just starting to go down, spreading delicate light over the Pacific ocean as a few remaining surfers chased the last few waves of the day. She caught sight of Joe; he was having drinks with a group of business friends on the veranda overlooking the ocean. Okay, so *not a date*.

"Hey, here she is! Guys, this is Deborah Stark, the woman who transformed my son into a champion."

"Stop it. Craig was already a champion, I just pointed him back in the right direction."

It was a pleasant evening. The group talked mostly about their business and clients and Deborah mostly listened. She laughed at the jokes and smiled at their stories, then when it was time to go, she started to say good night.

"Please let me drive you home," offered Joe.

"It's okay, it's just a short walk to the Canals from here."

"Then may I walk with you?"

They walked along the boardwalk down to Venice Beach and then up one of the quaint beach alleys into the Venice Canals where Deborah lived. Sheldon, her neighbor, was on his deck, so she introduced them. Sheldon gave her a wink but she laughed it off. When they reached her deck, she decided to just come out with it and ask him. The up and down of not knowing was becoming unbearable, and she knew she had to say something. The suspense was too much and she wanted to know where she stood before he disappeared back to Sydney in a couple of weeks.

"I want to see you again," said Joe. Deborah was still forming the words in her head but he had beaten her to it!

"Uh, yes, I'd really like that."

"Can I pick you up at 6 p.m. tomorrow?"

"Sure."

"Dress warm."

"What does that mean?!" cried Abby when she called later to see how it had gone.

"*I don't know!*"

Deborah followed directions and put on her 'third-date' big, cuddly, warm sweater. Joe picked her up promptly and they drove to Santa Monica airport.

"I don't have my passport with me," she quipped as they parked near one of the runways.

Joe laughed, "You won't need it, we are only going to Santa Barbara."

"What?!"

"This is my buddy Eric, he's going to fly us up there. Did you know they have an Italian restaurant at the airport? Signorina, your carriage awaits."

Joe opened the door of a small 4-seater plane and she started to get into the back seat.

"Here, get in the front with Eric, I want you to experience it all. I'll sit in the back."

They all put on headphones and the little plane made its bumpy way out onto the runway.

"Ready?" asked Eric.

"I guess!"

The engine started to roar as they sped up faster and faster along the runway, and then *whoosh* up into the night air. They climbed higher and higher and then took a sharp turn. The left wing dipped down and suddenly the little plane was totally on its side! Deborah was now looking straight down out of her side window! There was nothing between her and the busy 405 Freeway 500 feet below except a piece of glass! Her heart was pounding as they straightened out and then flew up the coastline to Santa Barbara. It was exhilarating seeing the Malibu hills and the cars on PCH from high above in the night sky. The waves were crashing on the sand under the lights of some of the beach homes, and even though it was chilly, she couldn't feel it. They glided along in the cool, quiet darkness over the mountains and then along the coast again. The ride lasted 40 glorious minutes, then they softly bumped onto the landing strip at Santa Barbara. After turning the plane around, it soon came to a stop. Joe helped her out and they followed Eric into the restaurant.

On the flight home, Eric let Deborah take the controls for a few minutes. It was a perfectly magical night.

"Thank you, that was very special," whispered Deborah as they walked back to the car.

"I thought you would like it."

"You are an extraordinary man. I'm so glad to have met you."

Joe hesitated and then looked very serious for a moment. "I was devastated after Craig's mom left. I'm an old-fashioned kinda guy and in old-fashioned movies, they would have called me a cuckold. But I refused to be defined by someone else's mistakes, so I worked hard and focused on the kids. Now they are grown and starting their own lives, I think I'm ready to live a little of my own life again now."

Deborah smiled at him. She felt such a warm connection and admiration for this man, how he had risen above the waves that had crashed into his life.

"Lunch tomorrow? I can pick you up at 12 noon, and this time, I promise no pilots or drivers, just us."

He kissed her hand and she melted inside. "I'd like

that."

Joe picked her up right on time for a stunning drive through Topanga Canyon and all the way out to the Point Magoo peninsula. "Where are we going to eat?" Deborah was sure there weren't any restaurants out there, just coastline and maybe a small naval base.

"I brought a picnic. What, you thought I'd bring you all the way out here to this gorgeous spot with nothing to eat?" There were smoked salmon sandwiches and exotic fresh fruit, sparkling juice, and exquisite handmade chocolates; he had managed to bring all her favorite foods. It was the most decadent picnic she had ever had. They talked and shared about their families and fears, their lives, and their dreams.

"I have to leave on Sunday…" Deborah's heart sank at the thought of him going away again so soon. "I want to stay in touch, I mean, I don't want to lose you."

Deborah smiled sadly, "How long will you be gone?"

"Well, we have a quick tour booked for Craig, you know, exhibition matches and sponsorship gigs in London, Europe and Japan, and then back to the States for the U.S. Open in August… If my son wasn't the most famous tennis player in the world right now, please know, I'd rather be here with you."

"I know, and I understand, really I do."

The next month was hard. She wasn't sure where this relationship was going, but she felt ready for it. Deborah had been single for a few years and had been intrigued to see who would come into her life next. She felt ready to share this new adventure with someone special, and Joe seemed to be, too. He called often. There were long phone calls from hotel rooms and airports, flowers arrived with messages of love and longing. It was painful for both of them to be so far apart, but timing and circumstances were running the show.

Deborah kept busy with her work. Clients were showing up now by word of mouth and she was getting inquiries from pain clinics and hospitals about her work. Someone from the Santa Barbara conference had even recommended her to appear on a local TV show. Finally, Joe and Craig were heading back to the States: first Miami and Houston, and then New York for the U.S. Open. Deborah had never looked at so many sports sections of the newspaper. Joe invited her to join him there, and they had the most romantic weekend doing all the romantic New York things.

"I don't know when I have ever seen my dad so happy." Craig was enjoying a chance to relax on a big, squishy sofa in the lounge of his hotel as he and Deborah waited for Joe to finish up some business calls. The smell of fresh coffee and freshly baked pastries floated in from the dining room where late risers were still having breakfast.

"He is so proud of you," offered Deborah, a little embarrassed.

"No. I mean being with you, he's so chilled out even though he's crazy busy. Between you and me, he used to get a bit uptight, you know, when business got intense. He seems to be handling it so much better."

Deborah grinned, "Maybe *you* are the one who has chilled out and you've stopped judging everyone and everything every moment of the day?"

Craig laughed.

"I just realized something." Deborah put down the magazine she was glancing through for a moment. "You must know Julia, Richard Sharpe's daughter?"

"Of course, we grew up together. Our dads were always good buddies so we did family stuff together, you know, birthdays, holidays. She's the same age as my sister. How do you know Jules?"

"It's because of Julia that I met Richard and got him to join my pain program in Sydney, and then Richard referred me to your dad!" Deborah smiled to herself as she reflected for a moment on how this extraordinary adventure had started. Her time spent with Julia had seemed so unbelievably crazy, and yet it had brought her here, right here sitting on this sofa in New York with a Wimbledon champion, waiting for the man she loved. How could she have imagined that? Walking into the unknown used to be the scariest thing for her, and now she *knew* it's just how life is. She had heard Syd Banks say it on a tape one time: 'Look for what is, not what isn't.' *That's why he taught that we should learn not to be afraid of our own experience*, she contemplated to herself. She was dying to tell Craig how it had all started with the crazy job in L.A. but hesitated, as she knew she couldn't say anything about Julia's personal story.

"I heard she was pretty messed up."

"Uh yeah, she did have a tough time for a while, but she is doing great now. Having her father up and about sure helped."

"Yeah, that was amazing seeing him in London. He was such an angry old bugger when we were growing up, you have no idea. The last time I saw him was probably at my sister's 18th. He was in his wheelchair yelling and screaming on the phone at some poor guy." Craig took a sip of his juice. "Seems like we've all had some insights, I just hope mine last through this next tournament."

"That's a thought you could watch go by," nudged Deborah. "Are you nervous?"

Craig shrugged his shoulders.

"But isn't that the exciting part? The not knowing?" He raised his eyebrows nervously at her. "If you knew you were always going to win, then what would be the point? That would be so boring! It's the same in the 'game of life', it's the not knowing that scares people and why we try so damn hard to control outcomes. But in sports, we somehow accept the unknown, and that's what makes the game so exciting."

"Sure, but..." he turned to her, almost begging. "But you always say something really helpful right about now, like, look beyond thought, or listen for a feeling. Come on, I need a new insight. Where am I going to find one this time?"

Deborah smiled and said slowly, "It's in the not knowing."

Craig shook his head and then jumped up as he saw his father come out of the elevator. He had seen some fans eyeing him near the front desk, so he high-fived his father and left Deborah to finish her coffee.

"Are you sitting down?" inquired Joe as he came to join her. Deborah patted the sofa she was sitting on and gave him an *are you okay?* kind of look. "Your amazing, selfless, hard-working agent," he pointed at himself, "has just got Craig a full, in-depth interview with the New Yorker magazine!"

"Wow, that's great, well done you! But I don't understand...why would *I* need to be sitting down for that news?"

"Well, I was giving the journalist some of the back story, about how you helped get Craig back on his feet...and he said he has a very special client for you to meet!"

Deborah hesitated. She gave him a long, quizzical look.

Joe cleared his throat, "Are you thinking…uh, Joe… *where's my passport*, or are you maybe thinking, *but what will I wear to the Palace?*"

But Deborah couldn't hear him, she was laughing to herself. She was already enjoying the *not knowing*.

Chapter Notes

4. Bondi Beach

1. Dr. John E. Sarno, MD, a pioneering rehabilitation medicine doctor at the Rusk Institute, New York, published several books about back pain and the Mind-Body connection.

2. Candace Pert, PhD, *Molecules of Emotion*, Simon and Schuster (1997): pp. 135–137.

5. Killarney Country Club

1. Javeria A. Hashmi, PhD, et al., *Shape-shifting Pain: Chronification of back pain shifts brain representation from nociceptive to emotional circuits*, from pubmed.ncbi.nlm.nih.gov (2013).

6. Pyrmont

1. The actual patient this character is based on had, in fact, had 14 back surgeries!

2. Dr. J. B. Moseley, "A Controlled Trial of Arthroscopic Surgery for Osteoarthritis of the Knee," *New England Journal of Medicine* (July, 2002).

7. Monday

1. Dr. Sarno called these "symptom imperatives" or "equivalents," as they are all symptoms of stress-related illness and often occur in people with chronic pain.

9. Tuesday

1. Between 1989 and 1994, 849,000 cases of Carpal Tunnel Syndrome were reported to the National Center for Health Statistics. By 2005, cases had fallen by half. *Where did they all go?*

2. All spines start to degenerate from age 20 and with the advent of digital technology, we can look so close inside the body that one will always find something imperfect on the scan of an adult's spine. Degeneration is normal, it's not a disease, does not cause pain, and definitely is not a reason for expensive, invasive surgery. Dr. David Hanscomb, MD, *Back in Control*, Vertus Press (2016).

3. Dr. V. S. Ramachandran is a neuroscientist known for his wide-ranging experiments and theories in behavioral neurology, including the invention of the mirror box.

10. Tuesday Afternoon

1. Javeria A. Hashmi, PhD, et al. *Shape-shifting pain: Chronification of back pain shifts brain representation from nociceptive to emotional circuits*, from pubmed.ncbi.nlm.nih.gov (2013).

2. Bulging discs or herniated discs almost never cause pain. Dr. David Hanscomb, MD, *Back in Control*, 2nd edition, Vertus Press, 2016.

3. Degeneration is not a disease, it's a natural sign of natural aging. A study published in 2020 showed "no association was found between baseline MRI findings and 13-year disability in Low Back Pain patients with severe Disk Degeneration of Facet Joint Degeneration. This highlights the limited prognostic value of a single baseline MRI scan on long-term disability." The same study also reported that "degeneration on MRI was a frequent finding in patients with LBP. None of the MRI changes suggesting degeneration were associated with a worse outcome at 13-year follow-up."

From

https://journals.sagepub.com/doi/full/10.1177/2192568220921391

4. There are differing opinions as to whether a pinched nerve can cause pain. Dr. Sarno said that if it's pinched it wouldn't be able to send a message to the brain, but Dr. Hanscomb and Dr. Norman Doidge seem to differ in their understanding.

5. "Chronic systemic inflammation, associated with chronic activation of the HPA stress response, is the result of chronic mental stress." Dr. William Pettit Jr., MD, Board Certified in Psychosomatic Medicine, Psychiatrist retired. Personal communication.

6. Prof. Peter O'Sullivan, professor at Curtin University, Perth, Australia. From pain-ed.com.

7. Dr. Dan Clauw, MD, professor at Michigan University. From uofmhealth.org.

8. Dr. John Sarno.

9. Frightening but true, according to a report in the *Spine Journal* (Sept, 2004) entitled "Cost-Effectiveness of Lumbar Fusion and Nonsurgical Treatment for Chronic Low Back Pain," Peter Fritzell, MD, Ph.D.

10 Drs. Hanscomb, Sarno, Schubiner, and Schecter are all in consensus about this. Various sources.

11. Wednesday

1. A 2006 Harvard Report contradicted the popular myth that excessive computer use will cause carpal tunnel. "Even as much as 7 hours a day won't increase your risk."

2. Michael Neill, from caffeineforthesoul.libsyn.com/the-

unreliable-narrator.

12. Wednesday Afternoon
  1. Sydney Banks, *Mind and Positivity*.
  2. As reported in the introduction of *The Mindbody Prescription* by Dr. John Sarno, Warner Books, 1998.
  3. Richard Webster, *Why Freud was Wrong*, The Orwell Press, 1995.
  4. Jody Gibbs, personal communication.

13. Thursday
  1. Dr. Harold G. Koenig, Professor of Medicine at Duke University, agrees. In 2012, he reviewed over 600 research studies and concluded that people who hold spiritual beliefs do significantly better with both medical and mental health problems. His research also showed that spiritual beliefs have a direct positive effect on healing outcomes, risk of disease, and activity of the immune and endocrine systems.
  2. Dr. L. Moseley et al., from www.tamethebeast.org.
  3. Elsie Spittle (3phd.net) and Linda Pransky (pranskyandassociates.com)
  4. From partner.sciencenorway.no/death-diseases-forskningno/leprosy-rages-still.
  5. Dr. Chauw's reference is to a movie, *This is Spinal Tap*, directed by Rob Reiner, about a 70's heavy metal rock band who were so outrageous their guitar amps went up to *11!* (Standard amps go to 10.)
  6. In 1995, *The British Medical Journal* reported on a 29-year-old construction worker who'd suffered an accident that involved jumping onto a 7-inch nail which pierced his boot clear through to the other side (Fisher et al., 1995). In terrible pain, he was carted off to the ER and sedated with **opioids**. When the doctors removed his boot, they discovered that the nail had passed between his toes without penetrating his skin! There was zero damage to his foot: no blood, no puncture wound, not even a scratch. But make no mistake: despite the absence of injury, his pain was real.
  7. The author has had the honor of meeting him twice. This is an example of true resilience, we all have it; it's our birthright.
  8. This term was first coined by Dr. Donald Hebb in 1949.
  9. Ivan Petrovich Pavlov was a Russian physiologist, known primarily for his work in classical conditioning.

14. Friday

1. Look for peer-reviewed research papers in recognized professional journals by Dr. Anthony Kessel, Dr. Jack Pransky, Dr. Thomas Kelly, Dr. Judith Sedgeman, "Beyond Recovery" prison programs, "The Spark Initiative" and iHeart school programs.

2. Emily Dickenson, *Tell All the Truth, But Tell it Slant* (1890).

3. Dr. Bennet Braun, psychiatrist at Rush-Presbyterian-St. Luke's Medical Center in Chicago.

4. Sydney Banks, *The Missing Link*, Lone Pine Publishing (1998).

5. Dr. George Pransky, arguably the best psychologist ever. pranskyandassociates.com

6. Anita Morjanis' book *Dying to be Me* gives an amazing description of her near-death experience. Hay House Books (2012).

15. Kings Cross

1. Alissa Roan Spray, personal communication.

2. This happened with 100% of the author's case studies.

17. Santa Barbara

1. In the 1700's, physician and philosopher Rene Descartes (of "I think therefore I am" fame) made a deal with the pope. Descartes agreed to uphold the belief that the mind is spiritual and therefore belonged to the church and that the body is physical and should be left to the doctors in order to get cadavers for his research. This biased divide led the medical world to see the body purely as a machine, and only very recently has the belief in the Mind-Body connection begun to reunite the physical and spiritual in our understanding.

2. Sydney Banks, *The Enlightened Gardener Revisited,* Lone Pine Publishing (2005).

3. Pallavi Schniering, personal communication.

4. Miriam Spiegel, personal communication.

5. Fictional treatment.

18. London

1. "*Motion is lotion*" and "*Sore but safe*" are "really cool" sayings from the really cool Dr. Lorimer Moseley. From www.tamethebeast.org.

2. Ibid.

19. Kingston upon Thames

1. Jacqueline Hollows and the "Beyond Recovery" program. From www.beyond-recovery.co.uk.

2. Sydney Banks, *The Washington Lecture,* from sydbanks.com.

Acknowledgments

I am so grateful to those who supported and encouraged me in writing this novel. Thank you to Ayelet Horwitz, Pallavi Schniering, Alissa Roane-Spray, Susan Marmot, and Lauren Weinberg for such valuable and insightful feedback and your generous encouragement. Deep thanks to Lori Capenos, Dr. Bill Pettit, and Ryan Green for their time in reading and reviewing the manuscript. Thank you to my editor, Sarah Rosenbaum, and to Aiden Wasserman for the quite genius title of my program and this book.

I would like to express deep gratitude and respect to my teachers and mentors; Dr. Bill Pettit, Dr. Dicken Bettinger, Dr. George and Linda Pransky, and Dr. Aaron Turner and to all my colleagues in the Three Principles Community.

Thank you to all my clients who trust me with their pain, their fears, and their dreams. You inspire me with your courage and determination to heal. Thank you to everyone who wrote to me after my first book for your support and encouragement, and to all the members of my Facebook group who are a daily inspiration. I especially want to thank Pallavi, whose sweet friendship is an invaluable support and whose insights keep us all inspired.

I want to express my sincere gratitude to all the pain scientists and researchers whose work contributed so richly to this book and my journey in understanding pain, especially Dr. John Sarno, Dr. Lorimer Moseley, Steve Ozanich, and Dr. David Hanscomb. To Eddy Lindinstein and his Health and Fitness podcast for setting me on the path of spreading this understanding in the world of pain management, and to Dr. Javeria Hashmi for her pioneering research and encouragement in the work that I do.

And finally to Mr. Sydney Banks, thank you for sharing your wisdom and for the joy and health that it is still bringing.

With love, Chana.

Resources

Chana Studley is a sought-after coach and mentor. She leads workshops about understanding chronic pain and the Three Principles in person and online. Her *Painless Program* consists of one on one personalized coaching sessions for individuals who want to get a deeper understanding of the Principles, the Mindbody connection, and address their physical issues. Chana also speaks at conferences all over the world and is available for consultations for businesses, clinics, and universities.

You can contact her at: chanastudley.com

Facebook Group:
TMS, Chronic Pain, and The Three Principles.

Recommended reading:
The Missing Link - Sydney Banks
The Quest for the Pearl - Sydney Banks
The Enlightened Gardener - Sydney Banks

Three Principles resources:
Sydbanks.com
3PGC.org
3pconference.org
Chana Studley - Youtube Channel

Printed in Great Britain
by Amazon